IN THE MIDST
OF
WOLVES

Also by Keith Remer

Run River Run

The Aristocracy of Caddo County

Blood City: Book Two of the Calamitous Breed Trilogy

Killing Bardoe: Book One of the Calamitous Breed Trilogy

The Hiding Place of Thunder

IN THE MIDST OF WOLVES

by

KEITH REMER

Honey Lee Press

Oklahoma City, OK

In the Midst of Wolves

First Honey Lee Press trade paperback edition December 2019
Manufactured in the United States
10 9 8 7 6 5 4 3 2 1

Print ISBN 978-1-7341015-1-5
EBook ISBN 978-1-7341015-2-2
Library of Congress Control Number 2019919293

For my precious and loving wife,

Jeanne Elizabeth Remer,

who constantly proves to be my greatest fan.

PART I
THE CRIME

ONE

avid Robbins reached with an unsteady hand and wrapped trembling fingers around the doorknob. The brass orb was not cold to the touch, yet it produced chill bumps on both his arms. After taking a deep breath and holding it, Robbins slowly turned the knob.

He reluctantly inched the door open. As the edge of the heavy paneled door cleared the door jamb, stark bright light erupted from the closed-off room. The rays of sunshine overpowered the darkness of the second-floor landing but had no effect on the gloom permeating David Robbins. Noisily exhaling the breath he held, Robbins moved on wobbly legs into the room and closed the door behind him.

Without benefit of the spryness that normally defied his forty years of age, Robbins fell back against the door. Puffy eyelids blinked to protect bloodshot eyes from the mid-morning sunlight radiating through the sheers covering the room's many windows. Anyone unfamiliar with the surroundings would think the terrible events of the past three days left this particular room unscathed. Robbins knew better. For him, the usually vivid room of splendid pinks, frilly lace, bows and ribbons had lost its sparkle. The Disney and Warner Brothers characters that once seemed to frolic on the curtains, wallpaper, and small bedspread, now appeared listless. The dolls lining the walls on shelves and the stuffed animals on the little bed no longer looked capable of inducing giggles and shrill shrieks of laughter.

An antique bureau with an oval-shaped mirror occupied space on the wall adjacent to the door. Knowing his olive complexion had paled and a face generally acclaimed as handsome was now badly swollen from too many tears, Robbins avoided looking into the mirror. Instead, his gaze fell on the little girl things cluttering the bureau top.

Barbie doll clothes, and the partially nude doll they belonged to, were strewn among stacks of coloring books. Toppled figurines from a vast assortment of children's movies intermingled with jigsaw puzzle pieces, costume jewelry and crayons. Positioned practically as a capstone to the pyramid of other items, was a hairbrush with strands of golden blonde hair intertwined in the bristles.

Motivated by something far from rational thought, Robbins took a first step toward the bureau. Like a man suddenly jerked from deep sleep, his movements were clumsy. In an uncharacteristically slumped posture – discounting his athleticism and making him feel much smaller than his five feet and eleven inches – Robbins stumbled to the bureau and picked up the brush. Lifting it to his nose, he inhaled deeply. Although faint, a scent still existed and it made David Robbins' knees buckle. After crumbling to the floor, Robbins curled into a ball and tucked the brush tightly against his chest. Once again, the tears began to stream.

* * *

David Robbins didn't move from his prone position until someone forcibly knocked on the door. After clearing his throat, he mumbled, "Just a second."

Robbins struggled to his feet and placed the hairbrush in the inner pocket of his suit coat. While wiping at his dark eyes with the back of his hand, he took a few more seconds to look around once again at the bedroom. Then, after a series of deep breaths, he managed a calm and clear, "Come in."

Lester Robbins came through the doorway and walked over to the nearest window. In doing so, he passed by David without as much as a word or glance.

"Hello, Dad," David Robbins said evenly.

With his back to his son, Lester Robbins pulled back the sheer curtain of the window and leaned forward to look down onto the expanse of manicured front lawn. "Someone egged the front of your house again last night and threw a bunch of garbage in your yard."

"Yes, I know," David sighed, as he ran a hand through his thick, black hair. "There were several more harassing phone calls last night, too."

Without turning around, his father just nodded his head and mumbled, "Yeah, well, you should expect as much…and then some."

The comment caused David to flinch, but it didn't surprise him. Lester Robbins had done little during the past three days to mask his new-found hostility toward David. This deep and sudden bitterness was very different from the emotions David normally invoked in his father. By far the most successful of Lester's four sons, David had become the vaunted pride of his father's life. Lester never missed opportunities to brag on David's thriving business or his elegant home in their town's most exclusive neighborhood. Although Lester Robbins cared little for church or church goers, he even verbally flaunted the fact that his son was an elder of the Highland Street Presbyterian Church. Now, however, David knew his father would never again have anything pleasant to say about his son's spiritual beliefs and practices. For the time being, David couldn't fault him for that.

"You know, Dad…" David managed before having to stop and clear his throat, "…you and I haven't had a chance to talk about…well…everything. Maybe if we could talk, we'd both…"

"We'd both what?" Lester Robbins interrupted as he spun to face his son. The look on the elder Robbins' face emphasized something volatile. "Feel better? I don't think so. Talking isn't going to stop this hurting. Talking isn't going to change a damn thing."

David Robbins dropped his head to avert his eyes. This was not the time and most definitely not the place for confrontation. After several seconds of strained silence, Lester walked past David but stopped in the doorway.

"I came up here to get you. It's about time to leave. Doctor Toliver gave Nancy another shot. She probably won't even know she's in a car, but Kevin says he won't ride with you. I told him he can ride with me."

In the life he lived before the past Friday, David reveled in his wife and fourteen-year-old son's love and respect. Now Nancy and Kevin detested him. So painful was the abhorrence shown by them, it seemed to more than compound the damage of the awful hurt that preceded it.

After David acknowledged his father's message with a nod of his head, Lester Robbins walked away. David lingered a moment longer and gave the bedroom a final once-over. With tears welling in his eyes, he reached up and gently touched the outline of the hairbrush in his pocket. Then he slunk away. It was time to bury his daughter.

* * *

Pottawatomie County District Attorney, Walter Spencer, leaned back in his high-backed leather chair and propped his cowboy boots on top of his massive oak desk.

"Come on in, Mike," Spencer said to the young man standing in the doorway.

"Thanks, Walter," Assistant D.A. Mike Pierce responded as he moved toward the two chairs situated in front of Spencer's desk.

"What can I do for you?" Walter Spencer asked with a weary smile. Mike Pierce was obnoxiously bullheaded and not very personable. But all in all, Spencer often reminded himself, Pierce was a damned good prosecutor. No matter what some might think, Spencer chose Pierce to be his number one assistant because of his abilities, and not because of his strong political ties. Although, when dealing with Pierce, Spencer could never afford to forget that the assistant's grandfather, a premier politician, stood only a phone call away.

"I figured you'd be going to Kayla Robbins' funeral in a little while," Pierce said as he settled into the chair on the right.

"You figured right, Mike. Why? You want to ride with me? Or, maybe, you want to chauffer me?"

"Oh, no, sir. I'm not going to the funeral."

It didn't surprise Spencer that the "chauffer" crack failed to tickle Pierce, but his response puzzled Spencer all same. "Seeing as how the Robbins family is so influential, not to mention how much publicity this death has received, I imagined the entire city of Shawnee would turn out for this funeral. Hell, half of the state of Oklahoma will probably show up. Why aren't you going?"

"Well, I don't know any of the family personally, and..." Pierce paused to take a deep breath, "...I wouldn't feel comfortable after asking what I'm prepared to ask."

Fighting off a sudden urge to rub his temples, Spencer exhaled, "What are you 'prepared' to irritate me with, Mike?"

Pierce shifted in his seat and leaned forward as if making sure no one else in the otherwise empty room would hear his next statement. "I want to bring David Robbins up on murder charges."

Spencer dropped his feet to the floor and moved his fingers to his temples. "You what?"

"Yes, sir," Pierce said more forcibly. "I want to prosecute David Robbins for murder."

Spencer shot up out of his chair and started to pace behind the desk that served every Pottawatomie D.A. since statehood. "Why would you possibly want to file charges against a man like David Robbins?"

"Quite simply, Walter, he committed a crime. The law has been broken."

Walter Spencer's arms flew into the air, and he wasted no effort on voice control. "Well of course. How damned stupid of me to forget who I'm talking with here! Ol' By-the-Book Mike Pierce! Shit, Mike, do you always have to play the role of a strict constructionist? Just this one unprecedented time, couldn't you put the spirit of the law over the letter of the law?"

Pierce stood up and leaned over the D.A.'s desk. "I've studied all the reports, Walter. I've talked to the detectives and every witness. I've been to the crime scene. For all practical intents and purposes, Walter, David Robbins killed his little daughter."

"That's the stupidest bunch of shit I've ever heard, Mike," Spencer growled. The D.A. would not coddle him. Never had. Even if his grandfather was Patrick Wayne Pierce. Still, Spencer always had to take that into consideration.

"Okay, Walter, he didn't pull the trigger of that .357 magnum," Pierce said, his voice rising uncontrollably, "but if he would have done what a reasonable, prudent person should, that little girl would be alive today."

"Can you, without a single goddamned doubt, prove that?" Spencer yelled, his booming voice rattled the old paint-chipped windows.

Mike Pierce calmly sat back down in his chair, adjusted the knot of his tie, and smiled, "I believe I can, and if I do, David Robbins will be found guilty of second-degree murder."

Spencer took a few moments to study the intelligent young attorney, and to recall some of the difficult cases Pierce prosecuted in the past, and won. Sitting back down, Spencer asked, "Have you considered the potential this has for ripping this city apart?"

The smile faded from Mike Pierce's face. Leaning forward in his chair, Pierce's voice softened. "I've done more than consider it, Walter…I've even prayed about it. I truly believe this is the right thing to do."

Spencer put his fingers back to work on his temples and nearly whispered, "What kind of case law do you have to support your position?"

After settling back in his chair and crossing his right ankle over his left knee, Pierce started with a smirk, "In 1999, in the hills of Pushmataha County, the pastor of the Apostolic Church of Christ's Disciples, Harold Cooksey, engaged in one of the beloved rituals of his denomination's worship services. Snake handling. Live, big ass, rattlesnake handling!

"During this particular Sunday night service, Cooksey emphasized what he called the 'believer's sign of salvation' with an added twist. After grabbing a snake and letting it writhe all over himself, he would hand it over to his nine-year-old son, Luke. The boy ended up with snakes wrapped around both arms, his neck, and a couple draped over his shoulders.

"Evidently all the shouting, singing and hand-clapping was too much for one of the big, nasty reptiles and it bit the boy. When Luke started screaming and jumping about, all the snakes started striking. He was bitten fourteen times before they could get all those damn rattlers off of him.

"After an hour's worth of praying and laying on of hands failed to produce a healing effect, the young boy was rushed to the nearest hospital. It was another hour away. Luke Cooksey died at noon the next day."

When Pierce paused, Spencer spoke up. "Did Cooksey offer a defense?"

"No. He took the fifth, and a jury sent him to prison. I think we can expect basically the same in a case against David Robbins."

"I think that's an awful big assumption. What else do you have?"

Mike Pierce pushed himself to his feet. "In 2009, in Garfield county..." Pierce said as he walked around behind the chair he had sat in, and leaned over to rest his elbows on its high back, "...Darvin Hensley was very drunk when his devout Mormon wife, Wanda, returned home from church with her four-year-old daughter from a previous marriage.

"Hensley deeply hated his wife's involvement in the church, and often harangued her about what he called her 'holier-than-thou attitude.' On this night his rantings and ravings turned to a tirade of how even Wanda Hensley, under the right circumstances, could commit the worst sin of all....murder. Saying he could prove it, Darvin walked into the bedroom and returned with a loaded revolver in each hand.

"He took one of the revolvers and removed all but one round from the cylinder. Darvin stuck this revolver in the waistband of his jeans and tossed the fully loaded pistol down at Wanda's feet. Then, for a second time, Darvin Hensley walked out of the room. When he returned he had his small step-daughter in his arms.

"Darvin spun the cylinder containing the one bullet and then stuck the gun to the little girl's head. The drunk bastard then told his wife she had to the count of ten to pick up the gun at her feet and use it to save her little girl. Wanda refused to pick up the gun. Darvin counted to ten and pulled the trigger. The chamber was empty.

"Darvin gave his wife another ten seconds to pick up the gun and use it on him. Again, Wanda couldn't do it. She screamed over and over about how she could not forsake the teachings of Christ. Darvin counted to ten again, pulled the trigger, and killed the four-year-old baby."

Walter Spencer leaned forward in his chair and started drumming his fingers on the desk top as he compared the two terrible cases to what he knew of David Robbins' plight. Before Spencer could comment, Pierce continued.

"Harold Cooksey and Wanda Hensley were both tried for second-degree murder. Both were convicted. In essence, the courts determined that the First Amendment right to freedom of religion does not nullify a parent's inherent duty to act in order to save a child from preventable death."

After plopping back into his chair, Pierce flashed a confident smile and asked, "Now, do you want to know how the courts ruled against seven cases involving Christian Scientists, who under the auspices of Christianity, failed to provide proper health care for their dying children?"

The D.A. inhaled deeply before saying sternly, "Bring me all the case citations and police reports, and set up appointments with the witnesses. I want to see them all this afternoon. I'm not going to promise anything, but I will consider it simply because both cases you cited were on point with the relevant fact and law at issue in Robbins' situation."

"Yes, sir. Thank you." Mike Pierce stood and started for the door. Just before exiting, he turned on his heels and said, "Oh, uh, Walter. I know you probably didn't know it, but I am uh, seriously, a praying man. I mean, I wasn't joking about praying about this."

Walter Spencer leaned forward, resting his elbows on his desk, and placed his hands finger tip to finger tip. After several seconds of contemplation, he responded, "I hope you are serious, Mike. Because if we do prosecute, I'm not really sure who will be our defendant…David Robbins…or Jesus Christ."

* * *

Jennifer Rhodes of Oklahoma City's KWTV Channel 9 News stepped in front of her cameraman, Josh Wadley. "I want you to be able to get the church and especially the hearse in the background, Josh. Just aim over my left shoulder if you can, and I want to start as they're loading the casket into the car."

Josh eyed the distance across the four-lane separating them from the church and then brought the camera to his eye to check the angles. "Move about a foot to your left. Okay. Good. I think it'll work," he remarked as he lowered the camera.

Taking care to stay in the same position, Jennifer turned around to face the Highland Street Presbyterian Church of Shawnee, Oklahoma.

"The service ought to be over in the next few minutes, and they'll be heading to the cemetery. Man, can you imagine what that David Robbins must be feeling right now?" she asked thoughtfully.

"Religious fanatics like him don't feel anything…" Josh said before switching to an impersonation of a television evangelist, "…expect for the love of ah Jeee Zusss!"

"You think he's a fanatic?" Jennifer asked.

"Hell yes. Don't you?"

"I don't know. Do you know Sherry Walker, the tall redhead who works in advertising?"

"No. I don't know her, but I think I know who you're talking about," Josh said as he made last minute level checks on Jennifer's microphone.

Jennifer turned back to face Josh. "When she found out I was assigned this story, she called me at home. She wanted me to know she went to college here at Oklahoma Baptist University, and she worked her way through school as a salesperson in Robbins' sporting goods store."

Josh looked from his camera to Jennifer. "Really?" He said, expressing a new-found enthusiasm for the conversation.

"Yes, really. Before I talked to her, I was kind of like you. I could just picture this Robbins guy standing on a street corner screaming scriptures at passing cars. Or, I thought he was, you know, one of those guys who's always talking about Jesus and trying to convert everyone."

"And he's not?" Josh asked with a skeptical arch of his eyebrows.

"Not according to Sherry, and I like how she put it. She said Robbins, and I quote, 'never talked about his religion. He just lived it.' She says he is the kindest, most caring person she ever met."

"It doesn't sound to me like the bastard was very kind and caring toward his little girl," Josh smirked.

Jennifer continued, "Sherry said something else that I really found intriguing. She said the way Robbins reacted, the choice he made, didn't really surprise her."

"Damn, she must be a flake too," Josh grumbled. "What he did…*or didn't do*… should surprise the hell out of any normal person."

"You would think so. The only explanation she could offer for not being surprised was that Robbins, and again I quote, 'just seems to walk a lot closer to God than most people.'"

"Yeah, well here they come. The service must be over. You know if what she says is true…" Josh said as he brought the camera to his eye, "…I just hope God doesn't have too many more nuts strolling around with him. Get ready, we're rolling in three, two, one…"

* * *

Walk away.

Don't walk away.

Everyone else had left the little girl's grave. David Robbins stood alone and contemplated the conflicting advice offered by his thoughts. The thoughts came from what he had long considered his two inner voices. Discord historically existed between his inner voices, but for the past three days, they embraced in bitter combat.

The child you loved so very much is not in that casket. She is in a much better place. Walk away, insisted the thought coming from what David accepted as his spiritual voice.

She is in there. You put her in there, David... countered the thoughts of what he identified as his carnal voice, ... *and when you walk away, they will put her in the ground.*

Robbins took a deep breath and brushed away the tears blurring his vision. Then he turned his head toward the funeral home's family car. His wife, Nancy, had been practically carried there several minutes earlier by her two brothers. Now, she and their son waited for him inside the car.

Your place is with those living on earth. Walk away. Go and be with your family.

Don't leave her, David. Don't turn your back on her... again.

He turned back to the small, silvery-pink casket. Bracing himself on one of the supports that held it suspended over the grave, Robbins bent over and kissed the top of the casket. Then he turned and walked away.

He followed the guidance of the spiritual voice. After all, the spiritual voice offered the only sensible alternative. The body of his daughter had to be buried.

But she didn't have to die. The other children didn't die.

In the deepest depths of David Robbins' soul, the battle raged on.

* * *

"I assume you had the conversation with Spencer," Pat Pierce said without looking up from his evening newspaper.

Mike Pierce took a chair next to his grandfather's recliner. He hadn't expected a warm greeting from the old man. It was just his way. Maybe, Mike considered, it was the way of all the truly powerful.

"Yes, sir."

"And?"

Still the eyes did not leave the paper. Newspapers kept Pat Pierce informed with not only what was happening in Oklahoma, but across the entire nation. The elderly statesman subscribed to and read nearly every word of seven papers each and every day.

"He's considering it."

A piercing gaze now fell on the grandson. "I expect him to do much more than that."

"I know, sir. I believe he will."

"This is the case that will give you the name recognition you need."

Mike nodded his understanding. And it was the case he wanted. No matter how unsavory some might consider his ambition, Mike Pierce intended to fight his way to the very top. To heights, he hoped, that would even eclipse the greatness of the man beside him. And there was more. David Robbins had been wrong. He deserved to pay. It was simply Mike Pierce's nature. When he believed something, he believed it with all his heart and soul. When he took on a cause, he took it on with a vengeance.

"Should I give him a call? Or, maybe, pay him a visit?" the old man asked sternly.

Mike had no qualms about using his grandfather's influence once he'd personally done all he could. He much preferred, however, making his own way and his own name. Again, simply part of his nature.

"No, sir. Not yet."

"Don't forget, Mike," the patriarch scowled, "I was not elected two terms as governor of this state and three as a U.S. senator by letting golden opportunities pass me by."

Mike Pierce would never forget.

* * *

D.A. Walter Spencer normally arrived home in time to watch the evening news. Not tonight. Twelve people witnessed the heinous murder of Kayla Robbins, and Spencer didn't finish the interviews Mike Pierce arranged until a few minutes after six p.m..

Knowing all three of Oklahoma City's major network stations dispatched crews to cover the funeral, Spencer turned on the television in his office and started flipping through the channels. Channel 4 was reporting on a three-alarm fire in downtown Oklahoma City, and Channel 5 was in the last few seconds of its update on the Robbins' story. Spencer turned to Channel 9 just before commercial break, and just in time to hear that they would return with their coverage of the funeral.

Assuming his favorite office position, he stretched back in his chair with his feet on his desk, and admired the taupe ostrich skin covering his boots. On the TV, a fast talking, good looking salesman tried to convince central Oklahoma his prices on new Fords couldn't be beat. While waiting for the commercials to end, the DA once again picked up and looked through the photographs taken at the crime scene. Once again, he cringed. When the news returned, Spencer tossed the photographs on his desk and turned his attention to the television.

The senior anchorman, a Dan Rather look-alike, stared out from the set with a saddened expression and said in a most somber voice, "Shocked citizens of Shawnee, Oklahoma, gathered today to say their good-byes to seven-year-old Kayla Robbins. Our Jennifer Rhodes was there and files this report."

"Although Shawnee is less than forty miles east of Oklahoma City," the pretty blonde began, "citizens here have long enjoyed a peaceful, small town atmosphere, free from big city crime statistics. That all changed last Friday night when little Kayla Robbins was slain in a bizarre shooting incident..."

Spencer glanced from the television set to the photos strewn across the top of his desk. His eyes fell on one in particular, showing a close up of what was once the sweet and angelic face of a very pretty child. As the reporter summarized the events of the past Friday night, the D.A. started back through the police reports Pierce provided. He wanted to peruse each and every document one more time. A decision he had made earlier – somewhere between his interview with the first and third witness – now needed to be reaffirmed.

The reaffirmation process was barely underway when Jennifer Rhodes finished reporting facts and started relaying public opinion. The elected official turned his attention back to the television reporter.

"Witnesses say David Robbins would not obey the demands because of his religious convictions. Although this city of 26,000 is home to both Oklahoma Baptist University and Saint Gregory College, it is believed David Robbins will find few, if any, advocates to condone his actions.

"Meanwhile," Jennifer said as the camera zoomed in for a close-up, "police have no further information on the identity or whereabouts of a suspect some might believe to indeed be the Devil incarnate...the man who shot little Kayla Robbins."

Jennifer Rhodes began wrapping up, and the District Attorney of Pottawatomie County bellowed, "Satan's roaming free and I'm going to prosecute a saint. It's a fucked-up world!"

Spencer solemnly nodded his head. He would allow the charge to be filed against David Robbins because of the public outcry, and because Mike Pierce's connections could impact Spencer's future political aspirations. And, lastly, he would give his approval because probable cause existed to do so.

* * *

David Robbins opened his eyes. It took him a second to realize he was in his study. Late in the afternoon he had slipped into the mahogany-paneled room to escape the tormenting stares and whispers of the family and friends supposedly there to provide comfort. Since that time, he somehow managed to fall asleep at his desk, enjoying the first real sleep he'd experienced since the night his daughter died. He didn't know how long he slept – daylight ruled when he sat down at his desk; now darkness stood its watch – but he felt thankful for the rest no matter how short or long, and he greatly appreciated sleeping, without dreaming horrid nightmares.

The house was quiet. All the mourners and supporters evidently left his home and returned to their own lives. It would be the first time since Kayla's death that he would be alone with just his wife and son.

The day Kayla died, David's wife had taken their son to a late afternoon orthodontist appointment in Oklahoma City. Afterwards, they stopped for dinner and mall-hopped until the stores closed. They didn't return home until a few minutes before ten. Kayla had been dead for almost two and a half hours. Prior to that, David chose not call her cell. What words could he have used over the phone? When they did arrive home, the pastor of their church, their family doctor, and David's father, Lester, stood by as David told them what had happened. Told them *exactly* what happened.

The pastor, Hershell Stewart, offered to deliver the dreadful news to Nancy. Lester Robbins suggested his son just give an abbreviated version, omitting David's "contribution" until after the initial shock subsided. David felt it his responsibility to tell his family precisely what happened, how it happened, and why it happened.

Sobbing, David started with the bottom line first. Their baby girl was dead. She had been murdered. Nancy fainted. Kevin screamed over and over that his father was lying. Doctor Marvin Toliver revived Nancy, and administered a sedative – the first of many. Through his tears, around his sobs, and over all the hysterics, David struggled through his story. By the time he finished, Nancy told him she hated him, and God would punish him. Kevin said he wished his father, not his sister, were dead. When David tried to embrace his son, Kevin struck him repeatedly in the face and chest.

The Robbins had barely spoken since. David Robbins didn't know how, but he had to reach out to his wife and son. He knew he could get through to both if they needed him just half as much as he needed them.

Robbins carefully made his way across the dark room and opened the door. A large entryway that housed a winding staircase separated the study from the living room. The entryway was dark, but a light shone from the living room. Robbins assumed Nancy or Kevin, or maybe both, were there. He made his way to the living room and was surprised to find his father pacing before the ornate fireplace.

"Hello, Dad," David said with a nod of his head. "I, uh, fell asleep in the study."

"Yeah, I know," Lester Robbins responded as he continued to pace. "I've been waiting for you to wake up."

Since first news of the death, the elder Robbins pulled no punches, but David now sensed the slightest touch of sympathy....and that worried him. Something else worried him, too. Something more tangible.

"Dad, everyone else has left. Why are you still here?"

Lester stopped in mid-stride and turned to face his son. "Nancy and Kevin went home to California with her parents. I stuck around to tell you that."

Lester Robbins walked past his son to the doorway of the living room. "I'm going now, David. I am sorry. But you know that you made this bed. Now you have to sleep in it."

He walked to the front door before stopping and looking back. "Oh, yeah, I almost forgot. Nancy and Kevin just want you to leave them be for a while. Maybe it won't be long." With a nod of his head, the father left his son's home.

David collapsed into the closest chair and dropped his head into his hands. Once again, the tears began to flow, and with great difficulty, he began to pray.

TWO

Mark Hogue pulled up between the oil well and the tank battery, killed his lights and turned off his ignition. The ancient Chevy truck sputtered, shook, and finally died. Only the crickets and the hum of the oil well's electric motor were left to assault the country quiet of the warm spring night. Brewing storm clouds hid the stars and a quarter moon, but reflected the distant lights of the Oklahoma City skyline and bathed the oil lease in a ghostly glow.

Twelve hours earlier, around ten in the morning, Mark received the phone call that now brought him here. He had been right in the middle of sleeping off a hangover and didn't appreciate the interference. He didn't care that his sorry older brother needed help, so at first, he refused to come. Then there had been the promise of money. Mark didn't like his brother, and he didn't like being alone out in the country at night. But Mark did like money. And he needed money. His ex-old lady threatened to have him thrown in jail if he didn't make good on some past child support payments. Mark wished the fat bitch would die of a heart attack.

Wonderful wishes of terrible ways his ex-wife could perish momentarily took Mark's mind off the lonely dark. A far-off howl brought him back, and he wondered if the noise came from a dog or a coyote. If it came from a coyote, would a coyote attack a lone man? Probably not, unless it had rabies. And, if a scrawny Oklahoma coyote with rabies would attack a lone man, what if the howl came from a not-so scrawny rabid Doberman, or worse yet, a fat, rabid Rottweiler?

The warm spring night suddenly turned too chilly for Mark. Stretching almost prone across the tattered bench seat, he grasped the passenger window crank and cranked like mad. Raising back up, he turned to his door, and into the lolling face that protruded through the open window. With a loud and high-pitched scream, Mark Hogue fell over in the seat and threw his hands up in front of his face for protection. The intruder exhaled a single, weary word.

"Boo."

"Goddamn you, Luke!" Mark screeched at his older brother. "That shit ain't funny!"

Luke Hogue reached in the window, grabbed the collar of Mark's shirt, and jerked him upright in the seat. "You're such a pussy," he said with a shake of his head.

"No I ain't, Luke. I just don't like the dark…" Mark protested with a shiver, "…and you know why."

Luke pulled his head out of the window and slowly scanned to the left and right, as if looking for someone. "Yeah, Mark," he finally mumbled. "I remember." Then he looked back to his brother and ordered, "Move over."

Mark scooted across the seat to the passenger side as Luke jerked open the door. The sudden illumination of the exposed bulb in the dome light had the blinding effect of a flash cube. With his eyes closed and covered by his hands, Mark groaned, "Are we going someplace, Luke?"

"Naw, man. I just wanna rest. I walked a good ways to get here."

Mark heard Luke grunt as he pulled himself into the cab, and he felt his weight hit the seat beside him. Seconds later Mark opened his eyes to find his brother draped across the steering wheel. Luke had left the door open, and Mark was shocked by what the light revealed. "Damn, Luke, you look like shit!"

Sunken, hollow eyes stared listlessly from a pale, thin face as Luke mumbled, "Yeah, Mark. I feel like shit, too. I need your help, man."

Mark thought of the money. "What kind of help, Luke?"

"I need a fix, Mark. I need you to make a buy for me."

"Oh, man," Mark whined. Dope scared him. People who did dope scared him. And people who sold dope really scared him. Why couldn't everyone just be alcoholics? "I don't wanna buy no dope, Luke."

The older brother reached into a back pocket of his soiled and tattered jeans and pulled out a wad of bills. He tossed the money on the seat between them. "There is two hundred bucks there. Get me three or four rocks of crack. You can have what's left of the money. Should be a little over a hundred bucks. When you bring me the shit, I'll give you another hundred."

Drawing on his experience with brotherly love, Mark grunted, "Oh, yeah? Where's the rest of the money?"

Luke rose up in the seat and thrust his left hand deep into his front left pocket. He produced another wad of bills that he tossed into Mark's lap. Mark snatched it up and counted twenty-eight hundred dollars mostly in hundred-dollar bills. Reluctantly, he handed the money back to Luke.

Mark knew when Luke called on the phone to expect trouble. That fact didn't even deserve thought or conversation because Luke Hogue was always in trouble. Besides, why else would he want Mark to meet him at ten o'clock at night in the middle of nowhere? Mark figured the two-bit thief was on the lamb for some small-time larceny or burglary. But two thousand, eight hundred dollars was a lot of cash for a two-bit thief.

"Damn, Luke," he said jokingly, "what did you do, hold up a bank?"

Obviously failing to see the humor, Luke closed his eyes and moaned, "I'm in big, big trouble, Mark. I'm really scared, man. I really need that goddamn dope."

Luke normally bragged about his escapades, and Mark could never remember him admitting fear about anything. Luke had piqued Mark's curiosity. "What'd you do, Luke?"

Luke opened his eyes and stared at Mark for a second before blurting, "Do you know about the little girl getting shot in Shawnee?"

Of course Mark knew about the shooting. Hell, everyone knew about the shooting. For the past three days it had been one of the main topics discussed in the bars Mark frequented. Just like everyone else, Mark questioned how any man could have executed that child in cold blood. And just like everyone else, he questioned *why?*

"Yeah, Luke, I fuckin' know about it." Mark felt his throat starting to tighten. "Why you askin'?"

"Goddamnit," Luke moaned as he reached into the small of his back and pulled a large revolver from the waistband of his jeans. "This is the fucking gun that blew her away, man!"

In a near daze, Mark looked away from the gaunt and pathetic creature that shared his up-bringing. Lightning was starting to stab at the eastern skies with wicked fingers. Shawnee sat to the east. Mark watched the skies for the next bolt of lighting, and mumbled, "Makes sense that it would be you, man. That sort of thing has gotta happen when Luke Hogue mixes crack and church people."

Luke Hogue dropped his chin to his chest and covered his face in his hands. "I wasn't that fucked-up, man," he moaned. "But I need to be now. Buy the dope for me, Luke. I wanna forget for awhile."

* * *

Tuesday morning proved to be a very productive one for Assistant District Attorney Mike Pierce. He started the morning by planting himself in his boss's outer office. When Walter Spencer walked in at straight up eight, Pierce quickly got the "go ahead" on the Robbins case. Knowing Spencer as well as he did, Pierce anticipated as much and had already prepared an affidavit of probable cause and the accompanying arrest warrant. Ten minutes later, he handed the affidavit to Special Judge Stewart Hackney.

Hackney was ancient. He had sat on the bench as the Pottawatomie Special Judge for forty years; five years longer than Pierce had been alive. Many attorneys, including the young Assistant D.A., considered a special judgeship as a stepping-stone to bigger and better robes. Hackney considered it home – his station in life. Pierce could not understand the man's apathy toward upper mobility. But today, Pierce felt good about Hackney just being Hackney. A more politically-motivated judge might find it difficult to issue an arrest warrant for such a wealthy and influential citizen as David Robbins regardless of whose grandson Mike Pierce happened to be.

As Pierce hoped, the old judge squinted at the affidavit for a minute or two and then signed the warrant deeming probable cause to arrest Robbins. Probable cause meaning, as Pierce hoped to one day point out to jurors, that it was more likely than not David Robbins' actions resulted in the death of Kayla Robbins.

* * *

Whoever kept ringing Larry Phelps' doorbell just would not give up. So, he gave in and struggled out of bed. Although it was ten in the morning, Phelps had only been in the bed for a couple of hours. He spent the entire night parked down the road from and watching the house of one Mrs. JoAnn Whitby. Hours upon hours he had sat and hoped that her son, Wally Whitby, would show up – like the cops in Oklahoma City said he would. But Wally Whitby, wanted for a string of burglaries in Oklahoma City, didn't pay a visit to his mama's house in Shawnee. And Larry Phelps, a Shawnee police detective, did not get to bust him. So, it had been a wasted night. A long, boring, wasted night. A night that put Detective Phelps in a very foul mood.

The couple of hours of sleep did nothing to change his state of mind, and the idiot whose finger was obviously stuck to the button of Phelps' doorbell wasn't helping either.

"Hey!" Phelps bellowed as he stumbled about trying to work one leg and then the other into a pair of jeans. "Give your finger a rest, asshole!"

But the obnoxious "ding-dong" continued – incessantly. Phelps, stilly clumsy with sleep, made his way as quickly as possible from his bedroom to the living room, forming choice words for his visitor as he went. When he finally made it to the door, he almost jerked it off its hinges.

Phelps had hoped for a salesman, or a campaigning politician, or a pair of those religious boys who wore ties and rode bicycles. Phelps hoped for someone he could really tear into and verbally annihilate for disturbing his much-needed sleep. Instead, he got a grinning Bobby Mann.

Phelps turned from the door without saying a word, shuffled to the nearby couch, and collapsed on it. Detective Bobby Mann stepped into the small apartment, pulled the door shut, and moved to a chair across from the couch.

"Did I wake you?" Mann quipped.

Phelps showed Mann the middle finger of his right hand and mumbled, "What do you want, Bobby?"

"I want you to go serve a warrant with me."

"I don't want to serve a warrant," Phelps yawned. "Get Ragsdale or Barcus to go with you." The Shawnee Police Department had four detectives, and he knew damn good and well that the other two were on duty with Mann.

"All of us are going," Mann said matter-of-factly.

Phelps set up in the chair and vigorously rubbed his eyes clear. "All of us are going?" he repeated. When all four of the department's detectives served a warrant, it had to be a really big case. It had to be *the* really big case. "We have a suspect in the Robbins homicide?" Phelps gasped.

Mann retrieved the warrant from an inside coat pocket and tossed it in Phelps' lap. "Well, I guess you could say that," he grinned.

No longer upset about being awakened, Phelps broke into a smile as he unfolded the warrant. When he read the name and the charges, his mind took him back to the past Friday night and the large building that sat behind the Highland Street Presbyterian Church. The smile disappeared.

* * *

The congregation called the building Fellowship Hall, the place where they gathered for socials, banquets, and their weekly, Friday evening covered-dish dinner. That Friday night was the first time Larry Phelps had ever been in the building. And he didn't care to ever go in it again.

All four of the Shawnee detectives normally worked the day shift, with each of the four being on-call for one week each month. The on-call detective would work his normal shift, and then work any call where a detective was needed between the hours of five P.M. and eight A.M. Phelps had been the detective on-call the night Kayla Robbins died.

When Phelps' cell phone started ringing at 7:50 P.M. on April the fourteenth, and displayed the police dispatch number as the calling party, Phelps cursed the phone and the caller. It was his next to the last night to be on-call, the first call he had received for the week, and the only night he had made plans. To make matters worse, his plans revolved around a first date with a very hot emergency room nurse. In fear of losing the opportunity to fulfill a fantasy or two, Phelps had angrily jabbed the answer button on the iPhone, preparing to administer a blustering tirade of "This better be good," to the calling dispatcher.

"You best hope this is a damned emergency," is how he answered the call.

"Detective Phelps?"

The tense, almost electrifying way the female dispatcher said only two simple words, convinced Phelps this was not going to be one of those many times a detective was called when a detective wasn't really needed. When the dispatcher immediately put a highly agitated supervisor on the line, Phelps knew he was right.

"A hysterical woman called about ten minutes ago. She just kept screaming for us to send an officer to Highland Street Presbyterian Church," the supervisor paused to catch his breath. "Ken Floyd arrived there a few minutes ago and got on the air and screamed for ambulances and detectives. We haven't been able to get the sonofa-bitch back on the air, and we're trying to reach him by phone now."

Phelps knew the seasoned patrol officer Ken Floyd wasn't the easily excitable type. Something terrible had happened at the Presby-terian Church. "I'll be in the car and on the air in two minutes," Phelps remembered saying.

Phelps pushed the unmarked detective cruiser to speeds that of-fended his survival instinct. He learned from the police radio that an-other patrol officer had arrived on the scene, and other units and at least two ambulances were also en route. The sound of distant sirens confirmed the radio transmissions.

Phelps was two blocks away when the second officer on the sce-ne, Bud Logan, blared across the air that shots had been fired, and at least two people were down. Logan, another level-headed officer, dis-played absolutely no composure over the air. The detective did not fault Floyd or Logan for being excited. A shooting in Shawnee, Okla-homa was a rare thing. In Shawnee, in the very heart of Oklahoma, people being shot while attending church was totally unthinkable. Wherein Phelps could excuse the excitement, the confusion pissed him off. Floyd screamed for detectives and ambulances – without tell-ing why they were needed. Bud Logan was not even sure how many people had been shot. Phelps could not understand the apparent cha-os – until he walked into the Fellowship Hall.

The building's front double doors opened into a very large room resembling a high-school gymnasium. The only things missing were the bleachers and highly polished hardwood floor. Two retractable basketball goals were suspended from the ceiling. One was located just inside the front doors. The other dangled in front of a small stage at the opposite end of the building. A gray indoor-outdoor carpet served to make the room more acceptable for socials and banquets while providing an adequate surface on which to dribble balls. Several doors opened off the large room. Phelps learned later that they led to classrooms, office space, restrooms, and a kitchen.

Looking back, Larry Phelps would use one word to sum up that Friday evening – overwhelming. When he first burst through those double doors, he was immediately inundated with the crying. He would later learn there were only fifteen people in the building when he arrived. He would swear there were at least twice that many – and all of them crying. The doors lining the walls of the large room seemed to be constantly opening and shutting with people coming and going. It took Phelps a while to realize it was the same people coming and going – going in one door and moments later coming out another door. They seemed to be people who just had to be on the move. People who could not stop crying.

A few merely wept. The others were more demonstrative. One woman wrung her hands and screamed at the top of her lungs. Another woman would burst from a door, pulling at her hair, and would trot to the opposite side and disappear through another door, all the while crying so hard she could barely catch her breath. A man who looked to be in his early to mid sixties, wearing Bermuda shorts and a polo shirt, frantically paced while hugging himself, and shaking his head, and shouting "Oh dear God," over and over and over. He seemed oblivious to a very nasty gash on the left side of his head.

Like this man, most of those crying shared another unusual characteristic – they were bloody. Some had blood just on their hands, or smeared on their faces. A few were coated, and they seemed to be crying the loudest. Larry Phelps soon understood why Officer Bud Logan had not been sure how many had been shot. Those covered in blood seemed to be in great, unbearable pain.

All the blood, all the crying, all the anguish, stopped Phelps in his tracks. He had no idea how long he stood in awe of the aftermath before spotting what had obviously been the nucleus of the storm. Strewn about the center of the room were a number of folding tables and chairs. Only a few of the tables and chairs were still in their upright positions. Paper plates and cups were scattered across the tabletops and on the floor. The most frantic of the frantic were huddled in the midst of the scattered furniture and debris, and among their numbers was Patrolman Ken Floyd. He and two of the civilians were kneeling. What they knelt before was obstructed from Phelps' view by one of the overturned tables.

Phelps hurried up to the huddle, and at first his mind could not make sense of the picture his eyes provided. Lying motionless and face down on the floor was an adult male. A small, bloodstained hand protruded from beneath the man's torso. It looked as if one corpse was lying on top of another, but Ken Floyd was gently patting the man on the shoulder – something police officers seldom do to a corpse. Phelps walked up just in time to hear Floyd blurt out, "I wish the hell that ambulance would get here!"

The detective concluded that the man was seriously injured. Just as he was about to inquire about the man's condition, and the condition of the small person beneath him, and about the condition of the entire, numbing, helter-skelter mess, someone grabbed him by the arm.

"The son of a bitch killed a little girl!" the someone nearly screamed in Phelps' ear.

Phelps turned to find Bud Logan hanging on to him. When they made eye contact, Logan released his grip.

"I can't believe this shit, Larry," Logan said with the dazed look of a shell-shocked soldier. "He shot her point blank, man. There's powder burns all over her little face and hands. I can't believe the son of a bitch would blow away a child point fucking blank. For Christ's sake, Larry, she's just a baby!"

Logan broke eye contact to look down at the little hand. Phelps followed his lead, and suddenly realized that the man was not simply lying on top of the child, he was covering her. Protecting her. In vain.

"Her father?" Phelps asked.

"Yeah," Logan grunted.

"How bad is he hurt?"

"He's not. Not physically. But we're afraid he may be in some type of shock. Maybe paramedics can help him."

Phelps, too, fathered a little girl. His nine-year-old Pamela lived with her mother in Dallas. He could very well imagine what the man was feeling. As a father, Phelps wanted to leave the man alone to hold his child and work through his pain. As a cop, he knew he was in charge of what would no doubt be the most notorious crime scene in the history of Shawnee, Oklahoma, and the crime scene had to be protected at all costs.

Phelps placed a hand gently on Logan's shoulder. "Get him off of her, Bud."

"He's liable to go crazy on us, Larry," Logan said with a weary shake of his head.

"Probably so," Phelps agreed.

But he didn't. When the uniformed officers, one on each side of him, reached down and carefully took him by the arms, he let them assist him to his feet without resistance. When they were sure the man could stand on his own, Logan and Floyd let go of his arms.

The bereaved father stood with his back to Phelps. By the position of his lowered head, the detective could tell he was staring at the mangled form at his feet. "Take him out of here," Phelps said to Ken

Floyd. "Make him comfortable in one of these side rooms." Then he turned to Bud Logan, "How many more are injured?"

"None," Logan said, "When I first got here, I thought there were several hurt because of all the…" Logan stopped in mid sentence. The way he grimaced and nodded toward the father, who Floyd had managed to move only a few feet away, conveyed to Phelps that he had stopped for the man's sake. He just didn't stop in time.

Phelps, looking towards Logan, did not know that the man had stopped and turned around until the man finished Logan's sentence.

"All the blood," the man said with a voice choked with emotion.

Phelps turned to face the man, and his knees practically buckled beneath him. "David?" was all the detective could immediately offer.

"All this blood, Larry," David Robbins struggled, "comes from just one little girl. My little girl."

Robbins' eyes moved from Phelps back to the spot on the floor from where he had been removed. Detective Larry Phelps did not follow his gaze. He could not, for several minutes look at the child who had called him "Uncle Larry."

* * *

Upon his mental return to the here and now, Phelps handed the warrant back to Detective Bobby Mann, and asked, "Did you initiate this?"

"No. I wish I could take credit for it, but I can't. This is Mike Pierce's doings."

"This is bullshit," Phelps responded.

Noticeably taken back by the comment, Mann huffed, "What's your goddamned problem?"

Pushing himself off the couch, Phelps walked to a nearby table and retrieved a pack of cigarettes. Only after lighting up an inhaling deeply did he respond, "David Robbins doesn't deserve this."

"You know Robbins personally?" Mann asked.

On the night of the shooting, Bobby Mann arrived at the Fellowship Hall only minutes after Phelps. After Phelps passed on what little information he had obtained, he took Mann aside and asked him to take over the responsibility as the primary investigator. Instead of providing the real reasons for the request, Phelps explained that he had the next two days off and intended to be out of town. Being the primary investigator would ensure him having to work right through his two days off. Mann jumped at the opportunity to head up the biggest investigation in the city's history and never questioned Phelps' motive for giving up such a golden opportunity.

Following two more deep hits off the cigarette, Phelps replied, "Yeah, I know him, and I knew Kayla Robbins, too. That's the real reason I asked you to take over the investigation."

"How well do you know the them?"

"Very well. His wife and my ex-wife are sisters."

"Damn," Mann responded with a sympathetic shake of his head. "That's bad. Sorry to hear it. So, I guess you won't want to go with us to make the arrest."

"No, I don't want to go. But I'm going. David will probably feel better with me being there." Then Phelps posed a question not to his friend Bobby Mann, but to senior detective Bobby Mann, the ranking officer who would be in charge of the arrest. "I don't guess you'd consider letting me go alone would you?"

"You know I can't do that, Larry," Mann groaned. "This is high-profile shit, man. We need to follow the book, and the book says that felony warrants will be served by no fewer than two officers."

"Damn, Bobby, David Robbins doesn't deserve to be treated like a common criminal. He didn't do anything criminally wrong."

"Yeah," Mann said with a smirk. "Tell that to his daughter."

37

THREE

David Robbins stood more than twenty yards from the trunk of the stately oak. Yet, high above his head, thick and twisted branches stretched well beyond where he stood. A gentle wind rustled thousands of brilliantly green leaves, which joined a league of vivacious katydids to produce the familiar sounds of country spring mornings.

Today, the tree offered refuge from the bright sunlight. In more violent spring and early summer weather, it would provide some shelter from pounding rains. In the winter, although bare, its impressive girth would serve to block portions of the piercing northern winds. Throughout the year, no matter what the weather, the ancient giant would stand as a reminder of life eternal and bring a comforting presence to an otherwise lonely place.

It was the tree that had sold David and Nancy Robbins on the small piece of land two years earlier. Since that time, they had both experienced some peace of mind just knowing they would someday retire to what they considered the prettiest plot in the Memorial Park Cemetery. Neither ever imagined the canopy of branches and leaves would one day crown a grave barely four feet long.

On this late morning hour after the day of interment, the lifeless hue of the freshly turned dirt seemed to mock the lively colors of the flowers adorning the small mound. No headstone was in place. It would be another week before it was completed. For now, the grave was marked by an eight-by-five placard that proclaimed only three words – Kayla Marie Robbins. The fact that the placard had so little to say contradicted and reinforced in David Robbins the reason he had come here. He had a lot to say.

During the three days of the burial process, Nancy had taken opportunities that David had not – that David could not. On that terrible Friday night, immediately after David explained to Nancy what had happened, she insisted on being taken to the body of her child. Since the remains were in the custody of the state medical examiner's office – undergoing a procedure that bereaved parents often consider an abomination – Nancy's demands were not met. But the moment the funeral director notified friends and family at the Robbins' house that Kayla had been "prepared for viewing," Nancy was rushed to the funeral home. In a room done in soothing earth tones with a few paintings of tranquil mountain scenery, Nancy leaned into the small casket and caressed the remains of her daughter for hours. In those hours, she said her good-byes.

David never went to the funeral home. Practically obliterating everything else in his mind were vivid, living-color impressions of his last look at Kayla. He wanted very much to replace the horrifying memories with more pleasant visions of his daughter, and he felt certain that seeing her in just a different, more dressed-up and cleaned-up version of being dead would not fill the bill. So, while Nancy loved on a limp form and whispered to a lifeless face, David looked for hours at dozens of photographs of a happy and beautiful little girl. As he studied the photos, often through blinding tears, he thought to himself the words he wanted to say to Kayla. His good-byes.

Until sometime in the middle of the lonely night before, that means of communicating his feelings had seemed sufficient. However, as he spent the entire night pacing through the large and excruciatingly empty home, hurting about all he had to hurt about, and obsessing over all he had to obsess over, he developed a great need to verbalize the many thoughts and emotions that were tormenting him. Had he a choice, he would have purged his soul to his wife. Since that was not possible, and since it all dealt with things not put to rest, things not said good-bye to, David decided to take his words to Kayla's grave. Of course, he realized, as his spiritual voice had been quick to point out, that if Kayla's soul could in fact hear his words, she wouldn't hear them from her body's place in the ground. David just felt that directing his words to the place her body rested just might make him feel a little better. It might just make him feel a little closer to the daughter be loved with all his heart and soul.

What David had to say was going to take a while. He lowered himself into a sitting position beside Kayla's grave. No sooner had he done so, he noticed an elderly couple walking in his direction. Until they were past him and out of sight, David would remain quiet. The words he had were for Kayla only.

* * *

"Stay away from me you mean bastard! I swear to God, I'll shoot you if you don't stay away from me!" Luke Hogue tried to steady the .357 magnum on the stern man in the black pants and white shirt, but the barrel of the gun danced to the frantic beat of Luke's heart.

"You're in big trouble, boy," the all too familiar voice growled.

"I know," Luke responded weakly.

"You're going to the hole, boy. But first I'm going to boot your ass real good," the man said through a sadistic smile.

Looking down, Luke observed in horror that the man had on his black cowboy boots, the boots with the toes as pointed and sharp as a pick axe. The toes were used to "boot" knees, thighs, buttocks, groins, or any other available body parts of those in need of disciplining.

"You ain't never going to kick on me and throw me in that fuckin' cellar again!" Luke screamed as he jerked the revolver's trigger three times in quick succession.

The gun's violent recoil and the thundering noise brought Luke back to his diminished senses, and he realized he had just wasted three bullets on thin air. The awful creature from his past had been no more than a withdrawal-induced hallucination. The gravelly voice, the coal black, greasy hair, the trademark white shirt, the black pants and the terror-inspiring boots had all come from the darkest recesses of Luke's memory.

After several fumbling attempts, Luke managed to secure the revolver into the crusty waistband of his jeans. He then collapsed to his hands and knees and crawled like a wounded animal into the dense thicket of underbrush he had called home for the past two days. Barely making it just the few feet to the spot he had trampled down and padded with leaves, Luke crumbled to the ground. He pulled his knees into his chest in an effort to ward off the slashing jolts of pain that tore at his guts. He didn't remember doing so, but an acrid stench suggested that he had soiled his den with vomit or shit, or maybe both. In addition to the cramps and nausea, a scorching fever had assaulted his body since the early morning hours, and it showed no signs of calling off the attack.

Lying in his nest of smelly and sticky leaves crawling with ants and spiders, Luke closed his eyes and tried to rest. At midnight he would have to walk the two miles back to the oil field to meet his brother, Mark, a second time. In his present state it would be a bitch getting there, but it would be worth it because Mark would have the panacea for all his ills. All he had to do – he tried hard to convince himself – was wait a few hours, walk a few miles, get a fix, and get right.

Sweet, sweet crack. It would chase away the pain and sickness and extinguish the fire. Better yet, it would send the son of a bitch with the pointed boots back to where he'd been for the past fifteen years. Sweet crack cocaine would send "Reverend Richard Lee" back to hell. And there could be no better place for the man who sired Luke Hogue.

* * *

The elderly couple, both with white hair and an unsteady gait, paused for only minutes at a grave site a couple of rows away from Kayla's. Neither said a word, and neither let go of the other's hand. David Robbins sensed that, like him, they belonged to the highly unfortunate fraternity of parents who had outlived a child. The fact that he might be in the presence of others who knew the pain of life's most terrible loss brought absolutely no consolation to David. Instead, it added to his crippling depression. It seemed the man and woman were performing a daily ritual, and the tombstone over the grave they visited looked to be decades old.

David waited until the pair hobbled out of sight before clearing his throat and calling to his daughter.

"Kayla?" His voice cracked over the single word, and he swallowed hard. He felt a need to say what he had to say in clear and concise terms, without breaking down. It took a minute or two before he could speak again.

"Kayla…I know you are now in a wonderful place, and you have a complete understanding of all things. That's the only two things I can find any joy in…"

Pulling out his handkerchief, David paused to dab at his eyes and blow his nose. "…because I know that for the last few minutes you were here you were so terribly, terribly frightened. And I know you didn't…couldn't…understand why I would not do what that man told me to do. Your last words…your cries…"

David dropped his head and emitted two breathtaking sobs before saying through gritted teeth, "…are burned into my mind, and still ring in my ears."

After a few deep breaths to help regain his composure, David continued. "Now you understand everything. Most of all you understand that I don't understand. I don't understand what God is doing. I did what I thought He wanted me to do. I did what I thought the Bible teaches us to do. I don't understand why I can't hold you in my lap anymore, why I can't hear your laughter and see your beautiful face anymore, and why I can't watch you grow up. I don't understand why God let that man kill you."

David didn't even try to blink back the tears welling in his eyes or attempt to calm his rising voice. "I want that man found. I want him arrested. I want him punished, and I don't understand why God is letting him run free. I don't understand why God let your mother and brother leave me. If this is all coming from a loving God, I just don't understand why. I don't under…"

David caught movement out of the corner of his eye. Looking up, he saw four men in jackets and ties walking toward him. Although they were a good distance away, he recognized detectives Larry Phelps and Bobby Mann, but not the others. Coming to his feet, David looked down upon the small portion of earth he held sacred and felt something he hadn't felt in days… a glimmer of hope. The detectives could only be bringing news of the man responsible for the mounded dirt at his feet.

* * *

"Hey, hold up a second, guys," Larry Phelps said as the group of detectives came within half a football field of David Robbins. All did so without questioning why.

"I got a question for you, Mister Follow-the-Book," Phelps, still a little piqued with his good friend Bobby Mann, said with a grimace.

"Yeah? Well, what is it, smart ass?" Mann shot back.

"You think if you guys stayed right here and let me go the rest the way alone, that it could be construed that you were present during the felony arrest?"

"Sounds good to me," Mike Ragsdale grumbled.

"Me too," Stanton Barcus added. "I don't want to arrest the poor son of a bitch while he's standing over his daughter's grave."

"Well?" Phelps grunted at Mann. "It's your case. Your call. I mean, hell you're close enough to see what's going on. You know, you're close enough," Phelps said with a smirk, "to be of help if he like…goes for his gun."

"Okay, Okay," Mann said with his palms in the air. "Go alone. I don't give a shit." He then dug the warrant out of an inside coat pocket and handed it over to Phelps.

"Thanks," Phelps nodded to Ragsdale and Barcus. Then deadpanned to Mann, "Cover me Bobby, I'm going in."

Leaving Ragsdale and Barcus chuckling and Mann calling him ugly names, Phelps started for Robbins and wished with all his heart that he didn't have to. If he ever dreaded anything as much as he now dreaded what had to be done, he damn sure couldn't remember it. A couple of years back, Phelps had to arrest a man for shooting another man for raping the former's wife. That had been tough, but it didn't start to compare to this. Phelps and Robbins hadn't just been brothers-in-law; they had been friends.

Phelps always felt that every cop should have a friend like David Robbins. That way, when they started thinking – as cops often do – that the world was made up of nothing but demons and fiends, they could go visit their friend and remember that, although few and far between, an occasional saint could still be found. David Robbins served as the patron saint of Phelps' psyche for the past ten years.

Although the last thing in the world Phelps wanted to do was arrest Robbins, he still had to admit that as a police detective, as a father, and as someone who had adored Kayla Robbins, he wished his friend would have made a different choice the night Kayla was murdered. However, no matter what he himself wished, Phelps did not feel qualified to point a finger at David Robbins and accuse him of doing wrong that horrible night. Phelps considered the decisions Robbins made as moral and spiritual decisions, and Phelps didn't know any jury of humans worthy of judging the heart and soul of David Robbins.

Phelps didn't think he could feel any worse than he already did, not until he got close enough to see Robins wiping at bloodshot, moist eyes. When only feet separated them, Phelps extended his right hand, and Robbins took it.

"I'm sorry to bother you here, David," Phelps said as the two men shook hands.

"How did you know I was here?" Robbins asked after clearing his throat.

"Just a guess. We already went to your home and business."

"You must have some really big news, since you've been looking that hard to find me," Robbins remarked, suddenly sounding more enthusiastic about the intrusion.

"News?" Phelps repeated. Then it occurred to him. Robbins thought they came with information about the shooter. Dropping his head to stare at the ground, Larry Phelps wished he was someone else doing something different in a place hundreds of miles away from Shawnee, Oklahoma.

* * *

David Robbins could tell by the expression on his old friend's face that there were no new developments in the efforts to identify and locate the man who caused all this misery. That could only mean one thing. Phelps and his comrades were there to ask more questions or quite possibly to ask again the same questions they had already asked repeatedly. How old was the man? How tall was he, and how much did he weigh? What was he wearing? What was the color of his hair and did he have any on his face? Did he have an accent? What, exactly, did he say? Detective Bobby Mann had asked dozens of questions, and Robbins – wanting the man apprehended – did his best to give the most accurate and detailed answers. As a matter of fact, he was asked so many questions and gave such good responses that he could not possibly think of anything that could have been missed and could not imagine anything that needed to be rehashed. Besides, for the moment, he just wanted to be left alone with his daughter.

"Larry, I don't want to be rude, because I really appreciate the effort you guys are making, but I really just don't feel like answering any more questions right now."

Phelps responded by screwing his face into a look of pain and exhaling a long, slow breath loudly through his mouth.

Robbins didn't understand the response, but it made him feel very uncomfortable. "You're not here to ask questions?"

Phelps reached inside his jacket and pulled out a tri-folded piece of paper. "I don't agree with this, and I don't like it, David," Phelps frowned as he handed the paper to Robbins, "but this is a warrant for your arrest."

As if he'd suddenly lost the use of them, Robbins' hand and arm that held the warrant dropped lifelessly to his side. The folded piece of paper fluttered to the ground and landed open and business side up on top of Kayla's grave. "You're here to arrest me?" he barely managed. "For what?"

Phelps knelt and gently lifted the warrant from the grave. He nearly whispered, "Second degree murder, David. The District Attorney is holding you responsible for Kayla's death."

Robbins felt as if the breath had been knocked out of him, and he struggled to stand on wobbly legs. Holding his head back and looking up at the network of branches high above him, he gasped for air and fought to hold back threatening tears.

Phelps cleared his throat and said, "David, tell me where I can find Nancy. I'll go break it to her in person, so it doesn't have to be done over the phone. I'll bring her to the jail to be with you while bond is being posted."

Robbins looked Phelps in the eyes and said, "She's in California, Larry. She took Kevin and left me."

"God, David," Phelps said in a small, helpless voice. "I'm so sorry."

Robbins dropped his eyes to the grassless mound, the flowers and the inadequate marker. "Me, too."

* * *

Phelps and Mann were in the process of booking Robbins into the Pottawatomie County jail when one of the jailers called out, "Got a call transferred from city PD for one of you two."

Phelps was quick to respond, "I'll get it." Before walking away, he patted David on the shoulder and assured him he'd be right back.

Walking into the small and cluttered office the jailors called home, Phelps picked up the receiver and mumbled, "Detective Phelps."

"You the cop in charge of finding who murdered that little girl?"

"I'm one of the detectives working the case," Phelps responded. "Who are you?"

"Don't matter who I am. Not right now, anyhow. All you need to know is that I know who killed that little girl."

The caller seemed very nervous, and he held Phelps' full attention. "How do you know who killed her?"

"I'll ask the questions right now. If you start askin' questions, I'll hang up."

"Okay. Fair enough," Phelps said, fighting to keep his voice calm. "You ask the questions, and I'll answer them."

The caller paused for so long that Phelps feared he had lost him. Finally, the voice asked, "Is there a reward for the murderer?"

Now, it was Phelps' turn to pause. There was no reward that he was aware of, but that wasn't what he wanted to tell this guy. "Hey listen, man. I think there is going to be a reward, but right now, I don't know how much it's going to be. You give me a number where I can reach you, and I'll find out and call you right back."

"You think I'm some kind of fuckin' idiot?" the caller bellowed.

"No. I don't think you're an idiot. Have you done something wrong?" Phelps calmly asked.

"Hell no. I ain't done shit wrong."

"Then what are you worrying about? Hell, man, we're going to have to see you and talk to you sooner or later if you want the reward. We aren't going to send the money in the goddamn mail."

Another pause and then, "I want ten thousand. If it ain't ten thousand, it ain't enough. I won't talk for less, and you'll never find out who I am."

"I'll find out how much," Phelps agreed.

"I'll call you back. You be there in one hour." Then the line went dead.

There were several organizations from which police agencies could request reward money, but none of them could commit to Phelps within an hour's time. Detective Phelps needed a pledge for ten thousand bucks, and he needed it fast. Only one source came immediately to mind.

FOUR

David Robbins could tell the jail cells were just past an open door at the other end of the room. He couldn't see them, but he could certainly hear the occupants.

At first, he could only hear one voice, but he could hear it loud and clear as it vehemently protested incarceration and proclaimed innocence. It bellowed for an attorney. It belligerently demanded to see the chief of police. It claimed to be a voice with influence, knowing everyone from the city mayor's sister to the Pope. It swore to have its day in court, its revenge, and everyone's job. It was extremely proficient in the use of profanity. It was profoundly obnoxious, and it had the endurance of a long-distance runner.

Eventually, it incurred the wrath of a second voice. A deep, serious, ugly voice threatened severe bodily harm if the first voice didn't shut-up and let the second voice serve time in peace.

The verbal battle that ensued caused Robbins to break out in chill bumps. The hate and anger in the inmates' malignant words painted a vivid picture of two rabid, caged beasts tearing to get at each other. The grossly overweight jailor working to fingerprint Robbins with the gentleness of a roustabout finally got his fill of the noise.

"Don't move," he growled at Robbins before waddling toward the door from where the din erupted.

Halfway to the door he stopped and bellowed, "Watson! Rains! Shut the fuck up! One more sound out of you assholes, and you'll lose your cigarettes, television, and next Sunday's visiting hours.

"They're a couple of real hard cases. Bad asses," the fat jailor huffed as he waddled back to Robbins. Grabbing the hand he hadn't printed, the jailor displayed a hateful grin and added, "They're both looking forward to having you back there with 'em. Seems that they don't much like daddies that help butcher their little girls."

The comment hit Robbins like a closed fist. The jailor was the first person to assault him face to face with what others had only communicated with their eyes and actions. Emotionally reeling from the blow, Robbins searched for words, both defensive as well as offensive. When no words immediately came to mind, Robbins registered his indignation by jerking his hand from the jailor's grip.

"Why you cowardly asshole!" the jailor fumed, raising a chubby open palm in the air. "I ought a give you…"

"What are you going to give him?" a voice behind Robbins boomed.

David Robbins turned to find Larry Phelps glaring at the jailor. Robbins greatly appreciated the timely arrival because of a sudden and terrible fear. A fury that far exceeded what the two men in the cells expressed had only been heartbeats away. Robbins feared that once the fury had been unleashed, the jailor would have suffered great physical damage.

* * *

Looking at David Robbins brought an age-old adage to Larry Phelps' mind – when it comes to fighting, don't worry about a man with a big, boisterous mouth, but keep a close eye on the silent types. Robbins definitely fit the silent-type mode, and Phelps had always suspected that his friend of average height and weight was not a man one would want to push too far. From the look in Robbins' dark brown eyes, and the way the muscles of his clenched jaw bones twitched, Phelps knew the jailor, Bill Coffman, had done just that. The brown eyes Phelps' ex-wife had always thought were the crowning glory of her brother-in-law's handsome face were normally soft, and compassionate. Now, they reflected the ugliness of the past week.

"Well?" Phelps growled as he turned his attention back to Coffman. "Let's hear what you're going to give him?"

The threatening hand now laid limp at the jailor's side. "I didn't say I was going to give him anything. I said I ought a give him something," Coffman huffed.

"Like what?" Phelps pushed. He had always heard Coffman was a bully, but this was the first time he'd witnessed the man in action. Larry Phelps hated bullies.

Coffman screwed his vast face up in a knot of obvious hate. "I ought a slap him around a little bit for what he done."

Phelps calmly moved to within inches of Coffman. "What you 'ought a' do is bounce your fat, beach ball ass out of this room. And you 'ought a' bounce it real damn fast."

"I ain't scared of you," Coffman said not too convincingly.

"I think I can change that," Phelps growled.

Coffman considered the comment for several long seconds before turning and waddling away. Just before going out the door he looked over his shoulder and mumbled, "I really ain't scared of you. I just need this job."

Phelps let the comment go unanswered, but said to Robbins, "I guess I should have stayed away a minute or two longer. Looked like you were on the verge of helping that slob lose a pound or two."

Robbins averted his eyes to the floor and ran both hands through his hair. "I'm glad you came when you did. I'm, uh, not a violent man by nature."

"I know that," Phelps said softly. "I'm really sorry for his behavior."

"It's not your fault," Robbins said as he looked back up. Then with a strained smile, he added, "Guess I better get used to people feeling the way he does."

Phelps knew Robbins was right. He already knew of several who felt the way Coffman did. Knowing this, Phelps sidestepped the statement. "I might have some real good news for you."

Robbins' expression lightened. "I could use some good news."

Phelps pulled up two chairs and invited Robbins to sit. "I just received an anonymous call from a man claiming to know who the gunman is."

Robbins' eyes widened, and he took a deep breath before asking, "Who is he, Larry?"

"I don't know. The caller won't talk without money."

"Money?"

"A reward, David. He wants ten thousand dollars, and he's calling back in less than one hour. There are organizations I can probably get the money from, but I can't get an answer from them in the time I got left."

"I'll give him ten thousand dollars," Robbins said without blinking an eye.

Phelps placed a hand on Robbins' knee. "I figured you would. The money, David, is rewarded for information that leads to a conviction. No conviction. No reward. So, this guy may not be anything but a nut or con-artist. If he is, then you won't have to spend ten-grand."

"This is ten-grand," Robbins said softly, "that I want to spend. I want to spend it very, very badly."

* * *

No real rest came for Luke Hogue. He could only manage to doze off for a few miserable minutes at a time. When the stomach cramps, or intense heat, or disgusting stench didn't wake him, she did. Sometimes she would just dance around on the outside of his underbrush hideaway, giggling, laughing, playing little girl games. Sometimes she would come into his den and cry and beg like she did the night she died. Sometimes she appeared whole and pretty and smiled sweetly. Sometimes she looked mangled and bloody with one side of her pretty face missing. Those were the times Luke woke up screaming the loudest. The last time he tried to sleep, she woke him up talking while on the outside of his den, conversing with a man wearing a white shirt and black pants and terribly pointed cowboy boots. After that, Luke Hogue decided he didn't really need to sleep.

At the same time, it occurred to Luke that having these dreams and hallucinations in broad daylight hurt bad enough. Having them in the dark while moving through dense woods would be unmerciful hell. In the dark, if the little girl and Reverend Richard Lee were qui-et, Luke wouldn't even know they were there – until they touched him.

Suddenly feeling the need to be bathed in sunlight, Luke rolled onto his hands and knees and scampered out of his burrowed place in the dense brush. The idea of making the trip to the oil lease under the cover of darkness no longer seemed like a good one. Luke didn't want his dead father touching him.

Striking out for the predetermined meeting place on weakened legs, Luke could not keep from remembering the last time Richard Lee did touch him. The external warmth of the bright spring sun coupled with the fever's inferno mimicked the August heat of that long-ago day and brought to life the awful memory.

Luke had been thirteen for two days when the Sacred Lamb's Temple kicked-off its annual tent revival. As customary, the founder and pastor of Wewoka, Oklahoma's only Independent Holiness Church, the Reverend Richard Lee Hogue insisted that the visiting evangelist and his family stay with the Hogue's during the week-long spiritual extravaganza.

That year's evangelist proved typically charismatic and possessed all the flash and style expected of a traveling preacher. Within the first hour of the first night of the revival, Brother Bob Harlow of Joplin, Missouri, whipped the flock of the Sacred Lamb's Temple into a holy frenzy. Thumping the well-worn cover of a theatrically large Bible, Brother Bob would spew forth the word to a congregation that responded with "Yes, Jesus" and "Amen, Brother!" All the while, Sister Mary Beth Woods ran up and down the aisles with both hands wagging high above her head, screaming at the top of her lungs in a sing-song, mumble-jumble tongue known only to the "Sweet Christ." On that very first night repentance was made and souls were saved. Brother Bob even laid hands on Delbert Johnson, one of Wewoka's most notorious drunks, and cast out the demons forcing the man to live his life in a bottle. All this and more happened, yet Luke barely noticed it. He had been too busy ogling the unusually large breasts of Brother Bob's twelve-year-old daughter, Michelle. Luke looked long and he looked hard, but he only looked when he thought Michelle didn't know he was looking. At thirteen, Luke had not yet developed his self-confident style of openly staring. Every time the girl would twitch, Luke would jerk his head straight forward and would take in the Brother Bob Show until he thought it safe to ogle some more breast. It wasn't until later that night, after the service ended, that Luke learned his fascination had not gone unnoticed.

The Hogue's and Harlow's returned to the small parsonage after the service. Once inside, Reverend Richard Lee and Brother Bob went immediately to the kitchen table and proceeded to divvy up the take from that evening's offertory. Meanwhile, the two wives – with Michelle in tow – set about preparing places for all to sleep. With little hope of stealing further unnoticed glances at Michelle, and in order to escape the bustling activity in the cramped quarters, Luke went out on the front porch and sat quietly petting a skinny, stray hound that he had adopted as his own. He wasn't on the porch long when Michelle joined him.

"What's your dog's name?" Michelle asked, speaking to Luke for the first time. Wanting to look up, but lacking the courage, Luke responded as if talking to the dog. "He don't have a name."

"What do you call him?"

"Nobody ever calls him. So, we don't call him nothing."

Several long, silent seconds followed. Michelle used the time to sit down within mere inches of Luke.

When she spoke again it was almost a whisper. "You like playing with titties, don't you?"

Gulping hard, Luke turned to look at Michelle to see if she intended on pulling his leg. She looked serious. "Yeah, I like playing with titties a whole lot," he assumed out loud.

"I'll let you play with mine if you want to."

The next thing Luke knew he was leading Michelle to the shed behind the house. Officially, they were going to look at his brother Mark's rabbits that were kept in pens inside the shed. Luke had been really careful to cut a wide swath around the parsonage's old storm cellar. The cellar scared Luke, as it did his brother Mark. Both boys' fears were well founded.

Luke and Michelle did look at the rabbits – for a few seconds. Then Luke got to look at something he immediately liked much better than rabbits. Michelle had not been the least bit hesitant about unbuttoning her blouse and pulling her white cotton bra up over her ample breasts. The sight all but took Luke's breath away.

"Do you think my nipples are too big?" Michelle asked nonchalantly.

Bending slightly at the waist and placing his hands on his knees, Luke gave the nipples a good eying. "They're big all right, but I like big nipples," he had just determined.

"Touch them." Michelle demanded.

"The nipples?"

"My whole titty. Both titties."

For support, Luke left his left hand on his left knee. Slowly, he reached out with his right index finger and touched Michelle's left nipple. Seconds later, progressing by instinct, he gently palmed as much of her left breast as he could. Quick blinks of an eye after that, Luke's left hand deserted its support role and joined in the action.

Not long after that, Luke started contemplating bringing his mouth into play. He later determined that it must have been just about that time that Mark quietly stuck his head in the door, and quietly pulled it back out again. Several minutes elapsed between the formation of the mouthing idea and the machismo to carry it out.

Luke had just gotten Michelle's right nipple in his mouth when the two holy men burst through the shed door.

Violence did not come immediately. As a matter of fact, Brother Bob inflicted the only pain that evening by loudly shrieking over and over in the small shed, "She's only twelve years old!"

Once Michelle got her exposed flesh covered – it seemed to Luke that she took her sweet time in doing so – Richard Lee turned his attention to his oldest son. With a strong grip on the back of Luke's neck, he guided the boy toward the house. As they passed the cellar, Richard Lee whispered, "After these people leave, you're going in the hole, boy!"

The threat ruined the rest of the week for Luke. It was one of the reasons he didn't even dare look Michelle's way for the remainder of her time in Wewoka but only one of the reasons. The other reason was because of what happened the following night at the tent meeting.

Nearing the end of the regular service, and only twenty minutes into a hard-sale, guilt-prodding invitational, Reverend Richard Lee joined Brother Bob at the podium. During the invitation the choir had been softly singing "Just As I Am."

Like Brother Bob had been doing, Reverend Richard Lee raised his voice over the sweet, soft harmony of the choir. "Brothers and Sisters," he began while holding his Bible to his heart, "Brother Bob has issued an invitation for those who are not saved to come forth and be saved. And they have come. The spirit of God is with us!"

A series of "Yes Jesus" and "Amen Brother," erupted from a teary-eyed tent full of followers.

"Yes, yes, praise be to God!" Richard Lee responded, and then continued. "Brother Bob has issued and invitation for those Christians who need cleansing, who need rededication, to come forth and be cleansed, to come forth and rededicate. And they have come. The Spirit of God is with us!"

More yeses and amens.

"But Brothers and Sisters…" Richard Lee screamed at the top of his lungs. "…Satan is here with us, too! For in this congregation of loved ones there are two of our own who are in his fiery grip at this very moment!"

The entire tent seemed to break out in groans of sorrows and a burst of "Help us, Jesus!" went to the heavens.

"Oh, Yes! Yes, Brothers and Sisters, Jesus must help us and he must help these two loved ones. If they will not come forward to seek God's forgiveness, then we must go to them!"

To Luke's disbelief and horror, Richard Lee rushed from behind the podium, jumped off the makeshift stage, and ran to where Luke was seated. His father grabbed him by the hand and dragged him onto the stage and before the people. Luke didn't stand there alone. Brother Bob retrieved Michelle, and she stood at his side. Michelle sobbed, and Luke wanted to, but didn't.

The congregation by now had worked itself into a frenzy. A majority of the people were praying out loud. All hands were held high in the air, and no one remained seated. Sister Mary Beth Woods enjoyed the company of others speaking in tongues this evening as the additional bearers of the gift chanted and babbled at the top of their lungs. The choir turned up their volume so as not to be outdone and also fired up their tempo to stay in step with the rest of Reverend Richard Lee's followers.

Back on the stage and behind his podium, the good Reverend now held his Bible high over head. "People of God!" his voice boomed, "these young believers have given in to the temptation of the flesh!"

The crowd roared disapproval.

"What these children need is for the people of God to gather around them and lay upon them the healing, loving and forgiving hands of Christ!"

The crowd roared approval.

"Come forth Brothers and Sisters! Come forth and save these sinners from the eternal damnation of hell!"

The brothers and sisters came forth – in waves. Luke and Michelle were jerked from the stage and engulfed in a sea of hands. Some of the hands just touched. Most didn't. Many gouged, slapped and clawed, and some even pinched. Luke feared the possibility of being torn in two.

Prayers were screamed in their faces. Warnings of damnation were spit at them. Clara Fuller, one of the church's most devout, threw ashes in their faces and declared that they should be forced to wear sackcloth. After what seemed like hours, the worshipers started returning to their folding chairs, but Luke and Michelle were forced to stand in front of the congregation while the offering plates were passed. That night the members of the Sacred Lamb's Temple gave abundantly as Luke studied their faces and wondered why the religion they practiced seemed so at odds with the Bible he often read.

For the rest of that week nothing else needed to be said about Michelle and Luke's indiscretion. Luke was actually foolish enough to think that even his father considered their debts paid in full. For that reason, Luke didn't fear Friday and the last tent meeting. That night, right after the meeting and the final splitting of the spoils, the Harlow's left Wewoka. Brother Bob was starting another revival in Fort Smith, Arkansas the next night.

Luke didn't stand out in front of their house and wave bye to the Harlow's like the rest of his family did. Instead, he went to the back of the house and stooped to pet the nameless dog. When the pointed boot landed just below his butt bone and sent him sprawling on top of the old dog, Luke thought it punishment for not saying proper good-byes to their guests. As he scrambled to get off the dog, who was trying to bite him, a second kick landed in his stomach and knocked the wind out of him. He tried to cry, but he could only manage to gasp. His dad kicked one more time and ripped skin from his left elbow. The next thing he knew, he was being dragged by his feet – toward the cellar.

"You embarrassed me terribly in a bad way, boy. You should have just let that little slut be!" his dad bellowed.

When they got to the cellar, Richard Lee dropped his son's feet to open the heavy wooden door. Luke had gotten back just enough of his wind to try and make a break for it. Before he could get all the way to his feet, a pointed toe collided with his testicles. Then he felt himself falling into the deep, dark, musty hole.

When he hit the ground, Luke curled into a tight ball and tried with all his might not to cry. Any noise at all always made the things that lived in the hole scurry, and Luke hated it when things he could not see scurried...

...The thought of things scurrying in the dark served to bring Luke back to the present and the task at hand. Before dark he had to travel two miles in a very weakened state. It was still a long time before dark, but Luke didn't want to take any chances. With all the strength he could muster, he stepped up his pace and tried to clear Richard Lee Hogue out of his mind. Trying to put his mind on more pleasant thoughts, he reminded himself that that had been the last time his old man booted him and threw him in the hole. Two months later, Harry Ward – a deacon in the Sacred Lamb's Temple – brutally murdered the Reverend Richard Lee.

FIVE

On the day of his arrest, David Robbins placed a call to Gene Lyle at two p.m. Fifteen minutes later the attorney sat at Robbins' side in the Pottawatomie County Jail. The quick response didn't surprise Robbins. The two men had been friends since high school, and Robbins was Lyle's largest commercial client.

Lyle had expressed shock over the phone as Robbins explained his predicament. By the look on the lawyer's face when he entered the jail, the shock had not subsided.

Lyle's first words were to Detective Phelps. "Thanks for not putting him in a cell, Larry."

"No problem, Gene," Phelps responded.

But Robbins knew it had been a problem. Larry Phelps had spent valuable time simply sitting with him just so he wouldn't have to be confined until the afternoon arraignment. Robbins deeply appreciated the friendship and concern. The fat jailor, however, had appeared to resent it. He had no doubt yearned to put Robbins behind bars with the beasts Watson and Rains.

"You doing okay, David?" Lyle used as a greeting.

"As good as can be expected. Larry's been a great help."

"I didn't do anything for you that you wouldn't do for me," Phelps said. "But I gotta get out of here now and help Detective Mann plan tonight's big adventure."

"Big adventure?" Lyle asked.

"David can explain it to you, Gene," Phelps said as he started for the door. "The conference room is empty, and arraignment is about fifteen minutes away."

"Yeah, we'd better hurry," Lyle agreed.

Once attorney and client were alone behind the closed door of the jail's conference room, Gene Lyle expressed further astonishment over the charge. "Second-degree murder? My God! What in the world has possessed the district attorney?"

Robbins responded by shrugging his shoulders and asking, "What happens next, Gene?"

"We go before a judge and get you arraigned. Then, we get you out of this horrid place."

"Which judge?"

"The same one who signed the warrant for your arrest, Stewart Hackney."

"I know Judge Hackney, but not very well," Robbins said with a shake of his head.

"He's a good and reasonable man. I think he will release you on your own recognizance."

"That means I don't pay the one hundred thousand dollars bond that was listed on my warrant. Right?"

"Right. But even if he doesn't release you on your own recognizance, I'm sure he'll at least reduce the dollar amount. If we have to pay money, you'll put up a cash bond that will initially cost you ten percent of the figure Hackney decides."

"After I'm out of here, what happens?"

Gene Lyle cleared his throat and started fumbling with the latches on his leather brief case. "First thing you have to do," he said, looking back up, "is get someone to defend you."

Up to this point Lyle showed no distaste for the circumstances that had put Robbins in the county jail. Robbins mumbled, "So, you can't bring yourself to represent me?"

"What?" Lyle said with his mouth falling open. "Damn, David I don't mean any such thing. Don't be ridiculous."

"I'm not being ridiculous. You won't be the first to shun me."

"I'm not shunning you, David," Lyle exclaimed. "I'm not a defense attorney. It's not my field."

"That's the only reason?" Robbins asked.

"That's reason enough, David. You are not in jail for some minor charge. Second-degree murder is serious business. In a worst-case scenario, you could get life in prison."

"Life?" Just repeating the sentence nearly choked Robbins. He knew his charge was serious, but not life serious.

"Yes. Ten years to life in the state pen at McAlester, David. That's the reason I won't represent you. You need one of the big guns. The biggest gun money will buy."

Opening his briefcase, Lyle retrieved a small black book that contained pages of business cards stuck in clear plastic pockets. After a few seconds of thumbing through the pages, he pulled out a card and handed it to David. "You need this gun, David."

Examining the card belonging to a Tulsa attorney, David responded, "Emerson Bailey?"

"One of the most prominent defense attorneys in the nation."

"I've never heard of him."

"You've never faced a murder charge."

"Good point."

"You need to call him, David. And no matter what you think of him initially, you need to hire him."

"What do you mean? What will I think of him initially?"

"You may not like him."

"Why?"

Gene Lyle stood and closed his briefcase. "Since we're in kind of in a hurry here, let it suffice to say you will have little in common with him."

"The implications of being represented by a person I have little in common with doesn't exactly thrill me, Gene," Robbins said dryly.

"I can understand that, but you must understand this. You need a hard-hitting, ruthless defense attorney. You need someone who can intimidate your opponents and romance a jury. You need someone with a record and reputation for winning. Emerson Baily is that kind of someone. He is a..."

"Okay, Okay," Robbins said with his hands in the air. "I'll call him. I'll give him a chance."

"Good," Lyle grinned as he glanced at his watch. "We'd better get down to the first floor. Court starts in just a few minutes." Then as an afterthought, "Hey, What's the big adventure Phelps mentioned?"

"They found out who shot Kayla, and he's hiding out in some woods in Oklahoma City. They're going to try to trap him tonight."

"Trap him?" Robbins responded.

"Yeah, they've worked out a pretty elaborate scheme with some type of special police unit there in Oklahoma City. I'll tell you about it on our way down," Robbins said with the closest thing to a smile he had worn in days.

* * *

"David Robbins."

The bailiff read the name out loud from the afternoon arraignment docket. Robbins' name had been the third called by the court official. In the past ten minutes, one car thief and a small-time burglar had been arraigned by Judge Hackney.

Gene Lyle had expressed relief that the district attorney's office was being represented by Assistant D.A. Judy Yarbrough. "She's not very tough," Lyle had smiled.

Now, as Robbins and Lyle stood to approach the bench, the door at the rear of the courtroom bounced open and a small, serious looking young man in a dark suit entered in a huff.

"Your honor," the young man hailed the court while striding down the aisle, "I'll be representing the people in 'State versus Robbins.'"

"Oh, shit," Lyle whispered.

"So noted, Mr. Pierce," Hackney said, seemingly not as impressed as Gene Lyle.

"Who's he?" Robbins whispered as he and Lyle moved toward the bench.

"Mike Pierce," Lyle groaned.

"Is he tough?"

"Very. He's a most capable prosecutor and former governor Patrick Pierce's grandson."

"Wonderful. Just wonderful," Robbins exhaled.

Pierce, Lyle, and Robbins stood before the bench for several seconds while Hackney squinted at some documents he held close to his age-wrinkled face. Finally, the elderly magistrate croaked, "Do you have a copy of the charges, Mr. Lyle?"

"Yes, Your Honor."

"Have you had an opportunity to discuss the charges with the D.A.'s office?"

Lyle got as far as opening his mouth before Pierce interrupted. "Your Honor, if I may, the state has no intentions of making any deals in this case. We will entertain no bargaining for a lesser charge."

Gene Lyle responded by attacking Pierce with his eyes and a grimace.

"Very well," Hackney nodded. "I guess that leaves us with setting a date for the preliminary." After minutes of fumbling with and squinting at a calendar on his bench, the old man said, "Okay, my first available date for a preliminary hearing is two weeks from now. Would nine a.m. on the first of May suit you gentlemen?"

Lyle retrieved a calendar from his briefcase and went through the motions of checking the date.

Mike Pierce beat him to a response. "I am available on that date and time, Your Honor."

"That's fine for me, also, Judge," Lyle lied a few seconds later.

"The first of May it is," Hackney confirmed. "Now we have the matter of bond. Mr. Lyle?"

"Your Honor, my client is a prominent citizen and a respected business and civic leader in this community. He has very strong ties to our city and state, and I think it is unreasonable to consider him a flight risk. Therefore, I move that the original bond of one hundred thousand dollars be set aside and Mr. Robbins be released on his own recognizance."

"Mr. Pierce?" Hackney barked.

"Your Honor, we feel the defendant is very much a flight risk. It is very possible that the emotional and psychological trauma that Mr. Robbins has suffered in the past few days has altered his judgment. If so, he has the resources to go first class to any country in the world. The original bond should be upheld."

Judge Hackney removed his thick-lensed glasses and rubbed at his eyes. When he put them back on, he looked at David Robbins for a long, silent moment. With a thoughtful nod of his head, the elderly judge turned back to the Assistant D.A. "Mr. Pierce, in this particular case, I would be negligent not to consider that which has been established over that which has not. Therefore, based on his honorable reputation, I will release Mr. David Robbins on his own recognizance."

* * *

Shawnee Police Detective Bobby Mann had been sitting on the deserted, dirt road less than fifteen minutes when the black Ford box van pulled up behind his unmarked cruiser. The boys from Oklahoma City were right on time.

The twelve men who filed from the back doors of the van were all dressed in OD green military-type utility uniforms. All wore black stocking caps and had their trousers bloused into black boots that resembled very high-topped tennis shoes to Mann. The exposed flesh on their face and hands was painted a very dark green. Six of the men carried Heckler and Koch G36K assault rifles, or "H&Ks" for short. The other six lugged bolt-action sniper rifles equipped with scopes. Four of the scopes were the very cumbersome, unusual looking starlight scopes for nighttime illumination. All of the men wore Glock .45s strapped into cross draw shoulder holsters, and radios with special microphone and earplug headsets that were held in place by the stocking caps. Every single one of the men looked very confident about the job they were there to perform.

One of the warriors broke from the pack and approached Mann, "Detective Mann?" he drawled.

"Yeah, Bobby Mann," he repeated with an extended shaking hand. After slinging his H&K, the very fit looking man grasped Mann's hand. "I'm Lieutenant Steve Cisco, OCPD Tactical Unit."

"Nice to meet you, Lieutenant. I appreciate you letting us get involved," Mann smiled, alluding to the fact that he was standing on ground well within Oklahoma City's limits.

"Call me, Steve, and we appreciate the help. It'll be nice just handing this puke over to you guys to take back home with you."

Yeah, Mann thought as he eyed the heavily armed squad, if there's anything left of him to take back home.

"Okay, guys," Cisco said as he turned back to his men, "gather round. Let's review this gig one more time."

As the others started ambling over and forming a loose circle around their leader, Cisco stuffed a wad of loose-leaf tobacco in his right cheek. Mann decided it must be standard issue, most of the other officers also sported bulging cheeks or gums.

"This road we're on runs north and south. The oil lease where the Hogues are supposed to meet is a mile and a half east of here. Luke Hogue told his brother that he's holed up somewhere further east of the lease. We'll move from here on foot through the woods just in case he's on the west side of it. There is another north-south section line we'll have to cross, and we could have started from there, but that's awful close to our objective. If he's in close proximity to the lease, he might have heard our engines."

Cisco paused and started looking around the circle until his eyes fell on a man studying a map. "Jenkins?" he barked.

"Yes, sir," the man with the map looked up.

"You got us good on paper…where we're at…where we're going…what azimuth we'll follow?"

"Ten-four. Also got us and destination on GPS," Jenkins confirmed.

"Okay," Cisco continued. "The oil well pumping unit and tank battery are sitting in the middle of a clearing that is about a hundred yards in diameter. We will move cautiously from here…in case we encounter Hogue west of the lease…to the east tree line. We'll use the dense foliage of the tree line to cover and conceal our movement and presence. We'll get there only minutes before dark. We'll use the remaining light to scan the clear area to make sure Luke Hogue hasn't already arrived…"

Cisco paused again – this time to spit. He aimed and delivered the stream of dark, thick juice at a space between the worn, scuffed boots of the biggest man in the squad.

A smile worked across the man's wide, stern face. "Don't fuck-up my spit shine, boss."

Cisco grinned at the man and started again. "If he's there, Smythe will move well beyond our left flank, Johnson beyond our right, and get a bead on him…"

The two men with the regular scopes attached to their bolt action rifles nodded in unison.

"…The rest of us will cut a path between Smythe and Johnson and go in for the assault."

"If he's not there, and he's not supposed to be until much later, we'll settle in and wait for dark. Okay, you guys with the starlights…Tinker will cover the sector of the clearing from twelve o'clock to three o'clock. Michaels will take sector three to six. Ables will take six to nine, and Bodine will cover from nine to twelve. When he's spotted, starlights will move out in front and lead us to him. Are there any questions?"

This time the big guy laid juice between Cisco's boots.

"Glad you brought me on this hunt, Boss..." The man grunted. "I have a seven-year-old daughter of my own."

"Good, Animal," Cisco nodded. "We'll let you do the honor of handcuffing the gentleman." Then Cisco turned to Bobby Mann. "Oh, yeah. It's policy that we handcuff...no matter what the conditions of the remains."

The Tactical Unit deployed from roadside to woods in a column formation. Following Lieutenant Cisco's instructions, Bobby Mann remained well behind the member "bringing up the rear." Mann had dressed for the occasion in jeans, a long-sleeve, brown shirt, and hiking boots, but a few minutes before the team pulled out, Cisco produced a camouflaged jump suit from the van and provided Mann with one of the radio headsets and camo paint. The big man with the seven-year-old daughter applied the paint liberally to Mann's face then chuckled about what a "bitch" it was to get off.

The team snaked its way across the first mile of heavily wooded terrain moving cautiously, yet at a quick pace, in the column formation. Forty or so yards short of the section-line road they had to intersect, Cisco stopped the team with a hand signal. Following another set of hand signals, the paramilitary group formed a line and crept up to the tree line at the edge of the dirt road. So far, not a single word had been uttered over the radio. Knowing there was no reason for radio silence, Mann assumed that Cisco was using the opportunity to practice the hand signals. The Shawnee detective was very impressed with how swiftly – and silently – the twelve men traveled across some fairly rough country.

Within seconds, Cisco's team buried itself in the available cover of the tree line's underbrush. Mann had no doubt that someone standing across the road would need a well-trained eye to detect the squad's presence. Mann had watched the officers take their positions, and now he had a hard time pinpointing them.

Moments later Cisco's voice erupted from Mann's earplug.

"Bowlin, secure the other side."

It was the big man who popped into view, sprang across the road and disappeared again into the far tree line. It was obvious to Mann that Bowlin was Cisco's favorite and most trusted subordinate.

"All clear, boss," Bowlin responded after a few minutes on the other side of the road.

"Squad," Cisco hailed calmly, "move out."

On line and with about ten yards between each man, the officers darted across the road. Like Bowlin, they were quickly absorbed into the woods. Mann followed practically on their heels. Having seen how quickly and quietly they could move without being detected, he didn't want to lose them.

As soon as Mann reached the tree line, he hit the ground using a small bush for concealment. At that moment, Cisco came back on the air.

"Squad, by bounding overwatch with Alpha team in lead…move out."

The left half of the line – what Mann assumed to be Alpha team – stood and started forward with their weapons at the ready. The right half – evidently Bravo team – remained in place with their weapons scanning the area in front of the men on the move. Alpha covered twenty to thirty yards, stopped, took up defensive positions and covered Bravo team as they came forward and "bound" past Alpha team. In essence – Mann figured out – the two teams were simply leapfrogging to the oil lease that was now less than half a mile away. This form of movement clearly offered more protection than the column they used for the first mile. Once again, the squad moved without as much as a single grunt, and radio silence was maintained until they were yards from the clearance that surrounded the oil lease.

"Squad," Cisco finally offered as a preparatory command. "Cease bounding over watch when on line, move to cover and concealment on tree line."

As they had done at the road earlier, the tactical unit crept into positions just within the tree line. After giving his men just enough time to dig in, he was back on the air.

"Smythe, Johnson…scope the area."

Bobby Mann sought cover closer to the left end of the line and could see Smythe slowly traversing the clearing through the scope of his bolt-action, sniper rifle. Mann couldn't see Johnson but felt assured that he was doing the same. After several long minutes, Johnson came on the air.

"Johnson to Cisco, looks clear from this angle."

"Ten-four, Johnson," Cisco acknowledged.

Several more minutes passed without a response from Smythe. Mann had been watching him and had noted that the barrel of his weapon had been scanning a very small area for the longest time.

"Smythe," Cisco barked. "What's going on?"

"Probably nothing," Smythe started, "but there's tall grass on both sides of the road between the well and tanks where the pickup is supposed to park. I'm just not…uh…comfortable with it."

"Are you uncomfortable enough that we should risk a recon of the area?" Cisco asked.

It took Smythe several seconds to respond. "Uh, no, I guess not. I've scoped it closely, can't see anything. Just don't like it."

Cisco took some time, too. "Ten-four. We'll call it secure," he said with an uneasy tone. "Squad, keep your eyes open. Make your-selves comfortable. We could be here a while."

* * *

Pacing around the rooms of his spacious home was starting to feel natural to David Robbins. Last night – after being informed that his wife and had son left him – he had paced out of pain, loneliness and a fear of what the future held. Tonight, he paced for the same reasons compounded with even more fear and a feeling of helplessness like he had never before experienced. The incident outside the court-house, after the arraignment, had not helped matters in the least.

After his arrest at the cemetery, one of the detectives had been kind enough to drive Robbins' car to the county jail. So, after the ar-raignment, Robbins planned to go by his sporting goods store to try to busy his mind and body with work. However, what waited on the courthouse lawn sent Robbins to hide out in his empty home.

The courthouse steps, lawns, and parking lots were teeming with television and newspaper reporters. Cameras and microphones seemed to come at Robbins from every direction and at every angle. Robbins' first response was to stop – like a rabbit caught in a headlight beam – but Gene Lyle grabbed his arm and kept him moving.

"Where are you parked?" Lyle screamed over the din of shouted questions.

Robbins pointed to the parking lot across the street. Pointing was all he could do. Lyle kept the grip on his arm and all but dragged him through the sea of people and electronic equipment. Every step they took produced more questions, delivered with escalating urgen-cy.

"Were second-degree murder charges actually filed?"

"Are you out on bond?"

"How much was your bond?"

"Will charges be reduced?"

"Will you plead guilty for a lighter sentence?"

Then, just as they were within steps of wrestling their way through the last of the reporters, one last microphone was thrust in Robbins' face. The pretty blond holding the microphone was Jennifer Rhodes of Oklahoma City's Channel 9 News. Robbins was not a regular viewer of television news and had not even had the television on since Kayla's death, but when he watched the news, he preferred to watch Jennifer Rhodes. The fact that she would be the one to ask the most painful, most piercing question seemed to compound the injury. So hurtful were the words that Robbins jerked his face away as if slapped. He tried with all his might to force the words from his mind, but they dug in. For sanity's sake he simply bypassed the entrenched question and continued in pursuit of a more strategic objective – his car. He knew that later he would have to face the question – did he feel guilty of murdering his daughter?

Gene Lyle had grunted the customary, "No comment" to Jennifer Rhodes as he had to the others, and continued the push to the parking lot. When they finally emerged from the tangle of reporters and were hurrying across the street and parking lot, Robbins noticed several cars brightly colored with call signs from Oklahoma City television and radio stations. He saw a couple from Tulsa and one from Dallas. Moments earlier, he thought one female reporter had identified herself as being from a newspaper in Fort Smith, but he wasn't really sure. She might have said Fort Worth or even Fort Cobb, a small town in the eastern half of Oklahoma. One thing was for sure; there were more than enough reporters to cover the scene. With that many reporters, the story of his arrest, like the story of the murder, was sure to make national news, and that really worried Robbins. That worry helped him further bury the question posed by Jennifer Rhodes.

Six hours later, Robbins paced and worried some more. He had tried with all his might to respect his wife's wishes and give her some time to sort everything out in her mind. He had spent the entire night before fighting off urges to pick up the phone and call. Now he was doing it again, but his reasons for wanting to call now were different than the night before. Last night, his motives had been selfish. He had wanted to talk to what was left of his family and, if necessary, beg them to come home. Tonight, he wanted to call in order to gently break the news of his arrest to Nancy. He wanted to spare her the shock and pain of hearing about the charges and seeing his bewildered face on the evening news. Or, considering what time it was in California, try to comfort her if she had already heard.

Finally, that line of thinking – calling for Nancy's sake – won out, and Robbins dialed his parents-in-law's number in San Francisco. As the phone rang, it occurred to him that Nancy would want to rush back to Oklahoma to be with him through this ordeal, and that would probably not be the best thing for her or his son, Kevin. As much as he wanted them back, he wanted them to be ready to come back. They would have to discuss this, and Robbins would have to insist that they stay until they wanted to come back.

The receiver at the other end of the line – hundreds and hundreds of miles away – was picked up on the sixth ring. Nancy's mother, June Decker, sounded as if she was just across town when she answered with a pleasant, "Hello."

"Hello, June. This is David," Robbins said, suddenly feeling sheepish.

"Hello David," she responded not so pleasantly.

"June, I have got to talk to Nancy."

After a slight pause, she replied, "She doesn't want to talk to you, David. She wants you to just leave her alone for awhile. We asked your father to explain this to you."

"He did, June, but things have changed. Have you seen or heard the news?"

"What news?" she exhaled as if put out.

Robbins felt relieved. "Something happened today that I need to tell Nancy before she hears it from some other source."

"David," she said with emphasis, "she will not talk to you. Besides, she's in bed. Do you know what time it is here? Right now, rest is one of the…"

"I was arrested for second-degree murder today, June," David forcibly interrupted. "They are charging me with our baby's death, and I want to speak to my wife."

A breathless "Oh, David," seemed to be all June could manage. Then, a few seconds later, "I'll wake her."

Robbins used the minutes of silence to plan his words. He would tell her about the attorney Gene Lyle had recommended, but wouldn't tell her about the information on the murder suspect. He didn't know how she would respond. In short, he would try to assure her that everything would be all right. He wasn't sure he believed it, but maybe he could make her believe it.

Suddenly, he could hear the receiver being picked back up, and the thought of hearing Nancy's voice brought a commodity that had been in short supply – joy.

"David?" It wasn't Nancy. It was June again.

"Yes?" he blurted.

"David, Nancy, uh, refuses to come to the phone."

"Did you tell her I was arrested. Did you tell her…"

"I told her, David, I'm sorry. I really am. I'm sorry about this whole terrible mess. Maybe with time we…"

As his mother-in-law talked, Robbins gently laid the receiver back in its cradle.

SIX

Luke Hogue woke up to a familiar sound in an unfamiliar place, and he felt something he hadn't felt for days. He felt rested — almost normal. He felt so different that he even had the presence of mind to lie still until he knew exactly where he was and what noise he was hearing.

Luke was lying on his back under a starlit sky. Thick, tall Johnson grass swayed with the light breeze. They towered over him, consumed him, hid him from the approaching headlights. Suddenly, he realized why the noise that woke him sounded so familiar. It was the sound of his brother's rickety old pickup. Hogue now fully remembered his exact location and exactly how he had ended up there.

The broad daylight trek to the oil lease had completely zapped Luke of what little strength he had left. So much so that when he reached the clearing surrounding the lease, he felt he dare not stop for fear of not having the strength to start again after dark. Taking chances, he proceeded to the well, planning to rest in the shade of the large metal tanks. However, just as he crossed the small lease road that separated the well and tanks, he stumbled into the shoulder-high grass and collapsed. Just before blacking out, he realized he was right beside the place his brother had parked the night before and the place he had been instructed to park when he returned with the dope.

Mark's pickup, badly in need of a muffler, was getting very close. Thinking of the fun he had with Mark the night before, Luke decided to remain hidden until Mark parked and put the suffering engine out of its misery. Luke had always derived great pleasure from startling his skittish brother. The fact that Luke now felt up to a little foolishness gave him even more encouragement. If Mark was on time, Luke had been lying in the grass for about eight hours. The very deep, almost death-like sleep did him a world of good. The stomach cramps and delirium had ceased – the withdrawal was letting up.

As Luke hoped, the old pickup came to rest only feet from where he lay. The passenger side faced Luke, and all he would have to do to scare the shit out of his younger brother would be to spring up and scream. Luke flexed his fingers and started to roll over on his belly when suddenly he heard someone talking in the cab. Luke couldn't make out the words, but that didn't matter. What did matter was that it wasn't Mark Hogue's voice. Catching his breath and holding it, Luke slowly retrieved the big revolver from the waistband of his jeans. He had been set up. His own, worthless, piece of shit brother had set him up. Whoever was alone in that pickup was either talking to himself or using a radio or telephone to talk to someone else. Luke was betting on the latter and was also betting that the lone man in the pickup wouldn't be alone for long. Help was either real close by or on its way. Luke had one thing in his favor – the element of surprise – and the longer he waited to react, the more his chances of escape dwindled.

Gun in hand, Luke eased over on his belly, and then sprang to his feet. Just two steps put him at the passenger door. In two seconds, he had the door opened. The man inside, wearing the same cap Mark wore the night before, reacted first with a startled gasp, then his right hand grabbed for the automatic Colt in the seat beside him. He wasn't quick enough. In one motion, Luke screwed the barrel of his revolver into the man's forehead with his left hand and scooped up the Colt in his right. In another motion he jumped into the passenger seat and pulled the door closed behind him – extinguishing the dome light.

"I'm a cop," the man gasped.

"No shit," Luke exclaimed, feeling as if his heart was coming up into his throat. Luke moved the barrel of his gun from the man's head to a point under his jaw bone. "Where's that goddamn radio you was talking on?"

The man was slow to answer but finally responded, "It's on the floorboard. Down by my feet."

"Reach down, real slow, and get it," Luke ordered.

Never taking his eyes from Luke, the man reached down and retrieved a small cellular phone.

"You got a choice, asshole. You can drive us out of here, or you can die here."

The man started the pickup.

"You drive real fast, man. You drive as fast as this old fuckin' truck will run!"

The cop did as told.

* * *

"Bowlin!" Lieutenant Steve Cisco shouted into the dark for his most trusted soldier.

"Yeah, boss," Bowlin responded from several yards to the right of where Cisco and Bobby Mann were standing.

"Switch your radio to headquarters' frequency. Alert the assigned patrol units of what's happened and get a helicopter out here."

"Ten-four," Bowlin responded.

"God damnit!" Cisco growled under his breath. For the third time, in as many minutes, he again used those two choice words to express his feelings.

Bobby Mann, feeling numb, as if in shock, had forgotten about the pre-positioned patrol units. According to the plan when the pickup parked in place, four black and whites were to take up positions on the rural roads to the north, south, east, and west of the oil lease. They were necessary in case things went bad, and boy had they gone bad.

While Cisco orchestrated calling in the cavalry, Mann closed his eyes, rubbed his temples, and relived the terrible past few minutes.

Mann had moved up beside Lieutenant Cisco earlier in the night. While the men with the starlight scopes scrutinized their assigned sectors, Cisco and Mann conversed in whispers. The other men on line with them remained so quiet and still that Mann often felt he and Cisco were sitting in the dark woods all by their lonesome.

The hours between dusk and twelve forty-five a.m. dragged by with no sightings of Hogue. Having nothing but dark to stare into, Mann had been practically blinded when the pickup's light first penetrated the night. The truck arrived on time, and parked in the right spot. Cisco wasted no time in testing his communications link-up with the truck. Moments later, all hell broke loose from the receiver plugged in Mann's right ear.

"My God, Cisco! He's there!" a voice screamed across the air waves.

The next couple of transmissions were garbled as two or more of the Tactical Unit cops tried to talk on their radios at the same time. It was right about then that the pickup's dome light came on and immediately went out.

Realizing they had "covered" one another's transmissions, the cops did what they had been trained to do – they cleared the air so the boss could dispatch questions and answers.

"Michaels!" Cisco hailed sternly. "What's going on?"

The same voice that started the whole mess came back on the air. "Hogue is in the truck, Cisco," Michaels panted.

"What are you…" Cisco started then stopped. The pickup's engine had struggled to life.

As it sped away, Michaels inserted. "He was in the grass, Cisco. He was there all the time. The entire fucking time!"

"God damnit!" Cisco screamed into the night.

From that point forward, he forgot the radio and shouted his commands angrily into the darkness. It all went to hell so fast that Mann still struggled to believe it happened, and he still had his eyes closed and rubbed at his temples when Cisco placed a hand on his shoulder.

"There's nothing else we can do here. We might as well start back for the van," the Lieutenant mumbled.

"Hey, boss," Bowlin's voice boomed from somewhere down the line.

"Yeah?"

"Headquarters and the units have been notified. The units are searching the area, and a chopper and more patrol cars are on the way."

"Ten-four. Maintain contact with headquarters."

"Gotcha."

"Jenkins?" Cisco yelled for his navigator.

"Right here," a voice responded from a few feet right of Mann and Cisco.

"Take the point and lead us out of this shit hole," Cisco barked. Then he placed his hand on Mann's shoulder a second time.

"Bobby, I don't know what to say. I feel like shit about what's happened. I'm sorrier than hell about your partner."

Bobby Mann felt the same. At that very moment, he didn't put much stock in ever seeing Larry Phelps alive again.

* * *

Mark Hogue had sat in the back booth of the truck stop's restaurant gulping coffee as long as he could stand it. For the past two hours he had been out on the front sidewalk of the busy establishment, pacing, and stopping about every other customer to ask the time.

The plain-clothes cop from Shawnee, Phelps, had met Mark at the truck stop at midnight – just like they had worked out over the phone earlier in the day. Phelps left his cruiser and took Mark's truck just sure he would be back with it before two a.m. – if everything went as planned. Now, at a little past three, Mark Hogue figured everything hadn't gone as planned.

The original plan called for Phelps taking Mark's place at the oil lease. When brother Luke made his appearance, some Green Beret-like cops from Oklahoma City would swoop out of the dark woods and arrest Luke Hogue. Mark was to wait at the truck stop located on Interstate 40 a few miles east of the oil lease and not many miles west of Shawnee. After the arrest, some more Shawnee detectives would drop by with Luke in tow for Mark to positively identify. That was the only part of the plan that Mark had not warmed to, but Phelps agreed to let him do the fingering from a distance and place where Luke couldn't see him doing it.

Now the plan had obviously failed, and Mark didn't feel so well. As a matter of fact, he felt down-right sick to his stomach. A small part of the problem was the many cups of black, acrid coffee sloshing in his guts, and none of the alcohol his system had built a dependency upon. The biggest contributor to his sick stomach was dread. Hogue felt certain that Phelps and his buddies did just exactly what the detective said they would try to avoid at all costs. Mark Hogue felt certain that Phelps and his buddies had gunned down Luke Hogue.

The thought of his only brother lying in a field, riddled with bullets filled Mark with rage and conflicting sadness. With Luke dead, Mark would not be entitled to the ten thousand dollars. Courts didn't convict dead people, and rewards were not given without convictions. Mark's dread, and rage, and sadness knew no bounds.

From his place on the sidewalk, Mark kept a close eye on the unmarked car that Phelps left in the parking lot. It was his only line to what was going on. If they had in fact killed Luke, the cops wouldn't go out of their way to find Mark on the premises, but they would come to get the car. When they did, Mark would be there to greet them.

Some minutes later, just as Mark was about to ask a truck driver dressed like a cowboy for the time, a car pulled through the parking lot, circled Phelps' parked car, and pulled back up in front of the restaurant. It stopped several yards from where Mark stood. Mark covered the few yards in a near sprint. The lone occupant of the car had his eyes on Mark and didn't bother to get out of the car.

"You're a cop, right?" Mark blurted when he reached the driver's open window.

"Right," the man responded dryly as he flipped a wallet open to reveal a badge and some kind of identification card.

"Detective Mann, Shawnee Police Department. Are you Hogue?"

"I damn sure am! Where the hell have you people been? Did you kill my goddamn brother?"

The detective responded by bouncing from his car. Mark sensed that the short and very stout man had taken exception to his inquiries.

"Do I have a happy look on my fucking face?" the detective growled.

"No, sir," Mark responded with much more respect.

"Then we obviously didn't get to kill the piece of shit, did we?" the bulldog-shaped man stormed.

"Uh, no, sir," Mark said meekly, recognizing signs of no sense of humor.

"Okay, then. Here's the deal. We fucked up. Your brother got away, and he's got Detective Phelps as a hostage. We've been searching the area with no luck."

Now Mark felt really sick – moments from throwing up sick. Worse than Luke being dead was Luke being alive and pissed off. If Luke had taken to killing defenseless little girls, the thought of what he would do to Mark left the youngest of the Hogue boys with weak knees. "Are you guys going to protect me?" he gasped.

The detective gave Mark a look and a grunt that seemed to imply disgust. Then he got back into his car and started the engine.

"Hey," Mark said as the man put the car in gear. "How am I going to get home?"

"There will be two more detectives here in a while to get Phelps' car. If they like you, one of 'em may give you a ride home. I suggest you go ahead and call a cab."

"Why don't you give me a ride home?"

"'Cause I don't fuckin' like you."

"Awwww, man," Mark whined. "I don't want to wait around for those other cops. Can't you call me a cab?"

"Sure," the mean-faced detective nodded with a nasty grin. "You're a cab."

With that, the detective backed out of the parking space.

"Oh! I get it! I'm a cab! That's real funny shit, man!" Mark hollered as he kept up with the car until the detective shot him the bird and pulled out of the parking lot.

"Bastard," Mark mumbled before running back into the restaurant. With Luke on the loose, he wanted to be in brightly lit places around lots of people.

* * *

David Robbins could hear the phone ringing through his sleep, but he was snoozing too comfortably in his large recliner to get up and answer it. Sluggishly, his mind questioned why sounds of running footsteps didn't accompany the ringing. Normally, every time the phone rang, a footrace ensued. A good ninety percent of the calls were for his son, Kevin, and at least fifty percent of the callers were younger girls. For the sake of having something with which to harass her older brother, Kayla always tried to beat him to the phone. Through his dense fog of sleepiness, Robbins couldn't understand why they weren't racing now.

Barely able to form the words, he mumbled, "Answer the phone, Kevin…Kayla."

Within a heartbeat of calling her name, he bolted upright in his chair, wide-eyed, and free from sleep's grip. It wasn't a Saturday or

Sunday afternoon, and he wasn't napping in front of the television, and there were no children to answer the phone. It was pitch dark, and he was all alone, and the phone rang and rang and rang.

With his heart racing, Robbins fumbled with the light switch on the table lamp beside his recliner. Squinting at his watch, he determined it was nearly four in the morning. As he wondered who in the world would call at such an hour, Larry Phelps surged into his mind. How could he have forgotten? How had he managed to fall asleep?

Bolting out of the chair, he darted to the nearest phone, nearly breathless when he answered, "Larry?"

"No, Mr. Robbins, this is Bobby Mann. I hate to disturb you."

"No, no," Robbins started before having to pause and clear his throat. "I've been expecting Larry to call. He said he would let me know the moment you guys got back with that…"

It was nearly four. Larry told Robbins that no matter what happened in that oil field – good or bad – he would call before two o'clock.

"What's wrong, Detective Mann?" Robbins finished.

"I know you and Larry are close, and I know he would want me to call…"

Robbins collapsed into a nearby chair. Bobby Mann had been so cold and aloof earlier in the day that Robbins knew he hailed from the camp that abhorred the actions that landed him in jail. Now his voice had a softer, kindlier edge, and it weakened Robbins.

"…The arrest went bad. This Hogue guy was already on the oil lease, hiding in some tall grass. He was able to jump in the truck, obviously taking Larry as a hostage, and they got away from us. They disappeared. We have no idea where they are. I'll try to keep you posted if anything comes up."

"Please do," Robbins managed before hanging up the phone. Slumping over to rest his elbows on his knees, Robbins dropped his chin to his chest and closed his eyes. He prayed – through gritted teeth.

"Why the hell are you letting this happen?"

* * *

Larry Phelps had no idea where they were. They had been over too many miles of dark, mostly dirt and gravel roads and had, on two occasions, driven cross-country over dozens of acres of pasture land. The best Phelps could determine, they had worked their way to the north, but there had been far too many orders of "turn left" and "turn right" for him to be absolutely certain about even that. Much of their trek had been made at high speeds without lights. That, too, had done its share to disorientate Phelps on the back roads of the unfamiliar countryside.

Phelps highly suspected that his captor was as lost as he was. He contributed Hogue's success at escaping the police – that Phelps had no doubt were out in force – to nothing more than luck, a commodity which Hogue seemed to keep on tap.

During the entire trip, Hogue had kept his revolver and forty-five trained on Phelps. He held the revolver in his left hand and kept his left arm resting along the top of the seat back. The barrel of the .357 never more than an inch or two away from the back of Phelps' head and neck. Hogue held the forty-five in his right hand and rested his right hand in his lap. He kept the automatic aimed at mid torso. A round from the powerful handgun would gut Larry Phelps.

The detective had done as told – certainly no more and absolutely no less. Although the thought of struggle and escape had never left his mind, any attempt up to this point and time would have listed him among the brave and stupid dead. Hogue had gotten an immediate drop on him, and nothing so far changed that. Until it did, Phelps intended to do what Hogue told him to do. A man who could murder a small girl in cold blood probably had no qualms of doing likewise to a cop.

Other than telling him when and where to turn, how fast to drive, and when to and not to use lights, Hogue remained silent. The silence had served to unnerve Phelps almost as much as the guns. If the man didn't talk, Phelps had no idea what he was thinking, what he was planning.

On top of everything else, Hogue reeked of illness. The smell of excrement and vomit was so strong in the small cab that Phelps struggled with nausea. If more of the old pickup's instrument panel lights worked, Phelps suspected they would shed light on a real sick-looking man. The detective in Phelps grew increasingly curious about what plagued Hogue. He hoped very much that whatever did so, left him physically weakened. An unarmed man needed every advantage he could get when it came time to attack a man with a gun in each hand. That time, Phelps realized with a start, was possibly growing very close.

They had turned onto a blacktop road at least ten minutes earlier, and Hogue was not having him turn left or right. He obviously felt no further need to zig and zag the direction he wanted to go. He obviously felt he had outreached any hastily deployed dragnet. If that were true, he would no longer need a hostage. By another mile or so down the road, this thought really started to work on Phelps, but then Hogue spoke.

"At the next road you come to, turn left."

The next road came only tenths of a mile later, and Phelps made his left turn onto yet another narrow, dirt road. He had less than a mile invested in the new road when Hogue spoke again. This time more urgently.

"Slow down! See that gate up there on your side?"

It wasn't actually a gate. It was a cattleguard. "Yeah."

"Turn in there."

Just past the cattleguard the dirt road dwindled into a deeply rutted trail. After a few acres of pasture land, the trail snaked down into a wooded depression. When they were well into the trees, Hogue ordered Phelps to stop the truck.

Sticking the barrel of the .357 behind Phelps' right ear and cramming the forty-five's barrel into his ribs, Hogue said calmly, "Leave the lights on. Kill the engine. Then, open your door."

Whatever Hogue planned to do, he didn't plan to do it in the dark. Phelps' stomach heaved an objection, but he followed the orders anyway.

"Stick your hands deep in your front pockets."

If this presented his last chance for a struggle, it offered a piss-poor one that wasn't even worth taking. So, Phelps took a chance on there being another chance and did as he was told.

"Now slide out, turn your back to me and take three steps away from the truck."

This was it, and Phelps had two choices. He could stand and wait for bullets, or he could run and try to dodge bullets. But what if this wasn't "it," and Hogue had no intentions of shooting unless Phelps broke and ran? Fearing he had less than seconds to do something – or nothing – Phelps took the deepest breath of his life and slid out of the pickup. Taking the first step, the detective deducted that if

Hogue intended to leave him standing, he probably wouldn't care if he wasn't standing stationary. The next step hit the ground at a run.

Phelps made it a good four feet before his left foot got tangled in vines. He struggled to free himself in mid-stride but only ended up losing his balance and stumbling backwards. He landed hard on his back and made no attempt to get to his feet. Hogue's dark silhouette towered over him, and he had both arms extended down toward Phelps. What little light the stars and slice of moon provided glinted off the metal that filled both hands.

"If you're going to shoot me," Phelps grumbled at the dark figure, "then why don't you fuckin' get it over with!"

"Cause I got something to say," Hogue responded with little emotion.

"Say it then," Phelps spat, feeling that any further attempts to stay on Hogue's good side would probably be a waste of time.

"You fuckers knew who I was and where I was going to be because I trusted that sorry-assed brother of mine, and told him a little bit about what happened to that little girl. But I didn't tell him the whole story, and I ain't going to tell you the whole story either. There's just one thing I want to say about it…"

Why would Hogue care to tell anything to a man soon to die? Phelps found knew hope of survival.

"…Not that it's going to do that little girl any good, or me any good, and it damn sure ain't going to do you any good. I just got to say it…"

Why? Maybe just to clear his conscience. All hope evaporated.

"…I showed my brother, that bastard, this here revolver I got aimed at your head right now. I admitted to him that it was the gun that killed that girl, but I didn't admit to killing her. So, what I want to say to you is that, yeah, it was my finger on that trigger, but I ain't the one that pulled it. That's all I got to say."

"That doesn't make any goddamned sense," Phelps grunted.

"Get on your fuckin' feet, turn around and get your hands in your pockets," Hogue responded.

Maybe the child killer had had another change of mind. Or maybe he just wanted to shoot Phelps up close and, in the back, an alternative to which the cop didn't necessarily object. Aiming close up at vital organs should ensure a quicker death. Phelps didn't want to lie in the woods and suffer. Taking it in the back just meant he didn't have to see it coming. One more time, Phelps followed Hogue's directions. As soon as he did so, one of the barrels was planted firmly in the middle of his shoulder blades.

"You know, you're right," Hogue said wearily from behind him. "It don't make any goddamned sense. But nothing in my world ever has."

Detective Larry Phelps never knew what hit him.

SEVEN

Nancy Robbins sat at her parents' kitchen table engaged in the process of finishing her fifth cup of coffee when her son entered the room.

"What's for breakfast? I'm starved," the boy said around a yawn.

"It's closer to lunch time," Nancy said with the closest thing to a smile she had managed since getting out of bed. The fact that her son slept late and woke up hungry pleased her. For the past five days he had shown no appetite and had been going to bed late only to get up early. Maybe he was healing. Nancy wished she could, too. She still took the maximum doses of the sedatives. The medication served to dull the searing pain, but it still penetrated like the needle-sharp teeth of a gnawing puppy.

"Wow," Kevin said after glancing at his wristwatch, "It is. So, what's for lunch?" he grinned.

The grin was nice, too. It had been practically nonexistent. It figured, that on the first morning her son had woken with no obvious pain, she would have more painful news.

"Tell you what," Nancy said, getting up from the table, "You tell me what you want. If we have it, I'll fix it."

"Pancakes?"

"I can do pancakes."

"Lots of them."

"Lots of them it is."

"Where's Grandad and Nana?

"They had to run some errands." Which was true. Nancy just didn't point out they planned the errands for that afternoon but changed their plans so she could be alone with Kevin to tell him about his dad's late-night phone call.

Nancy stepped into her mother's well-stocked pantry and scanned the shelves for baking mix and cooking oil. She wished her son had slept just a while longer. Maybe with a little more time she would have come up with the right words and the right way of using them to tell Kevin that his father could be going to prison for a long, long, time.

With the ingredients in hand, Nancy stepped from the pantry and opened her mouth to speak, but Kevin was no longer at the table. Nancy placed the items on the kitchen counter and started gathering the needed utensils. She had just started to prepare the pancake batter when Kevin returned with his face stuck in the morning paper. Nancy didn't have to look to know that the sports pages commandeered his attention. Kevin had a passion for baseball – just like his father.

Kevin selected the seat opposite of and facing the counter where Nancy worked to prepare his meal. He laid the paper out on the table and started moving his head and eyes at a quick pace from left to right as he no doubt took in every word on his favorite sport.

Nancy didn't wait for him to finish before starting her dreaded task. The fact that she wasn't starting with his full attention somehow made it easier. "Kevin, your dad called last night."

The young eyes momentarily stopped scanning, but didn't look up. "Oh," was all Kevin said before the eyes started moving again. It appeared to Nancy that they weren't as intent on the written word as they had been only moments earlier.

Within seconds and again without looking up, he muttered, "What did he want?" The words were acerbic.

Nancy took a deep breath and held it for a moment before using it to blurt, "He was arrested yesterday."

This time the eyes left the paper. "What?"

Nancy moved to the table and sat down beside her son. "He was arrested for…what happened to Kayla."

Kevin's mouth fell open and his eyes widened. "He was arrested for murder?"

"Second-degree murder," Nancy said gently.

"What's the difference between first and second-degree murder?" Kevin asked, his voice emphasizing the look of shock.

"I don't really know. I do know that the penalty for second degree is not as bad as for first-degree."

"Is he in jail now?"

"I think he called from home. I mean, I assume he has posted bond."

Kevin slowly lowered his head, and his gaze once again fell upon the newspaper, but he wasn't reading – just staring blankly.

Nancy reached out and placed her hands over his, and they both remained silent for several minutes.

Kevin finally broke the silence, but once again, he didn't look up. "Are we going home now?"

This was the part Nancy wanted to feel her way carefully through, the part she had dreaded even more than telling the boy his father was in trouble. "What do you want to do?"

After several long seconds of contemplation, Kevin responded, "I don't know. I don't want him to go to prison, but I'm still really confused and mad at him."

Removing his hands from beneath hers, Kevin propped his elbows on the table and dropped his forehead into his palms. Nancy could no longer see the eyes that looked almost identical to the eyes of David Robbins.

She could relate to her son's anger so much that she could not relate to his concern for his father serving time in a penitentiary.

"Kevin," she said softly. "I'm angry, too. So angry that I may never go back to live in Shawnee."

"You mean divorce?" a small voice asked.

"I think so," Nancy responded, wishing she could see his eyes.

After several more minutes passed in silence with Kevin still cupping his head in his hands, Nancy said with all the cheer she could fabricate, "I better get to making all those pancakes."

"I'm not hungry anymore," Kevin said just as the first large tear trickled from his face to the newspaper.

* * *

David Robbins drove the ninety miles between Shawnee and Tulsa in a little over an hour and a half. In that time, he convinced himself that Oklahoma City had to have lawyers as good as Emerson Bailey, and they would only be forty minutes away. Yet, since Gene Lyle went through the trouble to set up the appointment, and Bailey had been generous enough to clear his calendar, Robbins felt obliged to keep the appointment.

The law firm of Bailey and Associates occupied the entire nineteenth floor of a downtown high-rise. The two elevators that stopped on the nineteenth floor opened into a spacious lobby with raised panel cherry walls and highly polished hardwood floors. Persian rugs covered portions of the floor, and leather wing-backed chairs provided for clients' comfort. Brass chandeliers hung from the twelve-foot ceiling. Oil paintings in rich, wonderful frames, and lively ferns in large copper planters were placed aesthetically around the room. Bailey and Associates reeked of success.

The receptionist's large, ornate desk seemed better suited for a chief executive officer. The dark-haired receptionist seemed better suited for a glamour magazine. She first consulted a computer terminal and then followed up with a phone call to ensure that David Robbins had an appointment with *the* Emerson Bailey and not just one of his associates. After passing all tests, she directed Robbins to take the widest of the three hallways that branched off from the lobby. Mister Bailey's "offices" were to be found at the end of the hallway.

The hallway was at least a hundred feet long, but Robbins passed only four other offices on his way to Bailey's. It appeared the widest of the hallways housed only the highest brass of Bailey and Associates. The oversized double doors at the end of Robbins' trek opened into another reception area. It was smaller than the main lobby but just as luxurious.

Seated at another impressive desk was a blond lady who did not shy in physical comparison to the receptionist. A gold name plate on the desk introduced her as, "Mrs. Sloan – Executive Secretary." With a warm smile, Mrs. Sloan explained that Mr. Bailey would be right with Robbins, and she offered coffee or a cold drink. Robbins graciously declined the offer and selected a plush wingback opposite of and facing the closed door with gold letters proclaiming, "T. Emerson Bailey – Attorney at Law."

Robbins had just settled into the chair when voices became audible. They were coming from behind the closed door, so they were muffled and unintelligible, but they were obviously angry. Robbins looked to Mrs. Sloan for an explanation or reaction but got neither. She seemed not to notice. Moments later T. Emerson Bailey's door violently flew open, but Mrs. Sloan's expression never changed.

An overweight man of average height, dressed in a business suit appropriate for the extravagant surroundings, swished through the door and up to the secretary's desk.

"Call the police, Mrs. Sloan," he said in a high-pitched and effeminate voice. "I've had all the abuse I wish to take."

The order brought another man, powerfully built and of imposing height, storming out of the office. His apparel consisted of faded jeans, a denim shirt and scuffed loafers.

"Yeah, go ahead and call the police," he bellowed. "Tell them I'm being ripped off by a flaming little faggot!"

The richly suited man wheeled on the huge man and glided across the few feet of floor that separated them. If he had been tall enough, he would have been facing his opponent nose to nose.

A surprised David Robbins could not help but marvel at what unlikely opponents the two men were. The well-dressed gentleman looked to be in his late forties or early fifties and bore an air of financial success. His pudgy, pallid face was clean-shaven, and his hair looked to be professionally styled. The other man looked mid forties and dressed like one who had no interest whatsoever in any kind of success. His rugged face was deeply tanned with square jaws that were capped by a prematurely silver goatee. The top of his head was bald and perfectly round. The hair on the sides of his head matched the color of his sculptured goatee and was pulled back tightly into a small ponytail.

"If you call me a faggot one more time," the professional looking man huffed, "I will not be responsible for my actions!"

David Robbins admired the smaller man's tenacity but wondered about his common sense. The bigger man looked quite capable of taking the dandy apart piece by piece without wasting much effort and little time.

The man in denim bent low to look his challenger in the eyes. "Faggot!" he boomed.

Spinning on his heels, the older man strutted to the large double doors leading to the hallway, and jerked them open. "Okay, asshole! You can now expect a summons and a formal complaint!"

Then the man in the expensive suit really surprised Robbins. Instead of asking the huge man to leave, he himself left – slamming the doors shut behind him.

"I thought I was going to have to stomp that queer little bastard," the big man said to no one in particular. Then he turned to a set of icy blue eyes on David Robbins. The color of his eyes complemented his silver hair and contrasted sharply with his dark tan. "Who are you?" he asked with a scowl.

"I'm David Robbins. Who are you?" Robbins scowled back. No matter how big or powerfully built the man was, Robbins was in no mood to be intimidated.

"David Robbins!" The man's scowl melted into a captivating smile of perfectly straight and startling white teeth. "I'm Emerson Bailey!"

"*You're* Emerson Bailey?" Robbins mused, glancing at the doors the other man just exited through.

Bailey followed Robbins gaze and brayed, "Oh my God! You didn't think…"

"Yes, I did," Robbins interrupted.

"Hell man, that was a low-life divorce attorney. Of course, all divorce attorneys are low-life. They're what gives the rest of us such a bad name. You ever been divorced?"

"No."

"Well, I can tell you, divorce doesn't have to be an ugly experience. It's the divorce attorneys who make it ugly. My first three divorces were not bad at all. My fourth wife, however, has hired that little cock-sucking fairy, and he's trying to bankrupt me!"

Robbins fought off an urge to ask the man if he was really Emerson Bailey – *the* Emerson Bailey with the reputation of being a "Big Gun" – *the* Emerson Bailey of Bailey and Associates, a firm that by all appearances seemed to be thriving.

"Oh, well, hell!" Bailey chuckled. "I guess that slimy homo is just doing what he's capable of doing. We can't all be big time defense attorneys, David...You don't mind if I call you David, do you?"

"Uh, no. Go ahead,"

"Good," Bailey said, flashing another perfect smile. "You can call me, Emo."

"Emo?"

"Yeah, it's short for Emerson. I hate that name."

"What's the 'T.' stand for?"

"Don't ask," Bailey grinned. "I hate it even more. Well, I suppose we should get down to business. You need an attorney, and I need to make a small fortune to pay off that last bitch I was married to! So, come on in my office."

David Robbins was not impressed with attorney Emerson Bailey, but Emo intrigued him. The last five minutes had been the first time in seven days that his mind had been completely stolen away from the thought of Kayla's death. Just before stepping into the attorney's office, Robbins glanced at Mrs. Sloan. If anything unusual had been done or said, he could not tell it by looking at her. Robbins concluded that it took a very special person to be an executive secretary for Emo Bailey.

* * *

Wally Clayton guided his old John Deere toward the heavily wooded low area in front of him. The buzzards that caught his attention fifteen minutes earlier were still circling. Clayton had been feeding the calves penned up in the lot behind his house when he first noticed the scavengers. At first, he thought they might be circling a downed cow. Now that he could see they were flying their patterns over the hollow, he would have bet on it. Over the past forty years more than a few of Wally Clayton's cows had gone to the densely wooded depression to die.

Clayton ground the faded green tractor's transmission into first and let it idle down the steep trail. Creeping at a snail's pace, he couldn't help but notice the tire tracks. Someone else had been down the trail in recent hours, and Clayton breathed a sigh of relief. Whatever kind of carcass he was about to find had no doubt been dumped on his land. Such occurred on nearly regular basis. He didn't like sorry bastards who dumped on other people's property, but he felt relieved he hadn't lost a seven or eight hundred dollar cow.

Concluding that he'd soon find somebody else's cow, or horse, or maybe even a large dog, Clayton decided to head back to the house. He was in the process of turning the tractor around when he spotted the bright patch of yellow on the ground up and to the left of the trail. Clayton's eyes weren't bad for a eighty-six year-old, but they were by no means what they once had been. He had to get within ten feet of the yellow thing before realizing it was a shirt, and it was on a body.

It surprised Clayton that he didn't notice the blood before he did the shirt. It was everywhere. The body laid face down, and the blood clearly came from the back of the mangled head. Wally Clayton fought Hitler's boys many decades earlier and had seen his share of gunshot wounds. If he remembered right, they looked a lot like the hole in the back of this ol' boy's head.

The man was obviously dead. He lay too still, had lost too much blood, and the wound looked too fatal. Clayton didn't touch the body. He had seen enough television to know better. He did bow his head and utter a small prayer. Then, he started back to his tractor. The sheriff needed to be notified as soon as possible. The old man was just a few feet away when the dead man moaned.

* * *

Emo Bailey led David Robbins to the two over-stuffed chairs situated in front of his massive desk and let him take his pick. Robbins sunk down into the one on the right, and instead of moving to the large leather chair behind his desk, Bailey plopped down into the chair on the left. Robbins gave the vast office a quick going over and was most impressed by the picture window behind Bailey's desk. The plate glass started just inches from the floor and reached a point just below the ten-foot ceiling. It looked at least twelve feet wide and presented a spectacular view of downtown Tulsa. Three paintings with rich ornate frames adorned the walls. The paintings depicted New York City street scenes. One had the Statue of Liberty as a backdrop. Another used the Empire State building, and the third centered on the 9/11 Memorial on the sacred grounds where the World Trade Center once stood.

"You like New York City," Robbins observed.

"I hope this will surprise you," Bailey said as he turned to look at the Statue of Liberty. "I was raised less than a mile from that old girl."

"It does surprise me," Robbins smiled. Bailey acted and spoke one hundred percent Oklahoman. "You don't have the slightest trace of an New York accent."

"Well, I've been in the backwoods country for some time now, but time alone didn't rid me of an accent. I've worked hard to articulate like the natives. Oklahoma juries don't respond well to damn Yankee lawyers. I done learned myself that," Bailey chuckled.

"I bet you did," Robbins chuckled back. It felt good to laugh. He couldn't remember the last time he had. "How does a person reared in New York City end up practicing law in Tulsa?" The conversation felt good, too.

"Scholarships. I played football at the University of Oklahoma."

"You did?"

"You never heard of me?"

"No," Robbins grinned.

"Well, I wasn't all that good, so I didn't play that much, just enough to get me through school. By the time I graduated with a political science degree, I was enduring my first marriage. She was full-blooded Oklahoman who wouldn't even consider going back East. Something about the world being flat and fear of falling off the edge, if memory serves me."

Bailey paused long enough to settle back into his chair, crossing one long leg over the other. "So, I started law school at OU. By the time I earned my juris doctorate, I was fighting it out with my second wife…"

"Oklahoman?" Robbins interrupted.

"Oh, yeah. Looks like I would learn but I don't. Three and four? Oklahomans. Just something about you 'ens' women folk!"

"Will there be another one?" Robbins wondered out loud.

"Hell, David, I'm a hopeless romantic as well as a damned glutton for punishment. I can't help but believe that if I keep on trying, I'll find the right one. I like to say, most are bitches but," Bailey stopped mid sentence, and shook his head. "I just realized something. From what I know about you, which is what I read in the papers and watch on television, you are evidently a very religious man. Does my language offend you?"

Bailey's facial expressions and tone of voice did not suggest remorse or embarrassment. Robbins interpreted the statement as a challenge…or maybe a test.

"Does your language offend me? No. Do I approve of it? No. Do I condemn you for using that type of language? No. It is not my job to pass judgment. What is wrong for me, doesn't have to be wrong for you. What is right for me doesn't have to be right for you."

The answer seemed to please Bailey. "You're not a Baptist," he laughed.

"You're familiar with the Baptists," Robbins smiled back.

"Oh, yeah. Number three was a devout one. She didn't put up with me very long."

"I don't imagine she did."

Bailey pushed himself out of his chair and walked around his desk. As he situated himself in the big chair behind his desk he said, "Well, David, we better get to the matter at hand. First, and most importantly for both of us, I charge three hundred and fifty dollars an hour out of court, and five hundred for every hour that I'm before a judge or jury. This could easily end up costing you half a million dollars or more. I will want fifty thousand dollars up front, and you can work with my accountants on covering the balance."

Leaning back in his chair, Bailey raised his legs, crossed them at the ankles and rested two, large, bare feet on his desk, and grinned, "So, David, can you afford me?"

Robbins leaned forward in his chair, "Money is not an issue," he smiled, "but compatibility could be. Wherein I am not judgmental about the words you use, I am concerned about fundamental differences that might exist between us. Emo, I do not mean to be presumptuous, but I want an attorney with integrity and principles."

Bailey dropped his feet to the floor and sat up straight in his chair, "You want an honest attorney? God, don't we all!" Emo Bailey threw back his head and laughed robustly.

Despite how very serious he was on the matter, Robbins found himself laughing in unison.

When they stopped, Emo pushed back in his chair and scratched at the exposed top of his head, "David, I am arrogant and flamboyant and boisterous. I am not a saint…"

Emo leaned forward and stared hard into Robbins' eyes, "…but I'm no crook. I am bound by a code of ethics that I do not violate. And principles, as I'm sure you know, are relative. But in my world and by my contemporaries, I am considered a man of principle.

"So, David, as you wrestle with the question of to hire or not to hire, I'd submit that I'm about as honest an attorney as you are going to find. Furthermore, I am the very best money can buy. I realize that statement seems to clash with the noble ideas of integrity and principles, but that's life in the microcosm into which you've been suddenly thrust. If you want out of this microcosm, which I'm sure you do, then you want the best money can buy."

Robbins crossed his arms over his chest and stared into Bailey's confident eyes. "So, you can keep me out of prison?"

"All I can say at this point, considering what I know of your predicament, is that I'm not accustomed to losing. If I was, I couldn't charge such exuberant fees. However, in my line of business there are never any guarantees. You may very well end up paying me a fortune and then spend the next twenty years in jail.

"Of course, once I know exactly how and why your daughter died, then I can better assess the possibilities of proving your innocence. Keep in mind, David, that right now I'm just like the average, everyday Joe out there on the streets. I know only what I've read in the papers and watched on the television. Unlike the average Joe, I do realize that the media is full of shit. I do realize that just because my morning paper and my evening news have depicted you as a religious fanatic who basically offered your only daughter as a living sacrifice, does not make it true. But, David, I'm not the average Joe. I won't be seated on your jury."

"So, Emo," Robbins smiled wearily. "I tell you my story, and then you tell me if you can keep me out of prison?"

"More accurately, David, you tell me your story, and I will tell you how I plan to keep you out of prison."

"Fair enough," Robbins nodded.

"If you don't object, I want to record what you have to say. If you don't hire me, the recording is yours. If you hire me, then I will have it to refer back to."

"I don't object."

"Good. Do you object to me taking a piss before we get started?"

David Robbins watched Emo Bailey stride out of the room and tried to imagine him before a jury of average Joes.

EIGHT

"**P**lease bear with me," David Robbins said once Bailey was back behind his desk with the tape-recorder running. "I haven't had to talk about what happened since that night. I'm not sure I can do this without becoming emotional."

"I understand," Bailey nodded.

Robbins moved to the edge of the seat. "I would feel more comfortable if I was pacing. Would it hinder your recording?"

"Probably," Bailey nodded again.

Settling back into the chair, Robbins crossed his right leg over his left and sighed deeply. He began by describing the Fellowship Hall of Shawnee's Highland Street Presbyterian Church. Then he explained, "Every Friday night we have a potluck dinner there. It's not really a well-attended event. Normally the same families attend week after week. I would guess about twenty to thirty people are there on an average week. There's no service or anything. We just show up with a covered dish. Someone blesses the food. Then we eat and visit. When we're finished eating and visiting, we clean up and go home."

Robbins went on to explain that his family were Friday night regulars, and told why his wife and son were absent that particular Friday. "Nancy and Kevin weren't the only ones missing that night.

There were only fourteen of us there. I remember thinking that cleanup would be quick and easy.

I was one of the last to go through the serving line, and as I filled my plate, I stuck my hand in some ketchup that one of the kids had spilled on the table. So, I took my plate and set it at an open place on one of the dining tables, and then went to wash my hands in the men's room at the front of the building.

"When I came out, there was a strange man standing just inside the front doors. His back was to me, and he was watching the others eat. I don't think anyone else had noticed him. The guy was very poorly dressed with worn jeans and a dark, tattered jacket. He had on a grungy white T-shirt underneath his jacket. His hair was dirty, oily looking and hung down to his shoulders. I had no idea who he was or what he wanted, so to get his attention, I simply said, 'Hello.'

"The sound of my voice evidently startled him because he wheeled around in a very quick, aggressive manner. Which, in turn, startled me. I knew immediately that he was high on something or had been drinking. I could see it in his eyes. They had the crazed look of a wild, dangerous animal caught in a trap.

"He didn't say anything to me. He just bore holes through me with those eyes. He looked to me to be a vagrant, and I thought he might be hungry. I asked him if he wanted something to eat. I can't explain what it was, but there for a moment the look in his eyes changed. Maybe they softened a little...I don't know...Anyway, seconds later one of the ladies, Terri Horner, came out of the women's restroom, and she said something to the guy. I absolutely cannot remember what she said. I guess I don't remember because of what happened next."

Pausing, Robbins took several deep breaths, and let his head drop so that his eyes stared at the floor. All he had to do now was describe the horrifying events beginning to recreate themselves in his mind. "That was when the man reached into the jacket and…"

* * *

Terri Horner's scream reverberated throughout the gym-like structure. The stranger moved so quickly that Robbins could not intervene. In a mere second, he had pulled the gun from beneath his jacket, reached out and pulled Horner to him by the hair of her head, and had stuck the barrel of the revolver between her eyes.

"Shut the fuck up, bitch!" he screamed into her face while hanging on to a fist full of hair to keep her from getting away. Then he turned wild, angry eyes on Robbins. "Get in there, you son of a bitch. Get the fuck in there!" he screamed as he motioned toward the other church members with violent jerks of his head.

"Please don't hurt her," Robbins said while struggling to keep his voice from revealing his fear.

"Get in there!" he bellowed through gritted teeth, emphasizing his order by yanking Horner's head viciously to the left and then to the right. "I'll blow this woman's head off right here and right now if you don't get your ass in there!"

Robbins started to move on rubbery legs. Some of the others were by now out of their seats, and a few had started his way, but most of them remained seated and wore expressions of either horror or utter disbelief. Robbins frantically scanned the tables for his daughter. Finding her still seated, he headed towards her.

"You mother fuckers sit down!" the man screeched to those standing.

Taking longer strides now, Robbins continued towards his daughter but turned his head to look back. The man had spun Horner around and held her back to his front with a forearm tightly around her neck. The pistol looked to be screwed into her right temple. The two of them were moving as one toward the dining tables. One child was crying by now. A few of the women were near hysterics. Kayla wasn't crying, but shivered as if cold. Robbins took a vacant seat next to her and pulled her to his chest, draping an arm around her small shoulders.

"Who is he, Daddy?" she gasped.

"I don't know, baby," he responded.

"I'm scared."

"I know, Kayla. Just stay still, be quiet…and pray."

"Don't let him hurt me, Daddy."

"I won't, precious."

The table closest to Horner and her captor was empty. When they got within feet of it, the man shoved Horner. He used so much force that she ended up sprawled on top of the table. Folding chairs hit the floor with a clatter. Blood from a badly busted lip trickled down Terri Horner's chin. A woman at the closest table screamed, and then others joined in.

"Shut up, goddamnit! All of you just shut the fuck up!" the gunman roared as he waved the revolver in front of him for all to see.

The louder the man screamed for silence, the more frantic the women and children became. The other men in the room were antsy with fear as they fidgeted about in their chairs with their hands constantly on the move. It looked to Robbins as if his fellow captives were only heartbeats ways from jumping up and scattering in all directions. Robbins feared that such actions might bring indiscriminate fire from their obviously deranged guest.

In spite of the increasingly explosive atmosphere, the captor rushed to the nearest occupied table and grabbed fourteen-year-old

Chad Gains' left ear. Savagely, he used it to slam the boy's head down and hold it against the tabletop. Chad didn't struggle or make a sound. Robbins guessed he was too scared to do either. Chad's father, Harold Gains, leapt from his nearby chair but came to an abrupt halt when the barrel of the gun was stuck to his son's head. Letting go of Chad's ear, the man used the gun to pin the boy's head to the table. For a long second or two the clamor the man had tried to squelch only grew louder. Then he cocked the weapon. The ominous metallic click of the hammer being pulled back brought an immediate silence to the large room.

The absence of audible hysteria seemed to have a calming effect on the terrorist. For seconds he did nothing but survey his prey. When he spoke, his voice was low but still angry.

"Why didn't you people shut up when I told you to shut up?" When no explanation was offered, he said a little louder, "Why?"

Turning his eyes on the only other person standing, he asked Harold Gains, "You tell me. Why the fuck didn't you people mind what I was saying?"

"We're scared," Gains choked.

"You're scared?" the man mocked with a sarcastic whine before throwing his head back and cackling like an evil madman from some B movie.

"Aren't you people goddamn Christians? He grinned hatefully. "Ain't that the fuckin' reason you come to this place?" Again, no answers were offered for his questions, and again he turned a scowl on Harold Gains. "Well, ain't you fuckin' Christians?"

"Yes," Gains said with an exaggerated nod of his head "We're Christians."

"Then what do you have to be scared of?" the man growled at Gains.

"We're scared that you are going to hurt us," Gains offered without hesitation.

"Sit down you worthless piece of shit," the man spat. Then he scanned the room with a disgusted glare. "Well, now, you fine Christian folk have failed one test, so I'll give you another. You didn't do worth shit in putting your trust in the Lord Jesus. Let's see how well you do on giving to the poor." Again, he cackled.

"Yes, Brothers and Sisters," the man sung out like a old time evangelist, "I want you to reach deep into your hearts…and deeper into your pockets and purses…and pull out your wallets and give me your cash money, and I don't want none of you bastards holding out on me."

"You might not be *real* faithful Christians, but from the looks of all those Cadillacs and Lincolns in that parking lot, you must be some damn well-blessed Christians. Yeah, looks like the Lord has been good to you folks. So, now, you be good to me!"

The man seemed to be feeding off the pervading fear, growing more confident with every sob and gasp. He obviously started to have fun, and David Robbins didn't know if that was good or bad. He did know he wasn't about to provoke the man with greed. Robbins pulled out the two hundred dollars in his wallet and threw it on the table in front of him without the slightest hesitation. At first, Robbins thought everyone else was doing the same. Then he noticed Ted Blevens.

The retired Air Force colonel, who supplemented his government pension with a small but lucrative home repair business, was sitting two tables in front of Robbins. Blevens' hands were at his side, and Robbins could see his wallet in the back-right pocket of his Bermuda shorts. Being seated behind the older man, Robbins could not see his face but could imagine it exhibiting a look of unconditional distress. Robbins knew by experience that Blevens encouraged cash-only transaction in his home repair dealings, and it was a well-known fact that the repairman's wallet served as a portable cash register. Robbins did not care to guess how much money Colonel Blevens stood to lose.

"What's your name boy?" the man asked young Chad Gains. The gun still held the boy's head against the table, and it was still cocked.

"Chad," the teen rasped.

"Are you a good Christian boy, Chad? Can I trust you?"

"Yes, sir," Chad rattled.

The man removed the gun from Chad's head and carefully let the hammer down. "Sit up, boy."

Chad Gains did as he was told. Robbins could see the boy shuddering, and his heart went out to him.

"Is this your daddy, Chad?" the man asked, using the large revolver to point out Harold Gains.

The son turned a set of terrified eyes to the father, eyes that no doubt prompted the elder Gains to respond for his son. "Yes. I'm his father."

"I ain't talking to you, asshole!" the man exploded, as he assumed a two-handed grip on the pistol and took aim at Harold Gains' face.

"Please!" Chad Gains screamed as he jumped to his feet. "Please don't hurt him," the boy begged.

"If you don't want me to hurt him, then you better do exactly what I say and answer me when I ask you a fuckin' question."

"Okay," Chad quickly agreed.

"I guess that's your mama," the man said, nodding his head at the small woman clinging to Harold Gains, on whom the sights of the gun were still trained.

"Yes, sir," Chad moaned.

"Well, I'll tell you what, boy. I'm going to stand here and keep a real close eye on your ol' mamma and daddy while you go around this room and collect all my money. Can you do that?"

"Yes, sir."

"Well do it fast and just get the green backs. I don't want no damn coins."

Chad Gains moved about the large room with an urgency one would expect of a child whose parents were being held at gunpoint. Robbins noted that he paused a second in front of Ted Blevens but moved on without a word being exchanged. It wasn't until Chad took Robbins' money that David saw the tears in his eyes and on his cheeks. By the time he made it back to the armed robber, Chad Gains had accumulated a healthy stack of bills.

"Hey, you do a damn good job at passing the plate, Chad," the man grinned as he took his support hand from the weapon's grips to take the wad of bills. Once the money was secured into the front left pocket of his jeans, his left hand went back to help steady the gun on Chad's mother and father. "Did everybody contribute to my cause, boy?"

"Sir?" Chad asked. Robbins wondered if the teen wasn't trying to buy time, hoping his tormentor wouldn't bother to repose the question.

"Did they all give me money, man? And don't fuckin' lie to me, or I'll blow your mom and pop straight to hell!"

From where Robbins sat, he could see Chad Gains' head and shoulders start to shake and bob. It wasn't until the boy spoke that

Robbins realized he was crying. "Two people didn't give me any money," he sobbed.

"Which two?" the man growled.

"Mrs. Rivera and Mr. Blevens."

Before the man could respond, a female voice shaky with age but firm with confidence rang out. "Young man, I'm Ethel Rivera, and I don't carry cash. I do have a good amount of coins, but you said you don't want coins. So, you do whatever you feel necessary to me, but you leave that poor boy be."

The terrorist turned a surprised look on the ancient matron. After too many tense seconds of silence the man countered gruffly with, "Sit down, Chad." Then to the members in general, "Who's Blevens?"

"I am," Ted Blevens said in a voice that gave no hint of intimidation.

"How come you didn't give me no money?" the man frowned.

"I don't carry cash, either."

Just like he had the old woman, the man took a moment to study Ted Blevens. "Bring me your wallet."

"I don't carry a wallet," Blevens shot back in a convincing manner.

A few more seconds passed before the gunman ordered, "Come up here."

Now, Blevens initiated the pause. With a noticeable weaker tone of voice, he finally said, "I told you I don't carry a wallet."

"If you don't get your ass over here, old man, I'll come and get you. You don't want me to do that."

With what appeared to be great effort, Blevens pushed away from the table and started toward the man with the gun. Robbins couldn't help but notice how skinny and vulnerable the older man's legs looked in Bermuda shorts. By the time he got to the man, Blevens had his wallet in hand.

"You're a lying mother fucker, ain't you?" the man said as he jerked the wallet from Bleven's hand. The retired colonel offered no response.

With one hand, the man shook the tri-fold open, then threw his head back and whooped. "Pull that money out of there you old bastard," he grinned before tossing the wallet in Blevens' face. The wallet bounced off the solemn face and fell to the floor. Some of the bills spilled out beside it.

"There's almost two thousand dollars in there," Blevens objected.

The man whooped again. "That makes me so goddamn happy that I'm not even going to kick your ass for lying. Now pick that money up and give it to me."

"If you want it," Blevens snarled, "you pick it up."

The gun had been pointed in the general direction of the Gains. Now, the man slowly brought it up, inserted the barrel into Blevens' left ear and again pulled back the hammer. "You're too old and scrawny to play tough. Pick the money up, or I'll blow what few brains you have out your other fuckin' ear."

Blevens complied without further comment, and once again the man carefully let the revolver's hammer go forward. Once the money was crammed in his pocket with all the rest, the man dismissed Blevens with a shove. "Go sit back down you old son of a bitch."

Blevens stumbled backwards into a table and almost fell. Robbins could clearly see the bald spot at the back of Blevens' head and got a glimpse of the left side of his face as he pushed himself upright. The skin Robbins could see was a bright crimson, so he wasn't really surprised with Blevens' declaration.

"God will punish you for this."

Up to that point, the face of the man who held them hostage communicated primarily anger and disgust. Blevens' words brought a new message. The suddenly flushed cheeks and flared nostrils accompanied by a snarl of crooked, gritted teeth and an inflamed, squint-eyed stare clearly signaled unadulterated hate.

"You mother fucker!" the man raged without moving. "After lying in front of all these fuckin' people because of your love for money, you have the goddamn nerve to pass judgment on me?"

Then, he moved. One large step put him close enough to shove the .357's barrel underneath Ted Blevens' chin, forcing Blevens to sit back against the table he had stumbled into only seconds earlier. "And you call yourself a fuckin' Christian?" He blared.

"I am a Christian," Blevens said defiantly.

"The fuck you are! You don't even act like someone who believes in Jesus. You just say you're a Christian. You just borrow his name. That ain't fuckin' right, man. You ain't fuckin' right, but I wanna make you right. I wanna make your words match your actions. You say there's a Christ, but you don't act like it…So, you are going to admit right here and right now…that there ain't no such thing as Jesus Christ!"

"What?" Blevens gasped.

"You heard me, motherfucker. You live like there's no Christ, so tell me there's no Christ."

"I won't do it!" Blevens bellowed.

The revolver landed hard against the left side of Ted Blevens' head. Blood splattered across the faces and clothing of the Gains family. Chad's mother, Amy Gains, screamed as did others. Ted Blevens fell to his knees.

"Tell me there's no Christ!" the man thundered.

When seconds passed with no response, he raised the gun high in the air. Before he could bring it crashing down, Ted Blevens capitulated.

"There is no Christ," he said weakly, sounding dazed.

"You act like Satan…So tell me you worship Satan," the man pushed.

"I worship Satan," Blevens mimicked.

Stepping back and away from Blevens, the man turned a raging glare on the others in the room. "You worthless mother fuckers treat me like a piece of shit. You look down your noses at me. You hate me when you're supposed to love me. But the only thing you bastards really love is your money."

The large room was once again echoing hysterical cries, moans, and groans. Stepping up to and grabbing the table the Gains family sought refuge behind, the man turned it over and flung it aside. He crammed the gun into Amy Gains' crying face.

"Tell me Jesus Christ is dead."

"I can't," she managed between gasps for air.

"Open your mouth, Chad," the man demanded.

With the gun touching his mother's cheek, Chad obeyed. The man pulled the gun away from Amy Gains and stuck it in her son's mouth.

"Say he's dead, bitch."

"Jesus is dead!" she screamed.

"Now it's your turn, daddy," the man spat at Harold Gains.

"He's dead. Jesus is dead," the father rattled off.

"Do both of you worship Satan?" the man hissed.

Mother and father quickly agreed that they did, and the man pulled the gun from their son's mouth. Turning over two more tables, the man worked his way to Terri Horner.

Obviously thinking back to their initial meeting in the doorway, the man snarled, "This ought to be easy for you, slut."

It seemed to be. Terri Horner wrote Christ off and proclaimed Satan in the same breath – without encouragement to do so.

All along, since first laying eyes on the revolver, David Robbins had been silently praying. As the man worked his way closer to Robbins' table, he pulled Kayla even closer and bowed his head. While Kayla cried – she hadn't done so until Ted Blevens was struck – Robbins prayed out lout. He prayed that the man would grow tired of the nasty little game before he reached him. "Let this cup pass from me," he quoted from the Bible. And if couldn't be passed, Robbins prayed for empowerment to do what he knew was the right thing. "Strengthened with all power, according to your glorious might, for the attaining of all steadfastness," he borrowed again from the scriptures.

When Robbins looked back up, the man had just finished with Marlene and Doug Dolivo. While praying, Robbins heard the couple telling the man exactly what he wanted to hear. Barbara and Trent Carney followed in quick succession. The man passed by Mrs. Ethel Rivera, without as much as a glance. Martha Sugg and her eleven-year-old daughter Margaret were at the table directly in front of Robbins. The Suggs and Robbins were the only ones left, and the man was headed for little Margaret.

"Please don't put that gun in my baby's face!" Martha Sugg screamed. "I'll do anything you say, just please keep that thing away from us," she pleaded.

"Okay, bitch," the man said as he dropped the gun to his side, "Ask Satan to save you. Pray out real loud and real clear so everyone can hear you even over all this goddamn ruckus."

"Please, Satan," Sugg's voice rang out above all the crying, "please don't let us be hurt. Save me and my baby, please Satan!"

For what seemed like hours to Robbins, the man stood and stared silently at Martha Sugg, who had collapsed across her table in a pitiful, quivering, sobbing heap. When he finally turned his eyes on Robbins, the man suddenly looked tired.

"It's your turn, asshole," he mumbled with far less enthusiasm than he had used on the others. "Tell me there's no Jesus."

With much difficulty, David Robbins found the strength to come slowly to his feet. "I can't do that," he managed to proclaim. "I can't say there isn't when I know there is."

"I can make you do it, motherfucker. I can break you just like I broke these other sorry bastards," the man said with just the slightest tinge of his former vigor.

"No, sir," Robbins said calmly. "You can't."

With great deliberation the man brought the firearm up from his side, cocked it and took careful aim at Robbins. Then, cutting a wide, slow swath, he started to circle the father and daughter. Robbins stayed where he was but followed the man's movement by turning in place. At the completion of a half circle, the man stopped. Robbins back was turned to the other church members, and only a yard or so separated him from his tormentor. Robbins didn't realize that Kayla had gotten up and was standing at his side until she wrapped her arms tightly around his waist. Not daring to take his eyes from the man with the gun, Robbins didn't look down, but he could feel Kayla shaking, and he could hear her soft, frightened sobs.

With agonizingly slow steps, the man started to advance toward Robbins. "You're no better than these other hypocrites," the man said under his breath.

"No, I'm not," Robbins readily agreed.

The man's eyes twitched at the response, but he continued to inch forward, and for the moment he remained silent. For the first time since brandishing the revolver, the man seemed indecisive about his next words and action. Robbins took advantage of his silence. "Would you please just put the gun down?" he asked softly.

"Oh, you'd love that wouldn't you?" the man scowled. "You'd love a chance to get your hands on this gun, wouldn't you? Hell, you'd put a fucking bullet between my eyes in a heartbeat."

"I don't want anyone to get hurt," Robbins insisted.

With that, the man planted the barrel of the gun firmly underneath Robbins' jaw. "What if you had a gun right now?" the man practically whispered. "Would you use it on me if you could?"

Robbins' fear threatened to totally incapacitate him. His limbs felt numb – his breathing became labored. For a man who practiced honesty, the truth was the only thing that came immediately to mind. "I don't know," he admitted.

The forearm and elbow strike collided with Robbins' chest and took him by complete surprise. The force of the blow sent him tumbling backwards over his chair, and he landed face-up on top of the table. Dazed by the powerful strike, Robbins stared blankly at the ceiling until the terrible, shrill noise – that rose above all the anguished cries – cleared his head. Kayla was screaming.

Robbins sprang from the table and landed on his feet but advanced no further. The man held his daughter by the blond, curly hair of her head. The barrel of the gun twitched within inches of her lovely face. Tightly squinted eyelids concealed the child's dark blue eyes, and her normally creamy, white complexion flushed to a feverish red. A wide-open mouth of tiny, bright teeth emitted the tortured shriek. Small hands clawed at the empty air that separated father and daughter while gangly legs pawed for traction, but the man had Kayla stretched to her tiptoes.

"Let her go," David Robbins ordered in a shaky voice.

"If you had a gun now," the man responded, "you'd kill me."

"I'd protect my daughter," Robbins agreed loudly.

"Of course, you fuckin' would, and if you'd blow me away to save your daughter. Surely, you'd turn your back on God and worship Satan in order to save her. So, you best get to doing it."

A dense fog of near panic gripped Robbins' mind and dulled his senses, and maybe that was why he thought he suddenly sensed a change. Had the look of hate in the man's face somewhat subsided? Eyes that moments earlier reflected malice, now seemed more inquisitive. Did words that had been venomous now have a slightly softer edge? Depending on a hastily formed hunch, David Robbins spoke his thoughts. "You don't want to hurt my daughter. Please let her go."

"I'm tired of fucking with you, man. You got one more chance to tell me that there ain't no such thing as Jesus Christ."

Robbins could no longer sense conviction in the man's voice or manner, but little Kayla was growing more frantic by the second. She no longer screaming but now grasped to catch her breath. With her arms and legs still wildly active, her father thought she looked to be unsuccessfully treading imaginary waters and showing signs of drowning. He wondered how much had been inflicted on the seven-year-old's mind and emotions and considered the possibility of the damage being permanent. The thought of his precious child bearing hidden scars brought with it the conclusion that enough was enough.

"Listen, mister," Robbins said as he tried to contain his sudden anger by tilting his head to the ceiling and tightly closing his eyes. "If you just absolutely have to use that gun on someone here tonight," he said through gritted teeth, "then use the damn thing on me!"

"Noooooooooo…" Kayla's voice started in a scream. Before Robbins could open his eyes and lower his head, the gunshot erupted with a deafening roar. Looking to the spot where only moments earlier the man held his daughter, David Robbins saw nothing but blood. The source of the blood lay at least three feet away. Robbins took one step in that direction, and then collapsed face forward. The father's head came to rest at his daughter's small, still feet.

NINE

Robbins concluded his story with a series of sniffs, a hard sigh, and some quick swipes at his eyes with his finger tips. At the first mention of the gun, Robbins had moved to the edge of his seat. He perched there for the remainder of his rendition. Now, he settled into the chair's high and curved back and liked how its winged design provided the illusion of being hugged.

A number of times during the telling of his story, Robbins averted his eyes from Emerson Bailey. It proved easier to impart portions of the account while looking at something that couldn't look back. Each time Robbins returned his gaze to the attorney, he faced an emotionless stare from a stoic face. Robbins did look at Bailey when relaying how he had crawled on top of Kayla's body. As far as Robbins knew, that was the only time Emerson Bailey looked away. The soft, short whistle that followed was the only noise Bailey emitted during the entire chronicle.

At Robbins' conclusion, Bailey had, without uttering a single word, turned off the recorder and started scribbling on a yellow legal pad on his desk. Robbins did not interrupt the much-appreciated quiet time. Instead, he used it to reassemble his wits and emotions.

While the attorney scratched at the pad with a fat Mont Blanc, Robbins turned his attention to the elegant painting of the Statue of Liberty. His eyes locked on the object the grand lady held high over her head. Of all the souvenirs purchased during last year's vacation to the Big Apple, a small replica of the torch had been Kayla's favorite. The memory brought by the torch mercifully washed away Robbins' dark, mental image of how Kayla looked in death and replaced it with a recollection of how she looked in life at its fullest. For weeks after returning home from New York City, the invariably cheerful little blonde could be seen folding one of her Doctor Seuss books across her chest, hoisting the torch as high as she could and declaring in a squeal, "Give me your tired, your poor, your puddles and messes!" The facial expression the child dawned, like her oration, was never completely correct. Plump, rosy cheeks – that Dad took great pleasure in affectionately pinching between a thumb and index finger – and bright eyes that smiled even when the full little lips weren't, just couldn't master the statue's solemn dignity.

Robbins was several winding bends deep into Memory Lane when he realized the scraping sound of Bailey's writing had ceased. Turning from the painting back to Bailey, Robbins found himself under the penetrating gaze of the icy blue eyes.

"You were smiling at Ms. Liberty," Bailey stated in a quizzical tone.

"Uh, yeah," Robbins responded, suddenly aware of how strange a smile must have looked on a man who had just told such an awful story. "She reminds me of a trip my family and I took to New York City last summer. Kayla was very fond of the Statue and Battery Park..." With one more glance at the likeness, Robbins finished with, "...Your painting brings to mind better times."

"It does for me, too," Bailey emphasized with a slow nod.

Robbins pointed to the legal pad, "Is that your plan for keeping me out of prison?"

"Let's call it the first draft of my plan. It will need some tuning," Bailey said as picked up the pad and leaned back in his huge leather chair. "Two potential defenses come immediately to mind." Bailey held up the long, thick index finger of his right hand to represent the numeral one. "We can address your First Amendment rights to freedom of speech and religion in hopes of discounting depravity. That way…"

"Depravity?" Robbins interrupted.

"Yeah. Nasty sounding word isn't it?" Bailey chuckled as he lowered his finger. "You see, in your case second-degree murder has two elements." The index finger popped up a second time. "An act must be perpetrated that is imminently dangerous to another." The middle finger followed suit. "That act must evince a depraved mind."

"What's the legal definition of a depraved mind?" Robbins asked.

"In your case it simply means you intentionally engaged in conduct that was imminently dangerous to another, or, in other words, you knew there was a substantial risk to human life, but you disregarded that risk and perpetrated an act resulting in death."

"I take it that to perpetrate an act means to perform an act…to do something," Robbins frowned. "I didn't do anything. I refused to do anything. I refused to act."

"The courts have determined that an omission to act in the face of a duty becomes an act."

"In the face of what duty?" Robbins blurted.

Bailey's facial features softened, and he toned down his booming voice. "In the face of the duty to protect your minor child from intentional physical harm."

Robbins brought both hands up to massage his suddenly throbbing temples. While doing so he closed his eyes, inhaled deeply, and returned in his mind to the unfinished business of some twenty-odd hours earlier. The memory of the intent look on Jennifer Rhodes' face was still fresh enough to be vivid, and her poignant question had lost none of its punch. "Do you feel guilty of murdering your daughter?" With the exact words now rioting loudly inside his head, Robbins looked to an outside source to help quell it.

"Am I guilty of second-degree murder?"

"That's a jury's call," Bailey responded without missing a beat or batting an eye. He fielded the potentially disruptive question with the ease of a professional shortstop snagging a line drive hit.

"That is true, ultimately. But for now, I want your opinion."

"Fair enough," Bailey said as he tossed the pad back on the desk and folded his thick arms across a broad chest. "Let's first consider the facts. A man has a gun. The man commits armed robbery. The man then turns the gun on…" Bailey paused to lean forward and look at the pad, "…ten different people. These ten people are ordered to…" the big lawyer paused a second time, looked to the ceiling and scratched at his goatee while obviously choosing his next words, "…repeat mere words and phrases. They are…"

"Wait a minute," Robbins interrupted with a raised hand. "They were not mere words and phrases."

Bailey sat up straight in his chair, pulled close to and leaned across the desk, resting on his forearms. "Whose opinion am I giving here, yours or mine?" he grinned.

"I'll let you finish," Robbins nodded reluctantly.

"Thank you," Bailey smiled as he once again leaned back in his chair. "Any prosecutor worth a damn will go to any length, pull all plugs, push all buttons to convince a jury that what that man forced those ten people to repeat were simply mere words, no more. That's why I used that term. Now, back to the facts. Nine of the ten people repeated words and phrases, and those people were not harmed. Three of those nine people repeated those words and phrases because the man threatened their children. The two children belonging to those three people were unharmed.

"Finally, the most damaging facts. The man told you to repeat basically the same words and phrases that had, in essence, already saved the other nine adults and two children. The man threatened physical harm to your daughter if you did not obey his commands. Twice he verbalized his intent to cause her harm while holding a gun to her head. Twice you refused to repeat the words and phrases. The man shot and killed your daughter.

"Now, in my opinion," Bailey said as he pushed out of his chair and started to pace behind his desk, "up to this point in our outline of facts, your actions have pretty much evinced a depraved mind."

Hoping for a facial expression and tone of voice that would not betray his sudden internal upheaval, Robbins asked, "So, in your opinion, I am guilty."

Emerson Bailey took a few more steps and then stopped and turned to face Robbins. "If these were all the facts we had to work with, then yes, I would consider you guilty as charged."

"Those are all the facts," Robbins said dryly.

"No, they aren't," Bailey beamed. "We still have the fact of the unknown."

"The what?" Robbins asked with a scowl.

"The fact of the unknown. The fact that we do not know what would have actually happened had you repeated those words. We have no proof, no guarantee, that he would not have shot your daughter anyway."

"David," Emerson Bailey said with a gentle tone as he sat back down. "It was not your actions or words, or lack thereof, that murdered your daughter. It was a madman with a gun. By going with a defense of your First Amendment rights, our goal will be to engrave that on the minds and in the hearts of the jury."

Robbins found merit in Bailey's simple conclusion of the unknown fact and his madman with a gun theory, and Robbins had confidence in the attorney's abilities to sell conclusions and theories to a jury. Robbins just wished he could buy them – lock, stock, and barrel. If so, he could, in turn, offer them to satisfy the question posed by Jennifer Rhodes.

"You had two potential defenses. What's my other option?" Robbins asked wearily.

"Insanity," Bailey grinned.

"That is not an option," David Robbins sighed through a sad smile. "Up to the point and time that trigger was pulled, I was perfectly sane."

* * *

The firm didn't need the case. Business, as usual, was booming. But Bailey wanted it. Badly. He wanted the challenge. More so, he wanted the national recognition the case would most assuredly provide. Win or lose, the attorney who represented David Robbins would have his name and face on newspapers and television from Los Angeles to New York City. Now, he only needed to convince Robbins that he was the man for the job.

"David, are you familiar with Matthew 10:16?"

The mentioning of a Bible verse brought a curious look to the solemn face sitting on the other side of the desk. The abruptly off-topic question produced the effect Bailey hoped for.

"I don't have the gospels committed to memory," Robbins said with a semblance of a smile. "Do you?"

"Well, I can quote more than my fair share."

Robbins' curious expression escalated to a look of mild surprise.

"I was born and raised Catholic, David. Now, I don't profess to be a devout man. I, uh, haven't attended Mass since, well, since I can't remember when. But I did attend Catholic schools from the first grade on. Some things, you know, just stick with a man."

"So, are you trying to play on my spiritual sympathies?" Robbins asked with a taunting scowl.

"Would it help?" Bailey chuckled.

"Not in the least," Robbins smiled back. "But, you have aroused my curiosity. How does Matthew 10:16 apply to my situation?"

Bailey cleared his throat, "Behold, I send you out as sheep in the midst of wolves; Therefore, be shrewd as serpents, and innocent as doves."

Robbins silently considered the verse, and Bailey remained quite as he did so.

"David, if you don't know it by now, you've been literally thrown to the wolves. I sense by nature and choice that you are in essence a dove. I, on the other hand, can aptly provide the services of the serpent. I think our fundamental differences, as you would put it, will complement each other in this endeavor. I want to represent you in this case."

David Robbins' eyes slowly scanned the walls of the office and came to rest on the painting of the Statue of Liberty. After long seconds he turned back to Bailey.

"I'm willing to give it a try."

* * *

The sound of breaking glass disrupted the tranquil stillness of the rural darkness, and only the katydids seemed to notice. For a second or two their shrill, chirping chorus waned but quickly recovered, seemingly with revived vigor. The now accessible inside latch of the paned window did not easily give way to the twisting motion. After eternal seconds of exertion, it did break free but not without objecting with a high-pitched squeak. Somewhere in the not too far off darkness a dog barked and Luke Hogue's heart pounded a near drum-like beat.

Crouching into the shrubbery below the window, Hogue struggled to control his suddenly panting breath. Closing his eyes in a tight squint, he reminded himself of what a pre-dusk recon of the area had revealed. There were no residences within a quarter mile of the small country store he was now trying to break into. The dog, he tried to assure himself was, like him, a hungry stray searching for food. Still, he could not afford to take chances. A man wanted for murder, kidnapping and felony assault on a police officer could not afford to bungle a smalltime burglary. Despite agonizing hunger pangs and a mind-numbing weakness, Hogue opted to stay in the shrubs until the dog could be nothing but long gone, just like another dog that abruptly came to mind. Because he didn't have the energy to fight off the memory and because there were more horrid memories that could occupy his time, Hogue let the recollection play out in living color on the makeshift screen of his closed eyelids…

* * *

…Less than two weeks had passed since young Luke Hogue encountered the substantial bosom of Brother Bob Harlow's little girl, Michelle. It was still Oklahoma August, and the typically high humidity was on the offensive, making the air heavy and hard to breathe and assaulting skin and clothing with a syrupy dampness. Luke stepped out on the front porch that morning to find his brother Mark squatted on haunches and intently watching the activity in their overgrown and cluttered front yard. Ten yards or so beyond the porch and facing the house was the Reverend Richard Lee. Between the preacher and the house cowered the skinny, stray hound that Luke considered to be his pet – the dog with no name.

Richard Lee stood slightly bent at the waist and held his left arm exposed and extended toward the mixed breed mutt. He gently snapped the fingers of this left hand while verbally trying to coax the dog to him with sweet words, kissing sounds, and whistles. His right hand and arm were concealed behind his back.

"What's he doing?" Luke whispered suspiciously.

"He stepped in some dog shit around the back of the house," Mark snickered.

The short-haired, motley hound of brown, red, and black trembled and had its long tail tucked tightly between its bony back legs. When Richard Lee took a cautious step forward, the hound turned so that Luke got a look at its long-muzzled face. Large and brown eyes that were, even in better times, ceaselessly sad, were now watery and reflective of crippling fear. The dog looked like Luke Hogue suddenly felt.

In a squirming, side-winding fashion, the dog continued to move, but Richard Lee slowly and deliberately closed in. When mere feet separated man from beast, Richard Lee made a move that exposed his back to his sons. Looped in the father's right hand was a lariat of clothes-line wire. One more step put Richard Lee within desired range, and in a quick, smooth flick of the wrist, he managed to lasso the dog. Too late, the animal tried to run. A brutal tug on the wire cinched the thick metal deep into the flesh of the dog's neck and jerked it off its feet.

"I'll teach you to shit all over the place, you mongrel bitch!" the good Reverend bellowed as the dog jumped to her feet.

The pointed toe of the black boot connected first with the dog's left hip and sent her rolling. With a tortured, wailing yelp she scrambled back up and tried to scurry away, dragging the left rear leg like a limp rag. Another terrible jerk on the wire brought the canine back into striking distance. This time the kick went to the head, and again the dog rolled. This time she didn't get up. She just twitched and jerked like a fish too long out of water.

"Stupid, worthless bitch!" Richard Lee spat as he brutally stomped once and then twice on the dog's neck with his right boot.

Luke rubbed at the tears that filled his eyes and rolled down his cheeks as he watched his dog fight for its last breath of air. He wanted to scream at the man in the black boots. He wanted to cuss him. He wanted to do him harm. But more than anything else, Luke wanted not to end up like the dog.

The Reverend Lee Hogue dropped his end of the wire, and this time brought up his left boot as if to deliver one last stomp. Instead, he nonchalantly brought the boot slowly down and rested it gently on the dog's midsection. Then he vigorously rubbed the boot up and down and back and forth across the mangy coat. When he removed his foot, a dark, grainy substance remained on the fur.

"You boy," Richard Lee exhaled as he pointed a mean finger at Mark Hogue. "Take this mutt out in the back pasture and bury it."

Looking down, Luke observed his brother's eyes were wide with fright, but there was no sign of tears.

"It's Luke's dog, Daddy," Mark whined.

Turning a poisoned glare from Mark to Luke, Richard Lee responded. "Yeah, and you was the one always feeding the bitch. There's a world full of starving children, and you're feeding our scraps to a stupid animal. You take it and bury it, and maybe you'll learn a thing or two about the value of putting human life over ignorant animals."

Luke glanced down and into Mark's upturned and taunting face and shared his best I-hate-you look with his younger brother before stepping off the porch. Taking slow steps on wobbly legs toward his dead dog, Luke remembered that he still owed Mark for snitching on him about being in the shed with the Harlow girl. He would not forget again.

The dog lay so that her face could not been seen from the direction of the porch. As soon as the boy took the step that put him over the carcass, Luke grasped and stumbled backwards. He had not expected to look down into open and staring eyes. Eyes that still mirrored the awful events that lead to death. Eyes that looked…

* * *

…Like the eyes of the little girl. And once again, *she* rushed back to mind, and a grown Luke Hogue, hungry, weak and scared, grabbed his head in both hands and fought the need to start screaming, knowing that if he ever started, he wouldn't be able to stop until those little, dark blue eyes stopped staring. Jumping up from his hiding place in the shrubbery, Hogue grabbed the unlocked window and put his emotions behind the effort of opening it. The window practically flew open.

Before he could think more of dead eyes that continued to look and of the small girl who seemed to be lurking around every dark corner of his mind and in every closet of his conscience, Hogue scurried up and through the open window. He needed food; then he needed to go north. Canada was where he needed to be, and Canada was a long, long ways from Oklahoma.

* * *

David Robbins stepped out of the elevator and walked deliberately to the Intensive Care Unit's Nursing Station.

"Can you point me to room 345?" he blurted to a portly nurse who appeared to be quickly closing in on retirement age.

Robbins had not been in Oklahoma City's Baptist Medical Center in years, and as far as he knew, he had never laid eyes on this nurse. However, the nurse, like so many people were starting to do, held Robbins in a where-do-I-know-you-from stare.

"Uh, yes," she said haltingly. "It's to your right, end of the hall on the left."

"Thank you," Robbins said before wheeling right and striding away. Some people were standing at the end of the hall, and Robbins hoped one of them was Shawnee Police Detective Bobby Mann.

Robbins had not left Emerson Bailey's office until nearly six. Being in no hurry to get back to his hauntingly empty home, Robbins had opted for back roads over the turnpike and had taken his sweet time in getting back to Shawnee.

It was eight-thirty before Robbins listened to Detective Mann's message on his recorder – Larry Phelps was listed in critical condition.

Robbins made the usual forty-five-minute trip to Oklahoma City in thirty.

Bobby Mann was, indeed, one of the three men standing in the hall. Stanton Barcus, the Shawnee Detective who had driven Robbins' car from the cemetery to the county jail, and a uniformed Oklahoma City police officer accompanied Mann.

"Where the hell you been?" Mann greeted Robbins gruffly.

"In Tulsa," Robbins returned, and when that didn't seem to satisfy the obviously irritable, bulldog looking cop, he added, "Seeing an attorney." Robbins felt he owed the explanation. Mann had left the message about Phelps six hours earlier. "I would have been here much earlier if you'd called my cell."

"I didn't have your cell number with me," Man grumbled, and then said, "You know, Barcus, right?"

"Yes," Robbins said as he extended a hand to the other Shawnee cop. "Hello, Detective," Barcus took his hand with a smile and returned the greeting.

"This is Lieutenant Cisco, OCPD SWAT," Mann said, pointing to the uniform.

Robbins offered his hand to the big city cop. "Nice to meet you, Lieutenant."

"Same here," Cisco emphasized with an almost painful grip.

"Larry's in real bad shape," Mann sighed. "Kinda hangin' on by his fingernails."

"What happened? Was he shot?" Robbins asked.

"No. Knocked in the back of the head with something. Probably a gun. Then the asshole left him out in the woods to die. He's lost a lot of blood and has some sort of bad ass infection. He was unconscious until about two hours ago. He's been in and out ever since.

Every time he comes around," Mann said, looking hard into Robbins' eyes, "he asks for you."

The detective's eyes clearly communicated resentment, and Robbins could not fault the man's feelings. Robbins had not been spared the realization that Larry Phelps would not be where he was if not for him. That was not the only morsel of guilt Robbins had gnawed on during his high-speed trip to the hospital. Additionally, there existed the fact that Robbins had given Phelps, who only hours earlier had been missing and assumed dead, very little thought during the course of the day. He had done very little thinking of Larry Phelps and absolutely no praying for Larry Phelps. Of course, Robbins deduced, one could be excused for spending too little time thinking of a friend in need when one had a dead child, estranged wife, and life in prison on which to dwell. But he could find no excuse for not praying for his old friend. Robbins knew that just because he didn't feel like talking to God, didn't mean God wouldn't listen if he did. So, Robbins did. With a death grip on the steering wheel and tears blurring his vision, David Robbins had asked for Larry Phelps to be spared.

"Can I see him now?" Robbins asked, averting his eyes from the detective's scowl.

"Ain't nobody else in there," Mann grunted in the affirmative.

Robbins wasn't prepared for the sight that awaited him in room 345. A serious wrap, white and elastic looking, covered the top of Phelps' head. A tube that Robbins wished was not clear protruded from his nose and ran to a glass jug at which Robbins didn't care to look. Another two tubes ran down from two plastic bags, one with clear liquid and the other with blood. Both disappeared under the white sheet pulled up beneath Phelps' chin. He seemed to labor at catching shallow breaths, and what little skin he had exposed looked as pale and waxy as that of a man already dead. Some of the whites of his eyes – now yellowed – were visible through matted eyelids not quite closed. Three fingers of his left hand peeked from beneath the white sheet. Robbins moved to his bedside and gently took hold of the fingers.

With no little effort, Larry Phelps fully opened his eyes. A try at turning his head to look at Robbins resulted only in a despairing moan. Robbins leaned over the bed, so Phelps could see him without having to move. After several seconds of obvious difficulty, Phelps' eyes focused on the face hovering above him, and his dry, cracked lips formed into a slight smile.

"Hi, David," he managed in a raspy whisper.

"Hi, Larry," Robbins said as he gently squeezed Phelps' fingers. "How you doing?"

"Done better," Phelps said as the smile broadened.

"Haven't we all?" Robbins smiled back.

"David," Phelps said, the smile disappearing, "I'm sorry he got away."

The words affected Robbins' guilt like a lighted match affects gasoline. It took several seconds before Robbins could respond without his voice cracking. "You have nothing to be sorry about, old friend. I just thank God that you're alive."

"Me too, David, but," Phelps said, closing his eyes, and swallowing hard, "I'm really not doing so hot. I'm really scared, David."

"You're going to be just…" Robbins started.

"I ain't much of a praying man, David," Phelps interrupted. "You know that. Would you please pray for me?"

"I have been Larry," Robbins choked.

"I figured as much, but, please, say a prayer for me now."

David Robbins bowed his head and closed his eyes. The first part of his prayer was silent. *Hear me through my anger. Don't deny me* because of my bitterness. "Dear Heavenly Father," Robbins began as a tear worked its way from his closed eyelids. "Touch Larry with your strength. Heal him with your love. Let him feel your presence. Soothe his pain and take away his fear. In Jesus' Holy name I pray. Amen."

"Thank you, David," Phelps said in a voice weaker than before. "When I feel better, David, I'll tell you about…that man."

"Okay, Larry. I'd like that."

Larry Phelps' eyes slowly closed and he appeared to slip into unconsciousness. David Robbins let go of his fingers and whispered. "Take care of him, God."

* * *

The phone beside Robbins' bed started ringing for the second time since midnight. Thanks to sleeping pills prescribed by Doctor Toliver on the night of Kayla's death, Robbins once again found it almost impossible to orchestrate eyes, arms, hands and fingers well enough to find, grasp and deliver the receiver to his ear. This second time, however, Robbins had help in waking that he didn't have for the first call. This time he was angry.

Wrapping stiff fingers around the receiver and fumbling to bring it to his head, Robbins noted the time – 3:40 a.m. The last call had come just a little after one.

"Listen, pal," Robbins growled his first words, "if you want to call me some more names and make some more threats, then why don't you come and do it to my face!"

There was nothing but silence on the other end. This time the coarse voice didn't start off with "Did I wake you, you baby-killing son of a bitch?" And, it didn't jump right into calling Robbins a "fanatical asshole," and "hypocritical bastard." The voice didn't threaten

144

to burn down his house and his sporting goods store. It didn't promise to "Drop a hammer on you, just like you dropped that hammer on your own flesh and blood!"

The silence angered Robbins even more. Sleep was not something he recently had had in abundance. "Hey!" He nearly shouted. "Are you there?"

It wasn't the unknown's coarse voice that responded, "Is that you, Robbins?"

Instead, it was a voice David Robbins recognized immediately, and it brought him upright in bed, "Detective Mann?"

"Yeah. He's dead, Robbins. Died in the last thirty minutes. The infection got him. Larry was just too weak to fight if off."

The voice Robbins found to use sounded foreign and distant even to himself. The words that came to mind were the first he spoke. "But I prayed. I prayed that God would take care of him."

"Do me a favor, Robbins," a very weary sounding Bobby Mann responded. "Leave me out of your prayers."

TEN

David Robbins didn't hang up the receiver after Detective Mann disconnected. Instead, he held it tightly to his ear until it started beeping frantically. Then he simply let go of the device, and it fell on the bed beside him. Swinging bare legs off the side of the bed but remaining perched on the edge of the mattress, a dazed Robbins stared into the darkness and wished it would consume him into its nothingness.

After long, painful minutes proved the darkness would not swallow him up and could not engulf his torment, Robbins thought of something that could and would. Legs wobbling, he moved off the bed and out of the bedroom like a man in a slow-motion nightmare. After working his way tediously down the winding stairs to the spacious entryway, Robbins shuffled across the terrazzo floor. Reaching the double door entry to his study, he flipped the switch just inside the doors. The globed lights that hung down from the ten-foot ceiling drenched the room of mahogany panels and stuffed bookshelves in brilliant light. Robbins squinted and rapidly blinked assaulted eyes, but continued the trek to his objective. Once inside the door, he cut a diagonal path toward the rock fireplace in the center of the right wall. On each side of the fireplace were built-in cabinets stretching from floor to ceiling. Both had a bottom and top set of glass-paned doors that did nothing to conceal the inventory therein. It was the cabinet on the far side of the fireplace that housed what Robbins sought.

The contents of that cabinet had in the past evoked a wide range of responses from friends and associates, everything from good-humored wisecracks to warnings of damnation, from wide smiles to gaping mouthed repulsion. It was normally other Presbyterians, Catholics, and Methodists who either joked about, took in stride, or enjoyed the cabinet's ware. The more negative reactions usually came from Baptists and members of charismatic denominations who just could not fathom such a well-stocked liquor cabinet in such a devout man's home. For such people, Robbins never bothered to explain that the alcohol was seldom touched and was on hand mostly and truly for visitors and rare celebratory occasions. It would not have done any good. Such was life in the heart of the Bible Belt.

Robbins pulled a full fifth of Jack Daniels and a crystal shot glass from the cabinet and moved to his desk. Sitting down at the desk, he filled the small glass full of the whiskey and nearly tossed it into his mouth. The first shot went down like bitter medicine, burning all the way to the bottom of Robbins' empty stomach. The straight liquor brought tears to his eyes and terribly offended his taste buds, but it didn't stop him from repeating the procedure a second and third time in quick succession.

Robbins placed the shot glass on the desk and filled it a fourth time but didn't pick it back up. Pulling his right hand back from the bottle, Robbins formed it into a tight fist and moved it into his lap where it joined the left fist. Then he raised his head and turned a hard stare towards the ceiling, but it wasn't the tin ceiling tiles that drew his scrutiny.

"Ironic, isn't it?" Robbins mumbled angrily out loud. "Here I am turning to whiskey to dull my pain and give me refuge…to give me some comfort.

"Fifteen years ago, I turned to you and asked you to save a loved one's life. I promised that I would serve you and worship you in exchange for that life," Robbins had started in a loud voice, and it grew louder with each sentence. "You spared that life, and I kept my promises."

"That's what I was doing the night you let that man murder Kayla." Robbins was now sobbing. "You once saved a life for me, and now you take one away from me. Okay, I guess in some sick way that makes us even, but now Nancy leaves me, and Larry Phelps is dead."

Robbins slumped forward and crossed his arms over his head. He began crying so hard that he had to gasp for each breath, and as he did, he remembered the first time he cried as an adult.

He and Nancy had been two weeks into the second year of a thriving marriage when the car she drove was hit head-on by a drunk in an old Cadillac. They flew his all-but-dead young wife by helicopter to Presbyterian Hospital in Oklahoma City, and hours of emergency surgery were performed on the terrible damage to the top and back of her head. When Nancy did not regain consciousness after the surgery, her doctors officially listed her as comatose. Two days later, on a Wednesday, they hooked her to life support systems, and told Robbins that the love of his life would not make it to the end of the week.

Up to that point and time, Robbins had remained strong and tearless, just knowing the "fate" that produced such an unusually strong love wouldn't allow it to end in tragedy. But moments after the bearers of bad news vacated his wife's room, Robbins collapsed across her bed and practically dissolved into flowing tears and loud, breathtaking sobs. He didn't know how long he cried, but he knew he hadn't cried long enough, when a hand landed softly upon his shoulder.

Robbins turned and looked up to the gentle, concerned face of a man old enough to be grandfatherly. The man wore a black collar that Robbins thought only Catholic priests wore.

"Would you like me to pray for her?" the man asked softly, compassionately.

Robbins had been in one Baptist church or another for most of the Easters of his life and attended a few services during Christmas seasons past. He had been subjected to just enough Oklahoma Baptist influence to normally distrust any clergyman wearing a collar, but these were not normal times or circumstances.

"Yes, Sir," he said through his tears. "Please ask God to save her. Please."

"Is she a Christian?" the man asked as he moved around to the other side of her bed.

Nancy attended a Methodist Church regularly while growing up and sporadically since marrying David. They discussed Christianity on more than one occasion. Robbins was more secure with her salvation than he was with his own.

"Yes, sir," he responded.

The man picked up Nancy's limp and cold left hand with his right and reached across the bed and took Robbins' right hand in his left. Then with words that Robbins had long forgotten, the man with a collar asked Jesus Christ to spare Nancy Robbins' life. After he prayed, but before letting go of either's hands, the minister looked solemnly at David Robbins.

"Are you a Christian?"

"I think so," Robbins offered after a moment's hesitation.

"Would you like to pray for her?"

Robbins first nodded his head, then bowed it. The prayer he offered, he would never forget. "Please, Dear God, let her live. If you let her live, I will live my life for you. Amen."

The clergyman left minutes later but returned within the hour with a Gideons' New Testament for Robbins. The minister took the time to point out the pages at the front of the Bible that listed scriptures offering help in time of need, and passages that addressed some of life's more common problems.

The remaining days of that week found Nancy Robbins still living a life provided by machines and tubes and found David Robbins diligently studying his small New Testament. During those days he continued to pray for a miracle and constantly repeated promises of lifelong commitment in exchange for his wife's well-being.

Nancy didn't get well in a blink of an eye or even over night, but she did get well. One week after the doctors put Nancy on life support systems, they took her off. The next day she regained consciousness. Two weeks later, Nancy walked away from Presbyterian Hospital. She didn't need a cane or walker, had no speech impediment or loss of memory, and could see and hear just fine. The doctors had called her recovery phenomenal. David Robbins had called it a miracle. Until fifteen years later, he always believed it had been a special gift from God.

Robbins brought the shot glass up to toasting position. "This one's for you, Larry," he grumbled before swilling the contents of the glass. "Instead of praying for God to make you well…we should have drunk to your health."

Slamming the glass to the desk, Robbins angrily pushed himself up to stand on shaky legs. After taking a few seconds to steady his suddenly wavering vision, he shoved off in the direction of the bookshelves on the wall opposite of the fireplace. Unable to walk in a straight line, Robbins reached the bookshelves several feet to the left of where he intended. Using the shelves to hold him upright, he worked himself hand over hand until he could reach what he wanted to reach.

It took several fumbling attempts before his fingers locked onto and pulled from the bookshelf a very worn Gideons' New Testament. When the small Bible collided with the far wall, it came apart and pages went in all directions.

* * *

Luke Hogue had no idea what time it was, but the night had already lasted forever and surely couldn't go on much longer. He had spent the eternal night searching for cars belonging to trusting country folk who didn't bother removing keys from ignitions. So far, four out-back residences situated on eight to ten miles of dirt road failed to produce such vehicles. Hogue had slithered up to eleven different automobiles since leaving the rural grocery store, and all were locked up tighter than an Oklahoma liquor store on Sunday morning. It disturbed him that good 'ol country people had grown so mistrusting.

Hogue was working his way along the dark dirt road and practically came up on the next house before he even noticed it. Reason being, the house had no outside lights nor barking dogs to scare the hell out of him. The absence of the two basic, down-home security devices lifted Hogue's spirits.

A terribly abused Chevy sedan, an ancient Ford station wagon and a four-wheel drive Dodge pickup were strewn among a collection of other junk adorning the unkept front yard. Any one of the three would make a great replacement for Mark's old pickup that Luke hid in a hollow a half mile from the country store. Luke left the cop's gun on the front seat. On top of everything else he didn't want to be accused of stealing a police officer's sidearm.

Making his way quietly and cautiously over and around discarded engine parts, abandoned appliances and piles of ruined tires, Hogue pressed toward the Dodge. It was located furthest from the house and sat on an incline facing the road. If it had keys, Hogue could let it roll down to the road before starting it.

In spite of the night's previous disappointments, Hogue couldn't help getting his hopes up when he found the pickup's driver side window down. With a beaming smile he leaned into the dark cab and ran his hands along the column in order to find the ignition switch. There were no keys.

The old Ford wagon sat the next in line. Hogue went to the Ford's passenger side. Both windows on that side were up and both doors were locked. He moved on up to the passenger side of the dilapidated Chevy. The junk-mobile was parked four feet from an open window in the house and the other two cars had it blocked in. But its windows were down.

"Yeah, motherfucker," Hogue whispered out loud to no one but himself. "I'll climb in that son of a bitch and find keys. There'll damn sure be keys, and I won't be able to get the son of a bitch out."

Hogue climbed through the car window and reached for the column. But, again, there were no keys.

This time Hogue felt simply too discouraged to whisper filthy words. Perched in the middle of the old car's bench seat, Hogue exhaled a low moan and gazed wistfully out the windshield at the curtained window of the house. Luke Hogue wished he could trade his life for any given life living on the other side of that window. He was only minutes into his thoughts when the dark room inside the window burst into light.

Hogue found his will to move. With speed and agility, he didn't know he possessed, Hogue practically shot back out the window he had squirmed into. The next beat of his heart sent him scurrying on all fours back to the Ford. Careful to keep all body parts below the window line, Hogue plastered himself to the Ford's front passenger door and paused to catch his breath. From this position, Hogue heard the faint sound of a flushing toilet. Minutes later he slowly raised his head and peered through the door glass to the window and found it still throwing off light, so much light in fact, that it illuminated the interior of the old station wagon just enough for Hogue to spot the keys in the ignition. Just before the light went out, he also observed that the driver's window was only halfway up.

Hogue crept around to the other side of the car and lifted the multi-keyed ring from the ignition and found the pentagon-shaped head of a Dodge key.

Luke crawled through the pickup's open window to prevent noise and to keep the dome light from coming on. He just knew he would have to make several stabs at the ignition with the key but he didn't. He got it on the first try. Turning the key just enough to unlock the steering column and gear shift, Hogue put the truck in neutral and coasted it out of the yard and onto the gravel road. When it coasted as far as it was going to coast, Hogue held his breath and turned the key the rest of the way. The battered four-by-four started immediately.

Hogue waited until about a mile away from the small frame house before pulling on the headlight switch and lighting the road before him. The key had fit; the engine had started, and he had lights. Luke Hogue threw back his head and yelped joyfully at what was beginning to look like a streak of good luck. He grabbed the on/off knob of the radio and gave it a twist. Dwight Yoakam's voice filled the cab, and Hogue yelped again. It had been days since he'd heard any music. Dwight never sounded so good.

Luke Hogue crooned off key to help Yoakum tell about a long, white Cadillac. After that he hummed and whistled Hank Williams Junior through one of Hank Senior's old classics. Then a generic DJ announced it was 4:59 a.m. and one-minute shy of "news at the top of the hour." Hogue didn't want news, he wanted more music, but an upcoming intersection prevented him from immediately finding and twisting the tuning knob from the classic country station. He needed to decide to zig east or zag west. After a couple more zigs and a few more zags, Hogue would settle on a good blacktop and haul ass straight north. For now, he wanted to put lateral distance between himself and the good ol' boy who just lost his four-wheel-drive Dodge.

For no particular reason, Hogue chose west and made his turn. He was just reaching for the tuning knob when a deep-voiced newscaster opened with the words, "A Shawnee police detective…" Hogue slowly moved his hand back to join the other one on the steering wheel. As he listened, both hands gradually increased their grip on the wheel.

"…died early this morning from wounds received from an assault by alleged murderer Luke Gene Hogue…"

"Oh God, no!" Hogue groaned.

"…According to officials," the newscaster droned, "Detective Larry Phelps was kidnapped by Hogue early yesterday morning when an attempted arrest failed. Phelps was later found unconscious in a field south of Sparks, Oklahoma. Luke Gene Hogue was initially being sought for the April thirteenth murder of seven-year-old Kayla

Robbins in Shawnee, Oklahoma. A statewide search is now underway for Hogue."

Luke Hogue stomped on the brake pedal. The Dodge skidded first to the right and then to the left on the sand and gravel surface and came to a grinding halt mere inches from the bar ditch on the far side of the road. A tearful glance into the rearview mirror revealed dawning light in the eastern skies. Looking forward through the windshield proved night still ruled the west. Hogue did not fail to notice the analogy. Any bright spots in his life were now the most assuredly behind him. Only darkness lay ahead.

"I didn't mean to kill you," Hogue sobbed out loud, as he wiped tears from his cheeks with the back of his hand.

There was more he could say, but he didn't waste his breath. The dead cop couldn't hear him, and any live cops nearby wouldn't take time to listen anyway. Oklahoma cops weren't well-known for giving cop killers time to explain. Any encounter with the law from this point forward would no doubt start with them shooting to kill, and there would be encounters. It stood as a well-known fact in the circles Hogue traveled that Oklahoma cops hunting cop killers traveled in large, hungry packs. They wouldn't tire or give up easily, and their prey seldom, if ever, escaped the pursuit.

Canada now seemed completely out of the question. Even the dumbest police would soon deduce that Hogue was heading north. With the hoards of armed men searching every town and blocking every major intersection, Hogue knew he'd never make it as far north as Kansas.

Being a cop killer changed everything. It changed Hogue's chances for escape. It changed where he was going. Most of all, it changed his thinking and what he intended to do about it. One man, other than himself, could be blamed for the predicament Hogue now found himself in up to the armpits. To get to the man, he would have to go back south. Maybe the police would never expect him to backtrack.

* * *

Mrs. Sloan was already at her desk when Emo Bailey walked into his suite of offices at nine Thursday morning. "Have any dreams about me last night, Phyllis?" he asked without looking up from the front page of the Tulsa Tribune he was holding in his large and manicured right hand.

"Yeah. Nightmares," Phyllis Sloan smiled sweetly.

"You know," Bailey said as he paused in front of her desk to playfully shake a thick index finger at her, "I'm soon going to be a single man again. You might want to start trying just a little harder to win my affections."

"Oh, I so wish I weren't already married," she exhaled facetiously.

"Yeah, too bad," Bailey returned jokingly but sincerely meaning it. His gorgeous blonde secretary of ten years had been the starlet of more than a few of his torrid fantasies. "Of course, we could always just play like you weren't."

"Now, *you're* dreaming," Phyllis chuckled.

If you only knew, Bailey thought as he turned and started for his office. Times like this that made Bailey resent the hell out of Richard Sloan – her husband and one of his best friends.

Before going through the door marked with his name, Bailey stopped and looked back. "Oh, yeah. Has the media been notified of my little coup de theatre?"

"All local television stations have been alerted as well as channels four, five, and nine in Oklahoma City. They know your Learjet will land at Shawnee Municipal Airport at two this afternoon. I've set your appointment at three, and I'm still working on a limo to get you from the airport to the court house."

"Excellent."

"But of course."

Bailey entered his office but quickly stuck his head back out. "What attire?"

"Your charcoal suit with a white button-down and any one of your predominantly red power ties."

"Okay," Bailey nodded and then added, "What would I do without you?"

"Probably stay married."

Bailey nodded his head again and disappeared into his office.

* * *

As a general rule the District Attorney of Pottawatomie County didn't pace about nervously. Now, while he waited for his first assistant to come to his office, Walter Spencer made an exception to that rule. Spencer made about his sixth or seventh lap around the huge antique desk when Mike Pierce finally strolled into the D.A.'s office.

"I had hoped you'd sense the urgency in my voice and come quickly," Spencer barked.

"You snarled over the intercom for me to get in here. I didn't sense urgency. I sensed pissed off. I never hurry to get an ass chewing," Pierce said as he dropped into one of the chairs in front of the ornate old desk.

"I am pissed off," Spencer grumbled, stopping behind his desk. "And when I'm pissed off, everything becomes urgent!"

"Are you pissed off at me?"

"I'm pissed at the world!"

"Oh, I see. You're just going to take it out on me."

"I ought to," the D.A. said before collapsing into his chair. "David Robbins has a new attorney."

"Okay," Pierce responded with a nonchalant shrug of his shoulders.

"He hired Emerson Bailey."

Mike Pierce straightened in his chair but didn't lose his typically smug expression. "Bailey's a good defense lawyer."

"A good defense lawyer?" Spencer boomed. "Hell, Mike, what's your impression of Adolf Hitler? Just another German? Damn, man, Emerson Bailey is a premier defense lawyer. Don't make the mistake of playing down this development."

"I haven't missed the significance here, Walter, but all Robbins has done is hire another lawyer. He hasn't changed the facts."

"Naiveté, Mike," Spencer said with a shake of his head, "is not a quality that will benefit you in this endeavor."

"I'm not naïve, Walter. I just believe I can win this one no matter who I go up against."

Walter Spencer suddenly felt very stupid for expecting Mike Pierce to respond to the news with anything other than self-confidence. It now seemed painfully obvious that Pierce would not voluntarily ask Spencer to step in and take charge of prosecuting David Robbins. The controls of this runaway train would have to be jerked from the obstinate, young man's hands.

"You know I have the utmost confidence in you, Mike, and I believe this case can be won," Spencer said as he leaned forward across his desk and rested on his forearms. "But I just don't think you're ready to take on Emerson Bailey. I don't think you can win against him."

"Are you taking this case away from me?" Pierce asked incredulously.

"Yeah, I am, Mike," Spencer said gently.

"Then you can have my resignation with it."

"Don't be ridiculous," Spencer responded with a wave of his hand.

"I'm not being ridiculous," Pierce countered angrily. "The fact that I'm being removed from this case will be big news, and the whole state will see my face and hear my name in a context in which I don't want either of them used. So, if you don't have enough respect for me to spare me public embarrassment, then I will definitely quit."

One of the last things Walter Spencer wanted or needed was for his office to lose such a high-profile case as the State of Oklahoma versus Robbins. The very last thing he wanted was to lose his very competent first assistant, and the political fallout that would come from said assistant's grandfather.

"Mike, please try to understand… we're talking about Emerson Bailey here. Hell, man, it's not that I consider myself a much better prosecutor than you. It's just that I don't think Bailey will come at me as hard as he would a younger attorney who he will expect to be inexperienced and easily intimidated. More importantly, I think this is the type of case and Bailey is the type of defense attorney that the taxpayers expect the D.A. to personally take to task."

Mike Pierce pushed out of his chair and bellied up to Spencer's desk. His expression was intense but no longer angry. "If those are your only concerns, Walter, they why don't you just second chair the proceedings? You could be there to give me advice and help keep me on track. If I win, you'll share in the victory. If I lose, you'll have someone to lay the blame on should it become an issue during the next election."

The idea of being second chair appealed to Spencer much more than the idea of Pierce walking out on him. "I like it," he said after taking a respectable amount of time to imitate mulling. Then after leaning back and propping his exotic lizards up on the desk, he smiled. "And I'm much more relaxed now – not angry anymore. But you," he chuckled, "have to get ready to meet the infamous Emerson Bailey. He'll be here at three. Good luck."

With a laugh of his own, Mike Pierce started for the door and before going out he turned back to his superior, "I want you to know, Walter, Emerson Bailey doesn't intimidate me."

"And I want you to know, Mike," Spencer returned as his smile dwindled away, "I am very much intimidated by Emerson Bailey."

ELEVEN

Emerson Bailey remained strapped into his oversized comfortable seat and perused a Wall Street Journal while waiting for a special message from his pilot, Ralph Driscoll. Several minutes earlier the sleek jet taxied to a stop as close as possible to the terminal building of the Shawnee Municipal Airport. Shortly thereafter, Driscoll opened the door and lowered the steps. When the special message came, Bailey would go to work.

The lawyer didn't have to wait long. "Okay, boss," Driscoll's voice droned sarcastically over the intercom, "it's show time!"

From where Bailey sat, he could not see the door or the ground outside the door, but Driscoll had a good view of it from the cockpit. Driscoll just let Bailey know the news media was assembled on the tarmac, and the stage was set for the acclaimed counselor to do one of the things he did best. The time arrived for Emerson Bailey to make an appearance.

After serenely unfastening his seatbelt and coming to his feet, Bailey stretched, yawned, and slipped on his suit coat. He buttoned the coat with absolutely no sense of urgency, retrieved his aluminum briefcase and sauntered toward the door. Bailey didn't need a mirror to know he looked exquisite in his impeccably tailored suit.

Before stepping into the doorway, he asked Ralph Driscoll out of the side of his mouth, "Do I look humble?"

"You look like the pompous prick you are," Driscoll grinned.

"Good," he winked back to his employee and confidant. Bailey and Driscoll had been college roommates. The big black man served as the closest thing to a brother that Bailey ever experienced.

Being unusually tall, Bailey had to bend to get through the door and onto the first step. Then, while making an imperious production of straightening to his full height, he set his jaw, squinted his eyes and scanned those below him. As he knew it would, his stature and stern look brought all milling about, fidgeting, and chattering to an abrupt halt. Having gained the attention of the dozen or so news types, he relaxed his glare and offered a warm smile. Bailey held the smile until he felt sure the five video cams were zoomed in and the newspaper photographers had enough good shots.

"I appreciate you taking the time to meet me here today," Bailey started. "I am Emerson Bailey of the law firm of Bailey and Associates. I have been retained as council for Mr. David Robbins. I will defend Mr. Robbins against the preposterous second-degree murder charge filed by the District Attorney of Pottawatomie County. That concludes my formal statement. I do have a few minutes to answer any questions you might have."

"Mr. Bailey!" a young man at the front of the little mob cried out. "Can we anticipate any plea bargaining in this case?"

"None," Bailey said with a shake of his deeply tanned bald head. "My client is not guilty of any crime."

"What do you feel your chances are of winning this case?" asked a female reporter.

"The only way I can lose this case is by not showing up at the trial."

An older man wearing jeans and a western shirt fired the next volley. "Does David Robbins feel at all responsible for the death of his daughter?"

"Mr. Robbins feels the man who pulled the trigger is responsible for the death of his daughter."

"Counselor," a shapely and sophisticated looking redhead called out with a wave of her hand, "if this case presents no challenge to the defense, then why has your client hired one of the best and most costly attorneys in the state?"

Bailey responded first with a hearty laugh and then framed his answer with one of his toothiest smiles. "Because he can."

Another female stepped up and got about three words into a question before Bailey interrupted with a raised hand. "Sorry. I see my limo has arrived, and I do not want to be late for my meetings with the prosecution. There's no telling what type of charges they might file for such an infraction!"

Bailey bounded athletically down the steps and toward a waiting car.

* * *

Gambling on getting an exclusive, Jennifer Rhodes positioned herself and her cameraman, Josh Wadley, close to the parked Mercedes limousine. If Emerson Bailey refused her a personal interview, at least this vantage point would provide an unobstructed close-up of the prominent attorney crawling into a car that cost more than the reporter and cameraman combined would make in two years.

By virtue of Jennifer's choice of locations, the Channel 9 news team had not heard Bailey's statement or the questions and answers that followed. However, missing that exchange didn't concern Jennifer. She knew from the press release what Bailey intended to announce. If there were any unusual twists or turns, she would charm it out of one of the reporters who had gathered at the big-time attorney's feet.

When Emerson Bailey stepped out of his plane, it was the first time that Jennifer laid eyes on the man. According to reputation, Bailey was physically impressive and intellectually imposing. From fifty yards away, Jennifer could tell only that he was a big man, that his clothes fit him nicely, and that the top of his head reflected entirely too much of the bright afternoon sunshine. The latter observation, because of personal preference, somewhat disappointed Jennifer. Her mental picture of the famous attorney, based on comments from colleagues who had met him, had not included any physical defects.

Jennifer watched as Bob Michaels of Channel 4 approached Bailey at the bottom of the stairway at the conclusion of his announcement. Knowing what Michaels wanted and having seen the lawyer turn him down, extinguished what little hope Jennifer held of a personal interview. Still, she had to try.

Now, while Wadley readied his equipment, Jennifer kept her eyes on the approaching Emerson Bailey. Although he did not look exactly how she had expected, he did move like the man he was reputed to be. Bailey wasn't simply walking in Jennifer's direction. He wasn't merely covering ground. Emerson Bailey was devouring it – quickly closing the fifty-yard gap with a graceful stride that pulsated with self-confidence.

Turning to Wadley, Jennifer asked, "Are you ready?"

"I was born ready," her partner deadpanned.

When Jennifer turned back, Emerson Bailey was less than ten yards away. His brilliant blue eyes, rumored to be arresting, were locked on her. Looking into the eyes, Jennifer confirmed the rumor and felt powerless to avert her eyes until the man displayed teeth. Jennifer had never been able to resist a sensuous smile.

"Mr. Bailey," she smiled back. "I'm Jennifer Rhodes with Channel 9 News. I was hoping you might spare a moment of your time for an exclusive."

"I was hoping," Bailey said as his smile broadened, "that you might be my driver!"

"Sorry. I'm not licensed to operate a semi," Jennifer said with a sidelong glance at the limo.

"Are you insinuating you find my mode of transportation a bit pretentious?" Bailey asked with the smile still intact.

"I'm just a reporter, Mr. Bailey. The only thing I care to find is a story," Jennifer answered sweetly. "However, if I were a rural district attorney, I might find your choice of transportation more intimidating than pretentious."

Emerson Bailey responded with a wink and a chuckle.

"So, Mr. Bailey, do you have time for an exclusive?"

"I always have time for the press, Ms. Rhodes," Bailey expressed with a sly grin and a nod of his head. "However, you'll have to accompany me to the courthouse to get your exclusive."

With that, Bailey moved past Jennifer, opened the limo's rear door, and stepped aside. "Your carriage and your story await you, Ms. Rhodes."

Jennifer looked first to Bailey to see if he was teasing. When it didn't appear that he was, she turned to her cameraman, "Follow us in the van, Josh."

Jennifer looked into Bailey's face as she gracefully positioned herself in the limo's back seat. The bold and appreciative way the attorney averted his eyes to her legs was taken as a compliment. Jennifer liked the eyes. She liked the man. She even liked how he wore what little hair he had left.

* * *

Luke.

The single-word thought erupted from an alcohol-induced sleep and brought Mark Hogue's eyelids open with a jerk. In another involuntary and instinctive action, he employed his flabby arms and legs to untangle himself from damp, dingy sheets, so he could perform his poor interpretation of jumping out of bed.

Maneuvering through the filth and clutter of the smelly little bedroom was not easy for Mark even when he wasn't dizzy and badly hung-over, yet he made it to the closest window with only a few stumbles, no falls, and less than a dozen mumbled curses. The curse count tripled, however, when Mark pulled back dust-crusted curtains and didn't see what he wanted to see.

With his pounding head only slightly clearer, Mark hobbled out of the bedroom and padded over the unseen inhabitants embedded in the ancient shag carpet covering his living room floor. He turned into the kitchen off the living room and went to the window over the sink. This window opened on Mark's meager, weed infested backyard and the alley behind it.

Mark knocked over some of the weeks-old dirty dishes stacked haphazardly in the sink as he peered out the window. An already chipped coffee cup fell to the floor and shattered. Its contents of black, tar-like goo that had once been coffee, spattered on his feet and oozed in between Mark's crusty toes. Mark started with another string of obscene expletives but stopped in midstream when he spotted the khaki clad man checking gas meters in the alley.

First Mark smiled, then he laughed, then he started rapping loudly on the window glass. When the worker looked up and Mark was sure he spotted him looking out the window, Mark gave the other man a thumbs-up gesture. The man at the meters inconspicuously looked first to his left, then to his right, and then responded to Mark's thumbs-up with an extended middle finger of his right hand.

Mark moved from the window with a chuckle. He didn't care that the undercover cops watching his house didn't like him. Hell, they could absolutely hate his guts just as long as they stayed on their toes, kept their eyes open, and were ready when big brother Luke showed up. And he would show up. Mark had no doubt whatsoever. He would come looking for Mark, all right, and when and if he got his hands on him he would take care of Mark just…

"…like he did the rabbits," Mark mumbled out loud as the smile evaporated from his lips.

Mark was eleven years old at the time, and Luke was thirteen. Mark shared a bedroom with his brother, wore clothes that his brother had once worn, and played with toys that had also been handed down from Luke. The two rabbits were the only thing in the world that Mark could call his very own. Mrs. Dunfey, their closest neighbor, gave the rabbits to Mark as payment for tilling her garden spot. As he grew accustomed to doing, Mark went in to say goodnight to his pets on the night he spied Luke fumbling with the breasts of a Missouri preacher's daughter.

Mark thought it would be great fun watching how the two fathers would react to his brother's assault on those large tits. It proved to be great fun. For a couple of weeks after that, Mark practically died laughing when recalling the look on Luke's face when the preachers caught him with that nipple in his mouth. But after the old man kicked Luke into the hole then kicked Luke's mangy dog to death, Luke started kicking back.

On the morning after the dog met its demise, Mark woke to find his older brother standing over him. Luke was sporting a hateful grin and had his hands concealed behind his back. When he jerked his hands forward and flung their contents at Mark, the youngest Hogue first thought it was four long, fat and extremely furry caterpillars that pelted his face. Mark wasn't afraid of caterpillars no matter how big they were, and he didn't start to scream…until he realized they were bunny ears. Mark didn't get much of a scream out before a blood-sticky hand clamped tightly over his mouth.

"Stop screaming, or I'll cut your fuckin' ears off, too," Luke hissed. "And I won't even bother to stomp you to death before I do it!"

As if it only happened yesterday, Mark Hogue could still hear the hate in that voice and could still feel the sting of its seething anger. The memory pushed Mark back to his bed and beneath the fetid sheets. His brother Luke was not one to let a screwing go unanswered.

* * *

Emerson Bailey had never met a beautiful woman he didn't like – at first, anyway. So far, Jennifer Rhodes proved no exception. He liked her eyes, her smile, her hair, and especially her legs. He wondered if her toenails were painted with the same dark red that ornamented her splendidly long fingernails. He wondered even more about the sweet secrets housed at the opposite end of the remarkable legs.

While Jennifer readied a small tape recorder she pulled from her purse, Bailey moved up to the apparently perky breasts and gave them a good once over. Only when Jennifer turned her attention to Bailey did he slowly and teasingly move his gaze up from her breasts to stare intently into her eyes. If the reporter was put off or offended by the blatant optical exploration, it didn't show. What did show was self-confidence and an appreciation for admiration. Jennifer Rhodes fit well into the back seat of a limousine, and Bailey liked that in a woman.

"Okay, Mr. Bailey…."

"Emo," Bailey interrupted.

"Emo?" Jennifer smiled.

"Only friends ride in limos with me, and my friends call me Emo. It's short for Emerson."

"Isn't an Emo a big, ostrich-like bird?" Jennifer asked with a mischievous grin.

"That's an emu," Bailey smirked. "And, just for the record, they're much better looking than an ostrich."

Jennifer responded with a laugh before saying, "Okay, I'll call you Emo. Please call me Jennifer. Now, are you ready to answer some questions?"

"Fire at will, Jennifer," Bailey nodded.

"From what's been reported, David Robbins would not and did not give into the wishes of the gunman, Luke Hogue. He didn't, as some sources are calling it, *deny Christ*. At the time, did Robbins believe that Hogue would really kill Kayla Robbins if he didn't deny Christ?"

Bailey smiled his sly smile. Jennifer had brains as well as looks. The question was a good one that cut right to the heart of the matter. If Robbins believed Hogue would actually pull the trigger if he didn't repeat the "mere words and phrases," then it could be construed that Robbins intentionally acted in a manner he knew could result in the death of his daughter. Wherein, Robbins, during the telling of his story to Bailey, had alluded to the fact that there was a time he didn't think Hogue "wanted" to harm the girl – Bailey had purposely not belabored the point. If his client thought there was even the remotest possibility that Hogue would kill his daughter if he didn't give in, Bailey didn't want to know it. In some cases, it served best if an attorney didn't ask and, therefore, didn't know the thoughts, motives and intents of a client during the commission of an alleged crime. Knowing all could and often did limit available defenses, especially for lawyers who didn't particularly like committing perjury. Jennifer's question was definitely a good one and one for which Bailey didn't have a canned response.

"Without knowing my client," Bailey started carefully, "you cannot imagine the deep love he holds for family in general and for little Kayla in particular. I just cannot believe he would have ever intentionally put her in harm's way."

Arched eyebrows, quick nods of her head, and a smirk signaled to Bailey that Jennifer knew she was being sidestepped. He felt both relieved and impressed when she didn't push the issue. Going at the same angle only from a different direction was a ridiculous tactic that reporters often wasted time on with Bailey.

"According to police reports," Jennifer began with question number two, "Detective Larry Phelps used some of his last words to repeat something Luke Hogue said to him. According to Phelps, Hogue said it was his finger on the trigger of the gun that killed Kayla, but he wasn't the one who pulled the trigger. Could this mean Hogue felt Robbins goaded him into killing the child?"

"We have studied the report and its contents in detail," Bailey lied. His staff was obtaining copies of all police reports and witness statements as they spoke. This report would be one of the first that

Bailey would want to see. "We have concluded that Hogue is simply displacing guilt and responsibility for his actions. He may be blaming my client, but then he may be blaming his childhood or drugs. He may even be blaming the devil himself. The point is, we believe, he has admitted to the mechanics of the killing. Therefore, Luke Hogue should receive all blame and punishment for this abominable crime."

If Jennifer knew Bailey was tap-dancing his ass off, she didn't express it. Bailey feared she was just being considerate, or possibly, even coy. Like not knowing the difference between Emo and emu.

"Let's suppose, Emo, that Luke Hogue is captured, pleads guilty and is used by the prosecution against your client. How could this impact your case?"

It could send David Robbins to prison for a long time, but this wasn't something a defense attorney told reporters before a trial. "It can't. There are already twelve witnesses who will testify to the same facts that Hogue would have to offer. Facts, that no matter who presents them, prove my client to be innocent of second-degree murder."

Bailey assumed he had exceeded Jennifer's bullshit level when she smiled knowingly and slowly and just ever so slightly started shaking her head. Simultaneously, she turned off her recorder and put it back in her purse.

"Now, off the record, Emo," Jennifer Rhodes said with eyes squinted and lips forming a suspicious little smile. "Did David Robbins' choice to hire you have anything to do with your religious beliefs and practices?"

Quickly switching to his glaring, grave and earnest look, Bailey confidently reached for and took Jennifer's right hand into his left. "Of course, it did," Bailey exhaled in his most sincere voice. "I'm a real angel!" he concluded with a laugh.

"I'm sure you are," Jennifer laughed back.

"Let me prove it."

"How?"

"Go out with me tonight."

"Not a good idea, Emo," Jennifer smiled sweetly.

"Why not?"

"First of all, I'll bet you're married."

"Only in the eyes of God and according to the laws of this great state. However, I am currently engaged in the process of full-contact divorce."

"There's a lot of difference in getting divorced and being divorced. Besides, Emo," Jennifer said as she used her left hand to pat the one that held her right, "I never go out with a man just for the sake of a single round of wild, passionate sex. Your reputation, as they say, precedes you."

With his free hand, Bailey reached into his inner coat pocket, retrieved a business card and handed it to Jennifer. "Should you ever desire to lower your standards and need help, just call. I'm here for you."

"I'll remember that," Jennifer chuckled. "You know, Emo, there is another way you can prove you're an angel. I want to meet David Robbins. Completely off the record with no cameras or recorders, of course. Just him and me."

Working his eyes once more down over the perky breast and across a flat stomach to the pair of breathtaking legs, Emerson Bailey responded, "I'll see what I can do."

* * *

"Mr. Bailey has arrived, sir."

"Good. Show him in, please," Walter Spencer relayed to his receptionist over the intercom on his phone.

Spencer expected Bailey to perform the age-old waltzing-in-like-he-owned-the-place routine. Instead, Bailey strutted in like he held the mortgage on the entire damn county.

After pushing out of his chair, Spencer walked around from behind his desk and extended his right hand to Bailey. Two chairs were situated in front of Spencer's desk. Mike Pierce occupied the one to Spencer's left, and he wasn't bothering to get up. "Walter Spencer, Pottawatomie County D.A.," the prosecutor smiled.

Bailey grinned as he clamped on to Spencer's hand. "Emerson Bailey. It's nice to meet you, Walter," He said before letting go of Spencer.

At six feet one inch and two hundred ten pounds, the D.A. was not a small man but felt physically diminished standing beside Bailey. Spencer suddenly understood that his much smaller assistant wasn't remaining in his seat just to be rude. Had Spencer not been standing beside Bailey at that very instant, he would have gingerly rubbed his hand that Bailey just gripped and shook.

"Likewise, Emerson. This is my first assistant Mike Pierce," Spencer said as he nodded at his employee. "Mike will be trying the Robbins' case. I'll be his second chair."

Pierce leaned forward in his chair and offered his hand. If offended by the fact that Pierce didn't stand, Bailey didn't let on. He took Pierce's hand without hesitation. If Bailey squeezed the almost tiny hand with the same enthusiasm he had Spencer's, Pierce didn't let it show in his face or actions.

"Hello, Mike," Bailey's greeting was cordial.

"Mr. Bailey," Pierce's was much more official.

"Please sit down, Emerson," Spencer said, pointing to the chair next to Pierce.

"Thank you, Walter," Bailey said as he fell into the empty chair, crossed one long leg over the other and looked instantly relaxed. "Now then, Walter," Bailey began after setting his briefcase down beside his chair, "we've smiled and touched, and imparted civilities. Shall we spar?" Bailey's intense eyes were smiling. His lips were not.

With a chuckle, Walter Spencer presented his assistant with a palms-up gesture and said to Bailey, "Spar away!"

Bailey turned to Pierce, smiled amicably and said matter-of-factly, "Drop this ridiculous charge, issue a formal letter of apology to my client, and I won't sue for malicious prosecution."

"I will not drop or reduce the charge. Mr. Robbins will be tried for second-degree murder," Mike Pierce replied somberly.

Bailey turned back to Spencer. "How long has he been out of law school?"

Pierce beat Spencer to a response. "My experience is not pertinent to this case, Mr. Bailey. What is pertinent is the evidence, and I have enough of it to send your client to prison for the rest of his life."

Bailey looked again to Pierce and arched his eyebrows. "I assume you're referring to the testimony of the nine adults and two children who witnessed Kayla Robbins' death."

"I certainly am."

"How many of these witnesses profess to be Christians, Mike?"

"I haven't questioned my witnesses on their religious preferences and beliefs, Mr. Bailey."

"You should, Mike," Bailey snickered. "I intend to. And I think by doing so I will establish that each and every one of them profess Christianity. Then I will establish that each and every one of them denied their Christ on the night Kayla Robbins was slain. Then, I will establish that David Robbins, a pillar of the church and this community, a man whose tithes have basically paid for his church and whose civic and monetary contributions go unmatched in this city, actually followed the guidance set out in the Christian handbook. You do know what the Christian handbook is, don't you, Mike?"

With each "I will establish," Bailey drew a little louder and a little closer to Pierce. Spencer noted that as Bailey inched further out of his seat, Pierce inched further back into his. The young man's self-confident air was showing signs of thinning.

"The Christian handbook?" Pierce repeated.

Spencer thought, but wasn't sure, that the voice quivered just a tiny little bit.

"Yeah, Mike," Bailey nearly bellowed as he pulled his nose up to within inches of his opponent's, "that's the Holy fuckin' Bible! Have you heard of that?"

"I'm very familiar with the Bible!" Pierce barked back. His face now glowed red, as the arrogant façade all but eroded away.

"Of course, you are!" Bailey thundered, "And so is every other citizen within an eight-hundred-mile radius of this village. And therein lies your problem. You're in the middle of the Bible belt, brother, and you'll be trying a case that needs a jury of atheists. You'll be trying a case that you just cannot win. Give up now, Mike. Drop the charge and save yourself from the worst ass-kicking of your life!"

"I will not drop the charge!" Pierce spat through gritted teeth.

"Then I'll see you in court!" Bailey growled, his face contorted with rage. Then he turned to Spencer, winked and smiled broadly. "Always wanted to say that, Walter. Heard it on television a couple of times!"

Grabbing his briefcase with his left hand, Bailey stood and extended his right hand across the desk to Spencer. "If I can, Walter, I'll pick up a copy of the criminal complaint and preliminary hearing witness list on my way out."

Spencer stood and grasped Bailey's hand. "My receptionist has copies ready for you."

After letting go of Spencer's hand, Bailey reached over and patted the still-seated Mike Pierce on the shoulder. "If you liked me here...you'll love me in court!"

Spencer and Pierce sat silent for several seconds after Bailey left. The assistant finally broke the silence. "Well...what do you think?"

Walter Spencer leaned back in his chair and propped his boots up on his desk. After crossing one handmade calf-skin boot over the other, he exhaled, "That man went through you like a tornado in a trailer park. Like a maggot through a big slice of shit-pie."

Mike Pierce just nodded his head in agreement.

TWELVE

"You look like hell!" Emerson Bailey exclaimed when David Robbins finally opened his front door.

"I feel like it, too," Robbins sighed as he stepped to the side and motioned Bailey into his home.

"Are you sick?" Bailey asked, cutting a wide swath around Robbins. The last thing he needed with his schedule was a dose of some kick-ass virus.

"You could say that," Robbins said as he rubbed at his temples. "But I'm not contagious," he added, evidently picking up on Bailey's concern.

"Good," Bailey grinned as he took in the large entryway and the grand winding staircase. "With a place like this, I would expect a maid or butler to open the door."

"No maids or butlers," Robbins grunted as he walked past Bailey and motioned for him to follow.

Bailey trailed Robbins to the left side of the entryway, through two large, oak doors and into the study. Robbins went straight for a leather couch and collapsed on it. Two over-stuffed chairs upholstered in the same leather were arranged in front of the couch, and Bailey chose the one that put the greatest distance between him and his ailing client.

A quick glance around the impressive study revealed a desk at the other end of the room with a nearly half-empty bottle of bourbon and an overturned shot glass on top. The floor beneath the far wall of bookshelves, and just a few feet from the desk, was littered with pages from a small, destroyed book.

"No maids or butlers and evidently no housekeepers either," Bailey chuckled as he nodded his head in the direction of the mess on the floor.

Robbins looked first to the scattered debris and then back to Bailey. For seconds he silently studied his attorney, then responded flatly, "Most people I know, or maybe everyone I know would look at a torn-up Bible on my floor and do their best to act as if they didn't notice it. They certainly wouldn't make mention of it."

Bailey looked back to the pages and stated, "I didn't know it was a Bible."

"Had you known," Robbins said with a hint of a smile, "would you have acted as if you hadn't seen it?"

"Probably not," Bailey beamed shamelessly.

"I didn't think so," Robbins returned unpleasantly.

"But please don't consider me totally insensitive. I didn't mention the half-empty bottle of whiskey," Bailey laughed.

Robbins emitted a small laugh but then grabbed his head with both hands. After several seconds of vigorous temple massaging, he said without laughter, "You don't seem surprised that I destroyed a Bible while in a drunken stupor."

"I've experienced far too much humanity to be surprised by anything. Besides, I don't imagine boozing and Bible bashing is something you do in more normal times."

Robbins looked back to the small book, and as if addressing it, he mumbled, "I did have a housekeeper. She came in on Tuesdays and Thursdays to help out my wife. She called this morning and said she wouldn't be back. She at least had the decency to wait this long. My wife abandoned me on the day we buried our daughter."

Bailey had long ago learned there were some emotions an attorney could not let themselves feel for a client. Sympathy topped the list, but as Bailey gazed at the man staring at the Bible he could not help but sympathize. "I had no idea. I'm sorry," he said without his normal brashness.

Without taking his eyes from the scattered pages, Robbins acknowledged the words of condolence with a nod of his head.

"While we're sharing bad news," Bailey sighed, "the D.A. refused to drop the charge."

Robbins turned back to Bailey and shrugged his shoulders. "You told me not to get my hopes up. I didn't."

Bailey moved to the chair closer to Robbins. "Okay. Now we prepare for battle, and I have two proposed strategies we need to discuss."

"Go ahead," Robbins exhaled slowly.

"First, I recommend we delay the trial as long as possible in hopes that Luke Hogue is apprehended and tried first. This would facilitate the media's attention and public scorn being taken from you and placed on the rightful owner. Right now you're in the limelight. I want you out of it."

"Okay," Robbins nodded.

"That was easy," Bailey smiled. "You might not be so quick to agree with my second proposal."

Robbins scooted to the edge of his seat, leaned forward and rested his elbows on his knees. An intense, quizzical stare signaled Bailey to continue.

"I want you to take the stand and testify."

"Why?"

"Because you're a model citizen. You're a prominent businessman, a civic leader, and besides, juries love it. They will want to hear your version of what happened. If you don't testify on your behalf, they'll think you have something to hide."

"And," Bailey said as he recalled his earlier discussion with Jennifer Rhodes, "I can think of only one point of contention that could cause you harm. You must be able to testify you never at anytime truly believed that Hogue would kill your daughter."

"I didn't believe he was going to kill her," Robbins said flatly.

"Then you have nothing to hide."

"That's where you're wrong," Robbins barked defiantly.

The response caused Bailey to smile. Robbins showed signs of having balls. "How so?" he returned.

"I didn't believe he would kill her because I didn't believe he could kill her. I believed a loving God would never let that happen. What I have to hide," Robbins said through clenched teeth with anger burning in his eyes, "is I acted foolishly and did a very ignorant thing."

"We're in the Bible Belt, David. Oklahoma jurors will appreciate your faith and trust in God."

"Will they appreciate the fact that the faith and trust I inflicted on my little girl no longer exists? That it's gone? That it's dead? What will they think, Emo, of a man who once believed so strongly that he'd spare my daughter, but now struggles just to believe?"

David Robbins pushed off the couch and wobbled to the richly ornate desk. With a shaking hand he filled the shot glass with whiskey and tossed the contents to the back of his throat. Wincing, he concluded, "I do not want to testify before a jury on what I've been reduced to. I just don't think I could do it."

Coming to his feet, Bailey said gently, "Give it some thought, David. We don't have to decide here and now."

Bailey walked nearly to the study door when he stopped and turned back to face Robbins. "Oh, yeah, I almost forgot. Jennifer Rhodes is a reporter for Channel 9 in Oklahoma City. She wants to meet you – strictly off the record."

"Do you see a need for me to meet her? I mean, can it help us?"

"Having a sympathetic reporter on your side never hurts. I'd coach you on what to say and what not to say. Besides, it might make you feel better," Bailey said with a wink and a grin. "She's a very beautiful woman."

"Let me give this some thought, too, Emo," Robbins said as he brought the shot glass to his lips a second time. Following a hard swallow and a shutter he concluded, "Right now, I probably would not be very effective at meeting and befriending new people – beautiful or otherwise."

* * *

It wasn't serious war gaming, just the kicking around of possibilities. Later, closer to the trial date, Mike Pierce and Walter Spencer would in earnest plan their attacks and counterattacks. Normally, the D.A. insisted on having their little sessions. He believed bouncing ideas back and forth helped prepare for a case. Pierce generally found them to be a waste of time. Honestly, on big cases in the past he'd never felt as if he needed the help. But seeing how just hours earlier Emerson Bailey made him look and feel sophomoric, Pierce was a willing participant of this session.

They had already discussed the possible defense strategies. There weren't many. And they had both agreed that Bailey would want to put Robbins on the stand. And they both hoped he would. In most cases the prosecution could get more mileage out of a defendant's testimony than the defense could.

Normally, Spencer did the pacing, but this time he'd remained seated at his desk. Pierce, meanwhile, put the wear and tear on the carpet as he considered the last question posed by Spencer. What if Luke Hogue was arrested prior to Robbins' trial?

"It would not help or hinder our prosecution of Robbins," Pierce nodded after several treks around the spacious office. Hogue had done what he had done, and Robbins played his own special role.

For several more minutes they toyed with the idea and possibilities. The D.A. eventually drew the final conclusion.

"I think you're right. Hogue could not possibly help or hurt us."

It did Pierce's heart good to hear the confidence in his boss's voice.

* * *

"You can't do this! My taxes pay your goddamned salary!"

The plainclothes cop who'd agitated Mark Hogue, reached into his pockets and pulled out an assortment of coins. "Here," he mumbled as he selected a dime and flipped it at Hogue, "That's your contribution to my paycheck for the past ten years. Consider us even!"

"Hey, you're a real comical son of a bitch," Hogue blurted as the cop stepped off his front porch and started back to his unmarked cruiser. When the detective didn't turn back around or otherwise acknowledge the comment, Hogue cried out, "What did you say your name was?"

"Sergeant Maddox," the man called back over his shoulder.

"Well I hope you're happy Sergeant Maddox for just signing my fuckin' death warrant. I'm going to leave a goddamn note with your name on it. Yeah, that's what I'm going to do all right. It's going to say Sergeant Fuckin' Maddox is to blame for me being goddamned dead!"

Maddox just nodded his head, mumbled, "Go for it," and kept right on walking.

"Oh, act like you don't care now," Hogue squealed. "You won't be so cocky when you lose your job over me getting my ass killed. You won't be so smug when I reach up from my fuckin' grave and get your badge, asshole!"

As if he hadn't heard a word, Sergeant Maddox crawled into his car and started it up. Just before pulling off, he turned his face to Hogue, smiled, and flipped him off.

Hogue gave the cruiser a fifty-yard head start before mimicking the gesture and screaming, "Don't ever come back here, or I'll whip your sorry chickenshit ass!" Then Hogue bent down and picked up the dime Maddox had bounced off his chest.

"The joke is on that bastard," he grumbled out loud as he pocketed the coin, "I haven't paid taxes in the past ten years!"

Hogue remained on his front porch for several seconds just stewing over how much he disliked Maddox and other cops in general. From there, his mind took him to just how sorry they would all be when Luke Hogue really did show up and...

As if slapped back to reality, Mark scurried back into his house and frantically dead-bolted the door behind him. Just because Maddox and the Oklahoma City Police Department believed his brother was by now in Kansas and maybe even Nebraska, didn't make it so. Those clowns might believe Mark no longer needed protection, but he knew better. The cops didn't understand what Mark knew all too well – Luke Hogue didn't let screwings go unanswered. They didn't understand that discontinuing their stakeout reduced Mark Hogue to no more than a terrified defenseless rabbit in a cage. They had no idea how Luke Hogue dealt with defenseless rabbits.

* * *

I'm sorry I didn't come by yesterday," David Robbins said to his daughter's grave.

"A lot has happened since I was here Tuesday," Robbins felt detached from his voice. It sounded flat and monotonous and seemed to be coming from the far end of a long tunnel. "As you know, I was arrested, and your Uncle Larry died. Just a little while ago my attorney told me the murder charge would not be dropped. After he left, I had another visitor, and he threw the last straw on this camel's back."

Robbins did not know the man who'd appeared at his door. "Are you Mr. David Robbins?" he had asked cheerfully.

Somewhat numbed by the two shots of whiskey he'd downed ten minutes earlier, Robbins responded without consideration of the man's motives or intent. "Yes, I am."

"Then I believe this belongs to you," the man smiled pleasantly as he thrust a folded piece of paper into Robbins' hand. Without further hesitation, the man bound away.

Minutes later, Robbins stumbled out of his house to his car. Now, standing over Kayla's grave, he could not remember a single aspect of the fifteen-minute drive to the cemetery.

"Your mother is divorcing me."

The fact stated out loud had the effect of a dull, jagged knife being thrust repeatedly into the very core of David Robbins' being – ripping and tearing at the already badly damaged remnants of the man he was two weeks earlier. As if his feet had been kicked from beneath him, Robbins fell hard to his knees. The mournful wail that followed reverberated beneath the canopy of leaves provided by the ancient oak. It didn't stop until Robbins was left gasping for air and sobbing heavily.

Robbins' will to go on was gone. Dead. Just like his daughter, and just like his marriage. At that moment he didn't have the strength to get to his feet, much less to get through another night alone. For the first time ever, Robbins knew unequivocally that if the means were within reach at that moment – a gun, a rope, or even a pocketknife – he would use them to put an end to what had become an unbearable existence. In this darkest moment of the bleakest days of his life, when suddenly nothing in his world mattered any longer, someone placed a hand on Robbins' shoulder.

Turning and looking up, Robbins' eyes met those of a very old man. Snow white hair framed a deeply wrinkled face, and thin lips formed a concerned grimace framing ill-fitting dentures. The elderly man's left hand rested on Robbins' right shoulder. His right hand, gnarled by age, was extended down to Robbins.

Feeling as if in a trance or catatonic state, Robbins slowly moved his eyes from the man's face to the out-reaching hand. From that point, he only managed to stare at the appendage.

"Take my hand, Mr. Robbins. Let me help you up," the man said softly.

Robbins looked back to the face and applied as much attention as he could muster toward recognition. At best, the man just looked familiar.

"You don't know me," the man said as if reading Robbins' weary mind. "I know who you from the newspapers and television coverage, and my wife and I saw you here the day before yesterday."

With that, Robbins remembered. The old couple had visited a nearby grave that Robbins assumed belonged to an offspring. Thinking the woman would also be close by, Robbins turned to the burial site the couple had stood over. What he saw there made him jerk his head back to the old man "Who is…"

"It's my wife's," the man said as he looked to and nodded at a freshly covered plot adjacent to the one he had visited two days earlier. "She died early Tuesday evening. We outlived all our friends and family. I insisted the burial be quick as possible."

Robbins took the hand that was still reaching. It was bony and felt fragile, but the grip that helped him to his feet proved strong enough. Standing beside the older man, he managed a not so simple sentence. "I'm sorry."

"I am too, but it wasn't unexpected. We pretty much knew that Tuesday's trip out here would be our last together. She had cancer and was in really bad shape. The doctors had given her another two weeks, but she fooled them and went earlier."

The voice sounded strong and clear, but the eyes betrayed a deep sorrow. Robbins turned back to the fresh grave. It was easier to look at than the elderly gentleman's eyes. He had already said he was sorry and searched for other words, but the man spoke again before he could deliver.

"Mr. Robbins, my name is Leon Beck."

Looking back to the man, Robbins once again found his right hand outstretched. Robbins shook it and replied, "Nice to meet you, Mr. Beck."

"These are sad times and conditions to meet under," Leon Beck said with an amiable smile, "but, I too, am pleased to finally make your acquaintance."

"Finally?" Robbins responded.

"Ever since hearing of your ordeal, I've intended to contact you. I didn't want to impose on you Tuesday, and, well, I've had my hands full since. But, to the point, Mr. Robbins, I'm a retired Baptist minister and because of personal experiences, I might be one of few men who can understand some of what you must be going through. I might be able to help."

Robbins studied Beck's face for several long seconds. After finding nothing there to distrust, he looked down at Kayla's grave. "Mr. Beck, I need a lot of help."

Beck's following words seized David Robbins' attention. For close to an hour he remained a captive of the old man's tragic tale. The first words he spoke on the tragedy were emphasized by a crooked finger pointing at the much older and smaller grave that he and his wife visited regularly for nearly sixty-eight years.

"That's where our first born, Henry, is buried. He was four years old when he died. That was 1944..."

* * *

Little Henry Beck was a month away from his first birthday when his father sailed away as a Navy Chaplain. The small-town Oklahoma preacher spent the next two years ministering to the American boys fighting and dying in the South Pacific. He would have served longer but a mission to visit a detachment of marines on some long-forgotten island resulted in a sniper's bullet destroying Leon's right kidney. After months and months in a Navy hospital, Lieutenant Beck was sent home to his wife, Ramona, and by then, four-year-old Henry.

Soon after, a small Baptist church in Seminole, Oklahoma, invited the Reverend Leon Beck to serve as pastor. Leon borrowed a truck, loaded their meager possessions and left late on a Saturday afternoon on the four-hour trek to their new life. Since returning home, Leon had kept his son as close to his side as possible to facilitate and quicken the transformation from stranger to father. On moving day, little Henry rode in the cab of the truck with his daddy, and Ramona followed them in the family Ford.

Along the grueling route to Seminole, Henry taught his son new songs, words and phrases, and how to play "I Spy." The youngest Beck quickly grew fond of one of his dad's favorite monikers, and very quickly incorporated "Buster" into his conversational repertoire. When Leon Beck wasn't shifting gears, he kept his right arm draped over his son's small shoulders or held one of the little hands.

When they were within minutes of the Seminole city limits, Leon distinctly remembered saying, "It won't be long now, son. We're almost home."

"A'most home, Buster!" the four-year-old reemphasized with a giggle. The glow from the old truck's instrument panel lit the boy's tired but smiling face.

Leon was proudly admiring the lovely face when the truck collided with the two-thousand-pound black bull standing in the middle of the road. Leon Beck's head hit the steering wheel hard, and he was mercifully spared the sight of his son going through the windshield.

He wasn't conscious to feel first the front left tire and then the duals on the right-rear running over his only child.

* * *

"I didn't know who to blame most for my son's death," Beck said with a sad smirk, "God or myself. I felt at fault for taking my eyes off the road. I felt God was at fault for letting that bull be in the middle of the road in the first place. That sentiment was compounded by the fact that I was going to Seminole to do God's work. I expected special treatment."

"What you expected," Robbins almost blurted, "was for a loving God, one you were serving and worshiping, to protect your child. I don't consider that to be special treatment, and I don't think it's too much to expect."

"Is that how you felt, Mr. Robbins? Did you feel God should have protected your child?"

"That's exactly how I felt on the day my daughter was murdered, and the way I feel now, Mr. Beck. In addition, I feel betrayed. I feel God turned his back on me, and for that, I..." Robbins paused.

Beck finished for him, "Hate him, Mr. Robbins. Right now, you hate God. I know because I hated God, too."

"And you got over it?" Robbins asked incredulously.

"I did."

"How?" Robbins shot back.

"By realizing God is God. I had made the mistake, you see, of trying to bring God down to our level – to that of a man. I perceived him and approached him as one who thinks like a man, feels like a man, and knows only what a man can know. I forgot, Mr. Robbins, *He is God*. All seeing. All knowing. Omnipotent. I had to realize that as humans we see the here and the now. We can only see the 'little picture,' if you will. God sees the 'big picture.'

"I don't know why God let my Henry die. I don't know why he let your Kayla die. I'm not capable of knowing these things. But for the sake of my sanity and well-being, I have to believe that God – the Alpha and the Omega – had a reason for letting it happen. I have to believe what the Apostle Paul said in his first letter to the Church in Corinth – 'If we have hoped in Christ in this life only, we are of all men most to be pitied.'

"You see, Mr. Robbins," Leon Beck said as he placed a hand on Robbins' shoulder, "my hope in Christ extends into the next life. That's the only chance I have of ever being with my wife and boys again."

"Boys?" Robbins questioned.

"Yes, Mr. Robbins. Ramona and I had our only other child several years later. His name was Matthew," Leon Beck sighed heavily as his eyes started to moisten. "Sorry," Beck said under his breath, "It's been a tough day."

"I understand," Robbins nodded. He truly did.

"Tell you what, Mr. Robbins…"

"Please, David. Call me David," Robbins interrupted.

"Okay, David. And I'm Leon. So, David, I'm suddenly feeling my age, but there is more I want you to know. Just not now. Would you be willing to have some company in a day or so?"

Robbins quickly nodded his head, "Yes, I think I would like that."

He truly did.

THIRTEEN

There were no more pills.

The anguish raged unabated like torrents of cold wind and icy rain from a crippling winter storm.

The California doctors would not renew the prescription without a psychological "work-up." Nancy Robbins didn't need a doctor to tell her she hovered on the verge of losing her mind. She already knew that. All she needed from a doctor was the sedatives. A little shelter from the storm.

Nancy wished for downers and uppers and pain relievers and a very special pill she knew didn't even exist. One that would tell her what was right and what was wrong. What to do and what not to do. Because quite honestly, indecisions and doubts and conflicting thoughts worked at tearing her apart.

Her feelings brought to mind a memory of something she wondered why she would remember in the first place. Once, in a past that now seemed like a dream, Nancy stood at her kitchen sink of the grand house in Shawnee doing dishes and gazing out the window above the sink. The window looked out on the driveway. The small portion of drive that she could see was blocked in three directions by the house on one side, a rock wall on the other, and the garage at the end.

A fairly stout breeze blew that day. It came from the direction of the street and blustered down the drive. One of the children had evidently dropped a sheet of paper on the drive, and the wind found it. The motion of the wind in the enclosed area created a small cyclone, and the paper was caught in its grasp. The single piece of paper swirled and twisted violently around and around. It went up and down in a tight circle. It gave the impression of being trapped. The wind would not let it be. It quickly became tattered and soon thereafter it ripped in half. Then there were two pieces, battling both the wind and themselves. The struggle had held Nancy's attention, but at the time, it had no significance.

Now it did. The sheet of paper made her think of both herself and the man that was soon to be her ex-husband. And her feelings about David, like the paper had been in the wind, went around and around and up and down. Violently.

There was no single word to express her feelings for him because they were never constant. They swirled and tossed and twisted. And they were not consistent. Bitterness struggled against pity. She never wanted to see him again, and she missed him. Hate and…yes, love, both ebbed and flowed.

* * *

"This is ridiculous, Emo," Ralph Driscoll grunted, "We could have been home hours ago."

"What the hell do you have to get home to?" Bailey grinned. Ralph had been married and divorced almost as many times as Bailey and was currently unattached.

"I got a life, you know," Ralph said without conviction.

"Uh-huh, sure," Bailey chuckled.

"Hell, if it's just a woman you want, I got the numbers of some high-dollar call girls here in Oklahoma City."

"I know, Ralph, I gave you the damned numbers. Besides, this isn't just some woman. Something tells me this one is special."

"Uh-huh, sure," Ralph mimicked.

"No, really, this girl could be the one," Bailey nodded.

"Oh boy," Driscoll moaned as he stretched out on the couch in the television station's reception area. It was a large couch, but Driscoll made it look small. He made all things look small, even Emerson Bailey.

"Anyway, she'll be off the air in just a few minutes. We won't be here long," Bailey said as he examined the red roses he'd brought as an enticement.

Really, Bailey thought as he waited, Jennifer Rhodes could be the one. The one he'd change for. The one that would really and truly be the one and only. Maybe. He would never give up hope. And Jennifer seemed definitely worth the effort. Maybe.

* * *

"Are those for me?" Jennifer Rhodes asked upon stepping into the reception area. She loved roses, and she loved how Emerson Bailey sprang to his feet when she stepped through the door.

"They're certainly not for me," the large and deeply dark man on the couch sighed.

"Is this your bodyguard?" Jennifer smiled.

"Sometimes," Bailey spoke for the first time. "Mostly he's just my best friend."

"Mostly," the man said as he stood and offered his huge hand to Jennifer, "I'm just his *boy*. I'm Ralph Driscoll," he smiled pleasantly.

"Can't you go some place, Ralph?" Bailey grimaced.

"Sure. I can go wait in the limo that you're making me drive," Driscoll grimaced back.

"It was nice meeting you, Ralph," Jennifer said as Driscoll left the room. "He seems like quite a character," she said to Bailey.

"Best friend I've ever had," Bailey said sincerely, "And, yes, these are for you," he smiled while handing her the roses.

"They're beautiful," she said as she smelled them.

"Consider them a peace offering. I'm afraid I was a might presumptuous earlier today."

"Oh, really? I thought you were just playing the part of the big shot attorney," she teased.

"Well, sometimes I overdo things. I just wanted you to know there's another side of me."

"I like this side of you."

"So, will you have dinner with this side of me?"

"With all else you had to do today, did you find the time to finalize the divorce?"

"Oh, still hung up on that?" Bailey scowled.

"Yes. Still," she sighed.

"But can't we just go as friends?"

"Is friendship all you have in mind?" Jennifer giggled.

Emerson Bailey inhaled deeply and seemed to study her for a second or two. "No. Not at all."

Jennifer walked over to the receptionist's desk and carefully wrote her number on a piece of paper while cradling the roses in the crook of her arm. She then turned and handed the piece to Bailey.

"When you are divorced, totally and completely, give me a call."

He looked dejected. Before walking out the door, Emerson Bailey turned back, cocked his head and asked, "Are you a Baptist?"

"No."

The answer seemed to please him.

* * *

Her parents and Kevin had gone out for dinner. They had not been able to persuade Nancy to accompany them. The three had been gone only an hour when Nancy started wishing she'd given in. This was her first time to be alone in the house, and it was not a pleasant experience. It was too quiet. When the phone began to ring, she gladly grabbed for the receiver.

"Decker residence."

"Please don't hang up."

Nancy's breath caught in her throat for a long second before rushing out through her open mouth. Her next breath didn't seem involuntary. It felt as if she had to make an effort just to take it. In a split second and with only four words, David's voice took her places no others could.

And some of them were good places. Wonderful places from a past life that most people could only dream of having. Nancy had been all she had ever wanted to be – a wife and mother. David had been her only love, and it had been magnificent. She always believed there could be no other man as kind and loving and devoted as her David. He had in all respects been a model mate and…father.

And the other place his voice took her was to the funeral parlor and the tiny and still and wax-like body. Kayla had been a doll in life. And, in Nancy's arms, had felt like one in death.

She didn't hang up. The conflicting emotions all bore claws and they ripped and tore at her insides. When she could speak, her words were icy.

"My attorney doesn't want me talking to you. I don't want to talk to you."

"Please, Nancy, don't do this. Not now. Just give it some time, at least until after the trial."

"Why, David? The outcome of your trial will change nothing. Are you expecting something miraculous to happen in that courtroom David? Because that is what it would take to change anything for me. Something would have to come from that trial to make sense of what you did. Something truly miraculous to convince me that there was any good, any merit, in you letting Kayla die. And what could that possibly be, David?"

She only allowed a few seconds of silence before asking more harshly, "What, David? How, David, is your trial going to change a thing?"

"I don't know."

The desperation in his words softened her voice, but not her resolve, "I don't either, David, I really don't. So, there's no reason to wait."

Before he could say another word, Nancy hung up the phone. She didn't want David to hear her crying.

* * *

It took the longest time for him to recognize the sound penetrating the sluggish haze of alcohol-induced sleep. His eyes did not open without a cost. The pain throbbing behind his eyelids felt intense enough to be nauseating. The awakening sound was the doorbell, and although he'd hoped it wouldn't, Robbins realized that morning had come once again. After Nancy had hung up on him the night before, he'd drunk himself into a stupor and had at some point collapsed on the couch in his study. Now, he forced himself to wobbly legs. The room swayed as he made his way to the front door. An acidic taste of bile worked its way up his throat from his heaving stomach.

Robbins opened the front door to find Leon Beck, and embarrassment and shame overpowered the pain and nausea. He did not want to stand in front of this man hungover and still in the now rumpled clothes he'd worn to the cemetery the day before. But if the older gentleman found his appearance repulsive, it did not show in his expression. The aged eyes revealed nothing but kindness.

"I hope I'm not intruding," Beck said with a calming smile. Robbins invited him in and showed him to the living room. When both men were seated, Robbins brought his hands up to rub at his temples. "I've been trying to drink my way through this," he confessed.

"I understand," Beck nodded sympathetically, "As the younger generations says, been there and done that."

"It doesn't work."

"Yes, I know," Beck chuckled.

"My wife is divorcing me."

The revelation did not seem to surprise Beck, but his response did Robbins.

"When you married your lady did you expect it to be a temporary arrangement?"

"Of course not. I thought it was forever."

"Just like you think divorce is forever?"

"Right now, it has a definite ring of finality."

"David, people get married and they get divorced. Sometimes they marry each other again. Sometimes they don't. A long life has taught me nothing is forever and nothing is final. As believers, we have to know that this holds true even over death. We are born to die here so we can live on at someplace else. Nothing is final."

"I really want to believe that."

"I think you do believe it. I think you've just gotten off track. Or, more precisely, have been brutally knocked off track. I was that way when my little Henry was killed. And, many years later, I felt the same over my other son, Matthew."

"What happened to Matthew?" Robbins asked softly.

"I don't really know," Leon Beck responded with a sad semblance of a smile. "Matthew was a fine boy. A straight-A student and a star athlete. He was the kind of son every man hopes to raise."

"I have a son like that," Robbins thought out loud. "He won't have anything to do with me now."

"Sons never completely lose their need for a father. He'll come back to you, and no matter what's happening right here and right now, that makes you a very blessed man."

Leon Beck turned his gaze from Robbins to the mantel over the fireplace. It was apparent, though, that what he was looking at was not what he was seeing.

"If Matthew could have, I'm sure he would have come back to me. His mother and I took him to the bus station in 1968. We waved at him and he waved back until that Greyhound was out of sight. The bus took him to Fort Benning, Georgia, and from there, he was flown to Vietnam.

"Matthew was good about writing us. I think we got a letter about every week for the first six months he was over there. Then they stopped coming. The next thing we knew, there was a young captain and an army chaplain standing on our front porch."

Leon Beck sighed heavily. He continued to stare at a place and time beyond the ornate mantel.

"His company's base camp had been overrun. About half the company had been killed and the other half was either wounded or missing. Matthew was counted among the missing. They thought he was probably taken prisoner, but that was never confirmed. Nothing has ever been confirmed. He's still listed as MIA."

Robbins knew the words in his mind were trite and did not express what he was feeling for the feeble man sitting in front of him, but they were all he had.

"I'm sorry."

Beck slowly turned moist eyes from the mantle to Robbins, "Don't be," he smiled triumphantly. "I plan to see him again."

* * *

The now dilapidated and deserted old house had obviously once been grand. Signs that it served as the dwelling place of proud people of means lingered for the careful observer. In some places ornately carved woodwork was still in place. Strands of what appeared to be expensive wallpaper still existed in some of the rooms. Chunks of marble – though chipped and badly scarred – could still be found in the fireplace mantels and on a few of the first story windowsills.

The signs of a time gone by were still there but were few and far between. Signs of the here and now and of the transient occupants who often lurked within the dark old house were far too abundant. Beer and wine bottles – most of them broken – practically covered the floors. Rags and plastic baggies crusty with dried spray paint, along with the aerosol cans that had provided the crippling inhalant, could be found in nearly every room.

A home that had most likely been filled with fine furniture now housed nothing but an old ripped and stained mattress and two busted aluminum lawn chairs. Very few of the windows still had glass and a back door barely held to its hinges. Fires built outside the fireplaces to prevent telltale smoke from going up a chimney had more than once gotten out of control. An old house that had once been alive was now dead and decaying. Luke Hogue could not help but wonder what event or chain of events marked the beginning of the decline.

Maybe a father and breadwinner deserted his family. Maybe a loving mother and housewife fell ill with a crippling disease. Or maybe one of the happy and pampered children – the light of their parents' lives – suddenly died a terrible death. Maybe one of them had been shot to death. Maybe it had been a little girl. With blue eyes. And blonde hair.

People who killed such little girls were monsters or maniacs – deranged and incapable of feelings. At least that's what came over the four-wheel drive's radio from a call-in talk show. From the same program, Hogue learned the name and age of the little girl that had died. From that particular station he learned that her father was a wealthy and influential man, and that his name was David Robbins, and that he had been charged with murder.

The same people who called in and knew without a doubt the gunman was an animal, a cold-blooded reptile, an emotionless psychopath, also knew all to be known about David Robbins. They knew he was a religious fanatic, a zealot, a man who had done a terrible injustice to his family and to the image of Christians everywhere. How ironic, Hogue had mused, that so many people thought they knew so much, when they didn't know shit.

There was really much to know, so much that would absolutely astonish all the know-it-alls: the prosecutors, the defense attorneys, and especially David Robbins. There were two facts, in particular, if known would change a lot of people's mind about a lot of things. However, the only two people who could ever attest to the facts never would. One of them never would because she was dead. The other never would because he was a monster. A maniac.

The old deserted house, one of many in the heart of downtown Oklahoma City, had its fair share of dark, musty closets. Hogue selected the smallest closet and crawled inside to wait out the few remaining hours of daylight. When the sun had long set and the night was well into its shift, Luke would pay a visit to a relative.

Engulfed in the confined darkness of the closet, his thoughts turned – as they all too often did – to that night and to that moment Kayla Robbins died. Within seconds the emotionless creature started wiping at his eyes with the backs of his hands.

* * *

The day finally crept to an end, and Robbins sat at the desk in his study. A bottle and shot glass rested easily within his reach. After only seconds of consideration, Robbins filled the glass and raised it to his lips.

Leon Beck's early morning visit lasted less than an hour, but the old man and the fate of his son Matthew plagued Robbins throughout the day.

"How did you live through that?" he had asked.

"Just like you are now, David," Beck had responded, "and just like countless people do every day with tragedies that are forced upon them. We all live through our sorrows one painful breath at a time. Life, no matter how wretched, does go on."

Then Beck offered advice Robbins contemplated the rest of the long, long day.

"Go to the Bible, David. It does hold some answers. Some encouragement to simply keep putting one foot in front of the other, one minute and hour and day at a time."

Before leaving, Beck suggested a particular book of the Bible. Now, Robbins felt that reading it just might serve as a counterbalance to the glass in his hand. After several sips from the glass, he forced himself out of his chair.

The portion of the bookshelves that had housed the small Gideon's Bible, now resting in pieces on the study floor, contained an assortment of other Bibles and study guides.

Robbins selected a New Revised Standard Version reference Bible and walked back to his desk. Struggling against a powerful resistance not to, Robbins opened the Bible to the Book of Job. He would, he compromised, give Leon Beck's suggestion a moment of his time. A few minutes at the most.

An hour and several glasses of Jack Daniels later, Robbins continued to read on. Only when the words on the pages begin to blur, did he close the Bible. He marked the page before doing so.

And he didn't put the Bible back on the shelf, and he didn't put the bottle back in the cabinet. He left them lying side by side on his desk. Before leaving the study, he picked up the scattered pages of the small Gideons Bible, arranged them in the binder and put the Bible back in its place on the shelf.

FOURTEEN

Mark Hogue's first impulse upon waking was to scream, but he couldn't. Something was stuffed in his mouth – maybe a pair of socks, maybe a rag – and some type of strong tape held the gag firmly in place. The next frantic signal from his intoxicated brain told him to get up and run, but he couldn't do that either. He was hogtied – lying on his stomach with his arms behind his back and his hands tied to his upright ankles. Finding that he couldn't scream or move, Mark erupted into a frenzied squirming, tossing, and jerking medley accompanied by muffled cries and grunts. He kept this up until he couldn't do anymore, and when he couldn't, he simply lay still with his eyes exceedingly wide open and twitching to the left and right.

Mark Hogue did not go out the night before. He conducted his business from home. The business of drinking was not as much fun at home as in a bar, but proved just as effective. Well before midnight, Mark managed to get falling-down drunk. He thought he stopped short of passing-out drunk. Evidently, he had not. Sometime after midnight he blacked out, and by all indications his brother, Luke, found his way in.

His brother. Where was Luke? Mark lay on the terribly filthy floor of his tiny bathroom. A quick jerk of his head to the left found the bathroom door closed. Why would Luke close him up in the bathroom, and just where exactly was that son of a bitch, and more importantly, what was he doing?

Since he couldn't see Luke, Mark strained to hear over his labored breathing and the runaway pounding of his heart. Soon, he detected a noise coming from another part of the house. It took a minute or two for his terrified mind to make the noise out, and when it did, Mark's imagination really went wild but came up with nothing. Mark just could not imagine what or why Luke Hogue was sawing.

* * *

"By all means," Jennifer Rhodes blurted to the news station receptionist on the intercom. "I'll take the call!"

Then she calmed herself for a second or two, pushed the button on her phone that would connect her with the outside call and responded more professionally, "This is Jennifer Rhodes."

"Ms. Rhodes, this is David Robbins from Shawnee. I understand you wish to visit with me off the record." The voice sounded deeper than Jennifer expected and had only a trace of the twang common of native Oklahomans.

Jennifer took a deep breath and tried to contain her excitement. "I certainly would, Mr. Robbins."

"Would you by chance be free to meet me at my home at six this evening?"

Jennifer instinctively reached for her appointment book but quickly pulled her hand back. "If you'll give me your address, Mr. Robbins, I'll be there."

Jennifer couldn't invent a prior commitment that would take precedence over this meeting.

* * *

Luke Hogue laid down the handsaw and picked up the pry bar. He used the bar to pry lose the plywood flooring he'd cut in his brother's bedroom, revealing the ground less than two feet below the floor. The hole he created ran between two floor joists and measured just big enough for a man his size to squeeze through. Tossing the pry bar aside, Hogue picked up a shovel. Just like the other tools he found in the shed behind his brother's house, the shovel had seen better days. The wooden handle was splintering, and the spade practically rusted through in spots.

The dirt beneath the floor was soft and came up easily. Hogue deposited the extracted soil on a large piece of plastic sheeting he found in the shed. Once the plywood was put back in place, the carpet folded back over it, and the bed relocated over the hole, Hogue didn't want any traces of dirt left on the carpet. Although, he winced, it would take one damn sharp cop to distinguish the red soil from all the other filth in the disgusting shag.

The neglected old shovel was the first Hogue touched since burying the dog his father kicked to death years ago. The feel of a shovel in his hand and the smell of the dirt brought back vivid memories of that day. Hogue distinctly remembered wishing it were the Reverend Richard Lee's grave he was digging instead of the dog's. He didn't know it at the time, but his wish, or more accurately, a variation thereof soon would come true.

Late afternoon on a beautiful October day, Richard Lee brought his speeding car to a screeching halt in front of the small parsonage. Both boys and their mother, Ellen, had been sitting on the porch enjoying the father's absence. When Richard Lee bailed from the car short of breath and snorting like a bull, Ellen Hogue shooed her boys off the porch. The elder Hogue's face flushed a red deep enough to rival some of the autumn leaves just starting to fall. The good Reverend was, for some unknown reason, even in a more dangerous state than usual.

"It's all your fault," he bellowed as he stormed up the steps to the porch with a menacing finger pointed at his wife of nearly fifteen years.

"If you was the kind of wife you're supposed to be, I wouldn't be in such a mess right now," he screamed in her face as he grabbed a handful of her long red hair.

"The Bible says you women are supposed to be submissive to your husbands, and you ain't been submitting, bitch!" Richard Lee thundered as he jerked Ellen from her chair and pulled her into the house by the hair of her head.

His mother lay on the floor being kicked when Luke burst through the door. Ellen Hogue often intervened for her sons when their father tore into them and more than once paid a painful price for doing so. Both boys watched their old man beat their mother numerous times in the past, yet neither interfered. This time was going to be different. With the memory of what Richard Lee did to his dog still fresh in his mind, Luke Hogue sprang onto his father's back.

The wild ride didn't last long. Richard Lee – much taller and at least fifty pounds heavier than Luke – had little problem plucking the boy from his back and slamming him to the floor. Luke landed so hard it knocked the breath out of him. Rolling over and on to his knees, Luke struggled to catch his breath. Before he could, the pointed toe of Richard Lee's right boot caught him square in the mouth and toppled him over backwards. Luke sucked gushing blood from ruined lips down his throat as he continued to gasp for air. Richard Lee only wasted one more kick on Luke before turning back to his wife, but that kick landed between the boy's legs and left him withering uselessly on the floor.

Unable to get to his feet, Luke watched Richard Lee pull his mother from the floor and knock her back down again. Ellen Hogue cried, but she didn't scream. She never screamed. Richard Lee kicked the woman once in the face and positioned his foot to kick her again when a booming voice sounded from the front yard.

"Come out of that house, Richard Lee. I don't want to come in there and kill ya in front of ya family, but I will if ya make me!"

With a frantic curse, Richard Lee Hogue darted toward the rear of the house. Luke didn't know who was out front or what beef he had with his father, and he didn't care.

"He's going out the back door!" Luke cried as loud as he could manage.

Luke heard the man out front start to curse; then he heard running footsteps. A split second later he heard the back-screen door slam shut. On hands and knees, Luke scampered to and out the back door. He made it just in time to see Harry Ward, one of the deacons of his father's church, round the corner of the house at a full run. Ward carried a double-barreled shotgun, and when he spotted Richard Lee high-tailing it toward the barn, Ward didn't run another step. Instead, he brought the shotgun up to his shoulder and took careful aim.

Ward discharged both barrels at the same time, and both deer slugs found their mark. The impact of the pair of huge chunks of lead practically ripped Richard Lee in half. Luke always suspected that before what was left of the body hit the ground, the soul already burned in hell.

"The son of a bitch," Harry Ward said calmly as he lowered the shotgun, "was a' fuckin' my daughter." Before getting in his car and driving away, he informed Ellen Hogue, "Tell the sheriff he can find me at home."

Ward's daughter was thirteen at the time and one of Luke Hogue's classmates. Seven months after the shooting, she bore Luke a half-brother. The baby died a few months later.

Luke didn't shed a tear the day they stuffed his father in the ground. Now, as he lifted the last shovel full of red dirt from beneath the bedroom floor, he remembered how dark and fertile the dirt looked that covered the Reverend Richard Lee. That memory and the fact that the hole under the floor was now plenty deep enough, brought a smile to Luke's face. Time to drag Mark out of the bathroom.

* * *

"David, what a pleasant surprise," Leon Beck said upon responding to the knock on his front door.

"Hi, Leon. Have you got just a second?"

"I'm long retired. I have all day," Beck chuckled, "Please come in."

Beck sat Robbins at his kitchen table and offered him a cup of coffee. Robbins accepted the offer.

"Well, you certainly look to be feeling better than you did yesterday morning, David," Beck grinned with a wink. "Not a whole lot better, but some none the less."

"I didn't drink as much last night," Robbins responded sheepishly, "I actually fell asleep last night instead of passing out."

"One step at a time, David. Just one step at a time," Beck responded as he placed the cup of coffee on the table in front of his guest.

Robbins hooked an index finger into the cups handle, but didn't move it from the place on the table. For several seconds he simply stared at the cup.

"I started reading the Book of Job last night. I finished it this morning," Robbins said once he looked back up.

"Good," Beck nodded.

"He lost everything. Absolutely everything," Robbins said thoughtfully.

"Yes," Beck said as he settled into a chair across from Robbins, "He suffered greatly."

"But he got it all back, and a lot more on top of it," Robbins added while looking intently into Beck's eyes.

"He certainly did," Beck smiled.

"He lost much more than I did, and," Robbins paused and looked back down at his coffee, "so did you."

Leon Beck did not offer a response.

"It made me think, Leon. You lost both of your sons. I still have my boy. I can't see him, or touch him, but I know where he is. And your wife died. Nancy, well, she'll divorce me, no doubt, but at least I know she's alive. And, maybe, someday I can get her back. I hope I can."

"And I hope the same," Leon said softly.

"Anyway," Robbins said after clearing his throat, "it just made me think, and I want to thank you for that. Meeting you, getting to know you, has helped a lot. I'm still a long, long way from healing, but..."

Robbins didn't finish his sentence, but took a sip of his coffee instead.

Beck gave Robbins a few seconds while considering how to put what he wanted to say. He settled on being blunt.

"Have you been praying, David?"

The response came slowly. "No. Not really."

"You need to. Even if what you have to say is ugly, spiteful."

"Well, I've done a little venting," Robbins smiled wearily.

"Good. He has broad shoulders, David. He can take it. After all, He is God."

David Robbins seemed to consider the statement earnestly before taking another sip of coffee.

* * *

"Thanks for seeing me on such short notice," Robbins said as he walked into Emerson Bailey's office.

"You got lucky," Bailey said as he moved to shake Robbins' hand. "I was supposed to be in Dallas today selecting potential jurors, but the prosecution was granted a continuance. I got the bastards running scared!"

"It's good to know I've still got some luck left," Robbins smiled as he shook Bailey's hand and handed him a small stack of papers.

A quick glance revealed the papers to be a petition for divorce and a summons. Looking back at Robbins, Bailey was surprised to find the man so much more at ease and obviously less tortured than the last time they'd met. If anything, Bailey would expect Robbins to be ten times as depressed and downtrodden as he was twenty-four hours earlier. After directing Robbins to a chair, Bailey went back to his desk and sat down.

"You're taking this pretty well," Bailey said just to see how his client would react.

"I'm taking it, Emo. I'm just taking it," Robbins stated as a matter of fact.

"Do you want my firm to handle this?"

"Are you running any specials this week? Like, let's say, buy a murder defense, get a divorce done for free?" Robbins' lips smiled, but his eyes did not.

"You must remember, David," Bailey chuckled, "I'm counting on you to pay for my divorce! But my associates handle the divorces, and it will cost you far less than a murder charge."

"I would hope so," Robbins returned dryly. "That petition says I have twenty days to respond. Now that I've brought it to your attention, I'd like to wait a day or two before discussing actual fees and other particulars. I'd just like to forget about it for a couple of days."

"We have plenty of time. If you can put it out of your mind for a day or so, then do it. The woman I'm divorcing won't let me forget for a single minute."

David Robbins averted his eyes to the portrait of the Statue of Liberty. "I'm pretty sure my wife will want this over with as quickly and painlessly as possible."

"I'll assign one of my best associates," Bailey said kindly.

"Thanks," Robbins responded as he turned back to Bailey. "About our conversation yesterday…I've decided to testify."

Bailey studied Robbins a second or two wondering what factors played a role in changing his mind. "I'm glad. I think it will pay off for you."

"I've also changed my position on delaying the proceedings. I would like to have my case heard as soon as possible."

"Why, David?"

"My life right now hinges around the trial, Emo. I want it over with. If I'm going to be free, I want to be free as soon as possible. If I'm going to prison…Well, I want to get that over with, too."

Emerson Bailey could argue with the reasoning but not with the look of determination on David Robbins' face. "Okay, David. I'll push for an immediate trail date."

"One more thing," Robbins said with a scowl. "I'm meeting with Jennifer Rhodes tonight."

Emerson Bailey rocked back in his chair and burst into laughter. "From our last conversation, I didn't think you'd agree to doing this. Are you a different David Robbins than I visited with just the other day?"

The look of determination came back as Robbins mumbled, "Not yet. But I'm really working on it, Emo."

* * *

Mark Hogue had his eyes trained on the bathroom doorknob and noticed the instant it started to turn. One more time he struggled against the ropes binding his wrists to his ankles, and again it resulted in just a waste of energy. When the door swung open, Mark went through the mechanics of screaming. The noise he produced through the gag sounded similar to the whine of a far-off siren.

While he continued to squirm and gurgle, Mark took in the gaunt figure standing silently in the doorway. Luke had lost a noticeable amount of weight over the past four days and still wore the same clothes he'd worn when they met in the oil field. The once white T-shirt would never be white again, and the tattered jeans were soiled stiff. A scraggly growth of beard covered Luke's thin face, and his stringy hair was plastered to his head. The stench of his body odor permeated the bathroom. Luke Hogue looked to be well beyond the point of exhaustion, but he no longer looked deathly sick.

"Are you glad to see me, little brother?" Luke hissed.

Mark frantically nodded his head up and down and tried to grunt a yes.

"How does that old joke go? Let's see…How do you know when Mark Hogue is lying? When his lips are moving. Fuck, Mark, you can lie without even moving your goddamn lips."

Mark intended what came out as a string of guttural coughs to be apologies and pleas for mercy. Luke either didn't understand them or chose to ignore them. Without further comment, he bent and grabbed the rope tying his brother's hands and ankles. He used the rope to drag Mark out of the bathroom, down a small hall and into the shack's only bedroom. Mark turned, twisted and jerked all the way, but the resistance proved to be futile.

For a mere second after being pulled into the bedroom, Mark's mind was averted from his crippling fear by a rush of curiosity. Why had Luke moved his bed, and why was dirt piled up on the floor where the bed had always been? By the time Mark saw the piece of carpet folded back and the piece of plywood on the floor, Luke had him alongside the hole.

With a physical enthusiasm he never displayed before, Mark started to buck and kick and flip and flop. In spite of it all, he still tumbled into the hole, belly down. As he squirmed to get on his side so he could look up, Mark did the only two things left to do. He started to cry. And for the first time since very early childhood, he prayed.

He cried and prayed and watched wide-eyed as his older brother produced a revolver from the small of his back. He cried harder and prayed faster and squinted his eyes when Luke Hogue pulled back the hammer and took aim.

Then, everything went dark.

* * *

Jennifer Rhodes' ambition in life was to one day anchor a prime-time, network news show. When she reached that level of success, she hoped to live in a house like David Robbins owned. For several minutes after arriving at One Hundred South Willow Brook Avenue, Jennifer remained in her car and admired the Federal-style home from the circle drive. The reporter was not very familiar with Shawnee, but she doubted the town possessed many homes as elegant as the two-and-a-half story, red brick structure. Its white trim, door-sized windows with slatted shutters, and the four majestic columns of the front portico put Jennifer in mind of romantic plantation homes in the Deep South.

Suddenly, very anxious to get a look at the inside of the house, Jennifer hurried from her car to the front door. Thanks to those in her line of work, few, if any people in the state, wouldn't recognize David Robbins. When he opened the door, Jennifer Rhodes extended her right hand.

"Mr. Robbins. I'm Jennifer Rhodes," and before he could respond, "Oh, you have such a marvelous home!"

"Uh…nice to meet you Ms. Rhodes," Robbins said as he shook her hand. "And thanks. I've always liked the house, too."

Robbins wasn't averting his eyes from Jennifer's or showing any other signs of being bashful, but she could sense a little shyness all the same. Jennifer considered it a hobby to pluck the shy from their shells. "You must have paid a fortune for this place. Is the sporting goods business that good in Shawnee?"

This time Robbins smiled coyly. "The business has been good to me, Ms. Rhodes, and I've made some lucky investments along the way."

Robbins hadn't officially invited Jennifer in, but he was standing in the doorway holding the door open. That served close enough to

official for Jennifer. After walking past Robbins and giving the entryway a lustful once over, Jennifer looked back at Robbins. If he was
put off by her aggressive manner, he didn't show it. If anything, he
appeared to be amused by it. His next words, which he emphasized
with a grin, seemed to prove it.

"Please make yourself at home, Ms. Rhodes."

"It would be much easier for me to do so if you'd call me Jennifer," she returned with a grin of her own.

"Okay, Jennifer. I'm David," he said before raising his right
hand with palm up and motioning in the same direction.

"This is the living room. We can talk in there."

This time with a real invitation, Jennifer walked around Robbins
again and preceded him into the immense living room. The furnish-
ings of the room were extremely formal, but deep red walls and emer-
ald green floor-to-ceiling drapes prevented it from being austere. Jennifer could not determine if the Chippendale furniture adorning the
room was flawlessly restored antiques or wonderful reproductions.
Either way, she guessed certain the pieces had not come cheap. Jennifer chose to sit on a divan with a floral print of colors complement-
ing the walls and drapes. Robbins selected one of the two matching
armchairs across from the divan.

"I just love old houses," Jennifer said as her eyes worked their
way around the room. "How old is this one?"

"It's one-hundred and thirteen years old," Robbins said as he settled back in the chair. "My wife and I are only the second owners. A
Doctor Thomas Herring had the house built in 1906. He was, by the
way, the first physician to set up a practice in Shawnee. His family
owned the house until we bought it."

When Jennifer turned her eyes on Robbins, she found that he
too was looking around the room. She assumed that someone watch-

ing her as she looked around would have seen curiosity in her eyes. In his, she saw affection.

"I came from a large family," Robbins continued. "I had four brothers and two sisters, and it was necessary for all of us to go to work at young ages just to help buy food. My first job was throwing papers, and this house was on my route. I used to dream about living here. Buying it was a dream come true."

As Robbins imparted more information about his acquisition of the beloved structure, Jennifer turned her studies from the house to the man. She listened to his words but concentrated more on his physical appearance. To judge a book, Jennifer believed, you had to give due consideration to the cover.

By Jennifer's assessment, Robbins possessed much more than the average man's share of handsome qualities. She liked the close-cut style of his thick, dark hair but found his most endearing assets to be his large, brown eyes and cleft chin. His teeth were far from perfectly straight, but they were clean and bright and added a rugged touch to his otherwise pretty facial features. Jennifer guessed Robbins to be just at or slightly under six feet tall. His pleated khaki trousers and knit polo shirt covered a trim and athletic build.

When Robbins ran out of words about the house, Jennifer sent him in another ice-breaking direction. "I'm curious, David, how and why did you get into sporting goods?"

"The name of the store is Sports World, and it's been in business in Shawnee since the late fifties. I went to work there for the owner, a Mr. Edinburgh, when I was fourteen. I started out as a stock boy and janitor but was selling by the time I was sixteen. When I was nineteen, Mr. Edinburgh promoted me to assistant manager. I was in my early twenties when Mr. Edinburgh developed severe heart problems and offered to sell the store to me. He made me a great deal, carried the financing, and within ten years I owned it free and clear."

"This spectacular home and a thriving business," Jennifer concluded for Robbins with a smile, "makes you a very blessed man, David."

Robbins returned the smile, but his soft eyes narrowed. After a few seconds of apparent contemplation, he calmly stated, "Let's talk, Jennifer."

"Okay, David," Jennifer replied evenly, as if she hadn't been caught trying to bait Robbins into discussing things she knew he wouldn't want to discuss.

"Following the advice of my attorney, I can't discuss anything pertaining to the night Kayla was killed. I can't discuss anything I or anyone else did. I can't discuss anything I or anyone else said. I can't even discuss what I felt on that night, or what I feel about that night now. And most importantly," Robbins said with elevated forefinger and a stern look, "what I do say here tonight about myself or my life or my family is strictly off the record."

"Fair enough," Jennifer nodded.

"Okay, then," Robbins was smiling again, "if we can't talk about that night, and I'm going to assume that you have known all along that we couldn't, then why are you here?"

"Quite simply, David, I just wanted to meet you."

"You just wanted to meet me," Robbins repeated with a nod of his head. "You just wanted to meet a man capable of …doing what I did."

"Yes, David. You interest me. Me and thousands of others across the state and nation."

Robbins thought about the comment for a moment, and then started to chuckle. "Tell me, Jennifer, are you surprised I don't have pictures of Jesus and crosses hanging from the walls – that Bibles and religious pamphlets aren't on my coffee and end tables?"

Jennifer glanced quickly around the room again before answering. "Well, David," she smiled sheepishly, "I did expect at least some religious paraphernalia."

"Would you be even more surprised to learn, Jennifer," the look on Robbins' face as well as the tone in his voice turned playful, "that I only attend church once a week…that being the Sunday morning service…and that sometimes I even miss that one?"

"I'm familiar with Presbyterian churches, David. Enough to know most of them don't have Sunday and Wednesday evening services."

"Good. I'm glad you're familiar with my church. Maybe you'll understand what I mean when I say I consider myself to be a typical Presbyterian. I've never been baptized by submersion. I don't speak in tongues. I don't handle snakes while I worship God."

Jennifer interrupted with a laugh. Robbins joined her for a second or two and then plowed on. "I guess the only thing not typical about me, Jennifer, is that I'm a staunch rule follower. I play golf and tennis, and I always play strictly by the rules. If you were an employer and I was one of your employees, I'd follow your regulations and guidelines to the letter. I am the kind, Jennifer, who finds it extremely difficult to exceed posted speed limits."

"There's a point to be made here?" Jennifer laughed.

"Just this," Robbins grinned, "I'm a Christian. I'm not a fanatic or a zealot. I don't think I'd even qualify to be what we called in the seventies a Jesus Freak. I'm just a practicing Christian. As such, my rules and regulations, my guidelines, come from the Bible."

Jennifer took more than a few moments to consider all Robbins had said before responding softly, "I wish I could put the David Robbins I've found here on television."

"I wish you could, too, but you can't. I want to be tried in this county, Jennifer. I don't want to give the district attorney any reasons to request a change in venue."

"You asked me earlier why I came here. Now, tell me, why did you want me here?"

Robbins steepled his fingers, stared at them a second or two, and then slowly moved his eyes around the room. When his gaze finally made it back to Jennifer's eyes, he said, "I wanted to say what I said to someone very familiar with every aspect of this case. I just wanted that informed person to know at least that much about me. I am not the person that's been portrayed in the papers and on television. I just wanted someone in the media to know that."

"Well, David, now someone in the media does," she responded sincerely.

Only minutes later, as Jennifer Rhodes pulled away from the mansion on South Willow Brook Avenue, she pondered the man she'd met there. The terrible thing that happened at the church only blocks away, seemed now, more than ever, truly perplexing.

* * *

The piece of plywood covered the hole in the floor. The reapplied carpet concealed the plywood, and the bed, back in place, hid the entire project. Luke Hogue now lay spread eagle on the bed. Nearly six hours had elapsed since Luke covered the opening and what lay beneath it. Several times over the span of hours Luke thought about what he had done and then laughed out loud about doing it. He particularly liked thinking about taking careful aim…pulling back the hammer…and then quickly sliding the cutout plywood back in place with his foot. Just making Mark think he was going to be shot in the head brought great joy to the older brother.

Mark had really broken loose with some muffled cries and grunts when the board covered the opening. Then, when Luke threw the carpet back in place, Mark started banging on the floor with his feet, or maybe even his head. Not very much light at all could have made it through the slits in the plywood, but any light was better than no light at all. Especially if you were a son of the late Reverend Richard Lee Hogue and just happened to find yourself in a hole.

Mark really threw a good fit for the first thirty minutes beneath the floor. Then, his protests dwindled to only occasional thumps and groans. For the past hour, not as much as a single bump or gurgle wafted up from beneath the bed. After another fifteen minutes of complete silence, Luke began to worry that his brother might have strangled on the sock in his mouth or suffocated from an insufficient supply of oxygen. Making Mark think he was going to die was one thing. Actually killing him was quite another. Mark was, after all, Luke's own flesh and blood. More importantly, Luke needed Mark to help keep him out of prison.

Six hours earlier, Luke had made a noisy production of moving the bed back over the hole. He wanted Mark to hear the bed being moved and hoped his sibling would believe that his place under the floor was a permanent one. Now, Luke moved the bed out of the way quickly and effortlessly. Falling to his knees, he slung the carpet back and paused to take a deep breath. Then, he pulled up the piece of plywood. The sight that greeted Luke caused him to slowly expel the air in his lungs.

"You sure got awful quiet, asshole," Luke mumbled.

Mark Hogue lay still and silent as he stared up into the light and blinked like an owl. His face was caked with dirt and streaked with mud from where the tears had streamed.

"I didn't dig this hole for you, but I wanted you to spend some time in it. I wanted you to know what it's like because it's where I'll be spending a lot of my time," Luke said softly as he sat back on the floor and crossed his legs.

"Yeah, that's right, I'm going to be staying here a while, and this hole is where I'll sleep and go to when and if I need to hide. You being kin and all, I'm sure you don't mind putting me up, do you?"

Mark quickly jerked his head back and forth several times.

"Good. I mean, I wouldn't be here in the first place if it weren't for you. If it weren't for you snitching my ass off, I'd be long gone. Probably be in Mexico or maybe even Canada by now if you hadn't fucked me. You are sorry for fuckin' me, ain't you?"

Mark frantically bounced his head up and down.

"Good. That brings me to my next point. You know all that money I had?"

Mark nodded affirmation again.

"Well, I hid a good sum of it," Luke lied. "And if you turn on me again, and I go to prison, I'll meet a lot of boys coming and going that will kill your sorry ass over and over again for the amount I've got hidden away. See, I'll offer that money to someone that I know will get the job done. I'll explain to them that when I got proof of you being dead, I'll tell them where the money is. Believe me, it'll be easy to find someone that will jump on a deal like that. You understand me?"

Mark supported the frantic nodding of his head with a wide-eyed stare of terror and more tears.

"See, this should be the last place the cops look for me. If you don't fuck me again, I should be safe here. Don't fuck me again. You want outta there?"

Mark nodded a half dozen yeses.

"Okay. When I let you out, the first thing I want you to do is get this pile of dirt out of the house. I want you to carry it out in small containers and spread it around your yard. Hide it under bushes and other shit. When you get finished with that, I want something to eat."

Luke moved forward onto his hands and knees, reached down into the hole, jerked the tape from his brother's mouth and pulled out the sock. "You got any questions?"

After a few hard swallows followed by several seconds of spitting, Mark cleared his throat and moaned, "How long you going to be here, Luke?"

"I've got something I gotta do, Mark. Once I figure out how I'm going to do it, I'll be gone."

* * *

It was late, long after most working people were in bed, but Emerson Bailey was still in his office, just keeping his typical office hours. He jumped when the phone on his desk started to ring. Few people had the private number to his office, and those few never called at this hour.

"This is Bailey," he responded curiously.

"We don't have the whole story on David Robbins, do we?" a curt female voice responded.

"Now, that depends on who the stated 'we' are," he replied evenly. Bailey immediately recognized the voice. It was just more fun this way.

"You know who this is, but I'll play along. The aforementioned 'we' are the media and the populace. All of whom have a right to know what really happened to Kayla Robbins and why."

"Jennifer?" Bailey said with mock surprise, "Is that you, Jennifer?"

"Don't toy with me, Emo, I want to know what happened. I didn't spend much time with him, but I spent enough to know that David Robbins is not the type to stand idly or meekly by and allow Luke Hogue to execute his daughter. There is something that didn't show up in the investigation. Something you're not telling and I want to hear it."

"Okay."

"Okay? That easy?"

"Sure. That easy. I only have one thing, Jennifer, and that's the same thing you have, a feeling that there's something missing. The cops didn't find it. I haven't found it. The D.A. doesn't know what it is. And, now for the real kicker, David Robbins doesn't know what it is either."

"Are you putting me on, Emo?"

"No. I wish I were. By the way, will you have dinner with me Friday night?"

"Damn, you don't give up, do you?" Jennifer suddenly sounded tired.

"My divorce was filed today. Technically, I'm a free man."

It took a lot to make Bailey nervous, but the long bout of silence from the other end started to do so.

"Dinner would be nice," she finally allowed.

Yes, Emo Bailey's heart seemed to beat in Morse code – yes, it certainly would.

* * *

"I've been sitting here for an hour now just trying to come up with words," Robbins started. "I don't even really want to talk to you. I am so angry with you, and I'm not even sure you care. If you do, then I just wish to hell you'd start showing it."

Before concluding, Robbins rubbed at his eyes with both hands. "Okay. I've done my part. I've reached out. And, right now, I have nothing else to say. The rest is up to you."

He spent the next hour in silence, with eyes closed. Listening. Simply listening, to everything, and more importantly, to nothing. Giving the spirit of God a chance to intercede. And slowly, faintly, there somehow came a sense of tranquility. A hint of renewing. Just a flickering of hope. Far from what he longed for, but more than he expected.

PART II
THE TRIAL

FIFTEEN

David Robbins pulled his car to the curb across the street from One Hundred South Willow Brook Avenue. After putting down the windows and turning off the ignition, he settled back into his seat and inhaled a deep breath of the crisp October breeze that whipped through the car. He had always found the view of the old house from the street particularly wonderful in the fall of the year. It was the leaves of the ancient elms lining the circle drive that made it so. Brilliant shades of red and gold traditionally adorned thousands of branches and later blanketed the ground like a glorious patchwork quilt.

Being the latter part of October, there were more of those splendid leaves on the ground than remaining in the trees. To think that it was once again time to rake the yard amazed Robbins. On the one hand, it seemed as if he'd lived years without his wife, son, and daughter. On the other, it seemed mere weeks had passed since Robbins and his son had raked and gathered last year's harvest while little Kayla did her best to impede their efforts.

"Get ready, you guys," Robbins could remember Kayla squealing, "here I come!"

Kevin and David would pile the leaves high, and Kayla would fling herself onto the piles, giggling, kicking, and splaying her arms until the biggest portion of the leaves were redistributed.

"Daaaaad!" Kevin would protest in a whiney voice, insisting that Kayla should be stopped.

"She learned it from you," Robbins would laugh, as he thought back to a time before Kevin considered himself too old for such childish antics. "Besides, she'll get tired of all this running and jumping before too long."

And she did. Soon after, she started riding her bike through the piles. Kevin liked that even less and pointed out that he had never been so inconsiderate as to scatter leaves with a wheeled vehicle. Again, David just laughed. He remembered thinking that his little girl, like her brother, would all too soon think herself too mature to wallow in mountains of autumn leaves.

Now, as Robbins sat in his car, he thanked God that he had not stopped Kayla from having her fun. This year Kayla wouldn't run and jump and toss in the leaves, and Kevin wouldn't rake the yard. Neither would David Robbins. The house at One Hundred South Willow Brook Avenue, the house Robbins loved since his childhood, now belonged to another family. Robbins had sold it three months earlier. The money from the house went toward the settlement with his now ex-wife.

"So much has changed," Robbins mumbled under his breath as he started the engine back up. He had been divorced since June and had lived in a one-bedroom apartment since July. Having no need or desire for a social life, Robbins spent anywhere from twelve to fourteen hours each day in his store. He would return to the tiny, sparsely-furnished apartment only to sleep. Once a week, sometimes two, he called his son in California. Kevin would talk to him on the phone but strongly objected to meeting face to face. Robbins had decided not to enforce his visitation rights. He thought it best to give the boy as much time and space as he needed to adjust to the whole ugly ordeal of the past six months. Robbins never stopped wishing for reconciliation, and not just between his son and himself.

At least Kevin would talk to him over the phone on a regular basis. Robbins' ex-wife, now Nancy Decker, would seldom talk to him when he called, and when she did, it was never for more than a couple of uncomfortable seconds. Since Robbins did not contest the divorce, husband and wife did not appear in court together. David and Nancy had not seen each other since the day of their daughter's funeral. Nancy seemed clearly willing and able to stick with her earlier declaration. Something truly miraculous would have to come from his trial before she would even consider coming back to him.

As he pulled away from the curb, Robbins gave the old house one more glance in his rearview mirror. This was the first time he had been back to the place since the day he moved out, and he had no plans of coming back anytime soon. He had only come today because confronting the tangibles of the terrible, recent past was something he was about to do intensely. Within a few hours, Emerson Bailey and Assistant D.A. Mike Pierce would start selecting the jury that would decide his fate. David Robbins had not been given any indication or hope of a miraculous outcome.

* * *

"I wish I could go with you."

"Don't worry about it," Robbins responded as he held and patted the feeble hand, "I know your thoughts and prayers will be with me."

Robbins wished he'd visited more often. A month had passed since he'd last done so. Preparing for the trial and setting his business affairs in order…just in case…had occupied so much of his time. Still, he wished he'd made more of an effort. Leon Beck's health had taken a sharp downward turn and he was now confined to his bed.

"Are you ready?" Leon asked in a whisper.

"My attorney says we are."

"No," Leon smiled faintly, "are you ready?"

Robbins smiled back and nodded, "Yes, Leon, I'm ready."

"You're taking God with you?"

"Could I leave him behind even if I wanted to?"

Leon chuckled at the response, "Just checking."

Robbins knew he wanted to hear more. "God and I are doing okay, Leon. Not really great. Not like it was, but the relationship is mending. I have new perspectives. There is still so much I don't understand, but I guess that is to be expected."

"It is," Leon nodded just so slightly, "You know what I liken it to, David?"

"What's that, Leon?"

"The relationship between a loving parent and a child. You know, there are times when a parent takes actions for the good of a child that the child simply cannot even remotely understand. As parents we are older and wiser and know things a child can't be expected to know. We know what they need, but all they know is what they want."

Leon paused to take several quick, shallow breaths, "I remember a particular instance involving Matthew. He was a few months shy of his sixteenth birthday and getting his driver's license. A friend of his already had a license and a car. Matthew wanted to go with this boy and a few more friends to a concert in Dallas. I didn't want him traveling that distance with an inexperienced driver, so I refused to let him go. Matthew was devastated. He just could not understand. He did not know the things I knew about big city traffic and late-night driving, and drunks on the road and how boys will act when so far from home and on and on and on.

"Now, Matthew thought he knew, thought he had all the answers, felt he was old enough, and just thought I was absolutely terrible for not letting him go. But I was the parent. He was the child. Now, I know this is an oversimplification of what you've experienced, but please, David, try to always remember what I told you the first day we met. God *is* God. All seeing. All knowing. Omnipotent. No matter what happens from this point forward, cling to that. Don't ever forget it."

"I won't."

The frail hand resting in Robbins' palm suddenly gripped back with a surprising amount of strength.

"Promise me."

And he did.

* * *

Robbins did not expect to feel what he felt when entering District Judge Arthur Kazenback's courtroom. He anticipated a sense of familiarity spawned by experience. After all, this was his third time in court. First, there had been the arraignment, then the preliminary, but both had been presided over by Judge Stewart Hackney. Robbins had just not considered the impact unfamiliar surroundings and officials would have on his feelings. This was a different judge, not the amiable, grandfatherly Hackney. This was a whole new ball game. *The ball game.* And David Robbins had a case of gut-wringing pregame jitters. On wobbly legs he followed his attorney to the defense table while silently praying for strength and courage.

Emerson Bailey emphasized on an earlier date to Robbins what common sense already suggested – to win, they must have the right jurors. Absolutely everything hinged on the process Bailey called "voir diring a jury." If the critical task that lay before them caused Bailey any concern, it did not show in the least. The huge and, on this occasion, impeccably dressed attorney seemed his normal, arrogant self. He even maintained a smile. Of course, Robbins realized, Bailey wasn't the one facing a possible twenty years in prison. With that thought, Robbins reminded himself of his earlier visit with Leon Beck. Whether he understood it not, or liked it or not, his future clearly rested in God's hands.

The cavernous room was packed. The only empty chairs were the twelve in the jury box and the big one behind the bench. Robbins knew from a prior conversation with Bailey that eighty of the people in the courtroom were potential jurors. He imagined that well over half of the rest were reporters. Several television stations petitioned the court to allow cameras in the courtroom. With no objections from prosecution or defense, Judge Kazenback approved the petition.

Upon making it to the defense table, Bailey pulled out a chair and motioned for Robbins to sit.

"My legs don't want to," he responded in a whisper to his attorney.

"What do they want to do?" Bailey whispered back.

"Run."

* * *

Robbins and Bailey were in their seats for only seconds when a bailiff's call for all to rise brought them back to their feet. Without fanfare, the seemingly unpretentious Judge Hugh Kazenback slipped into his place behind the bench and asked in a soft, monotonous tone for all to be seated. To Robbins, the tall and very thin man didn't look old enough to be a district judge. The blond hair worn long enough to practically cover his ears worked in conjunction with the round-framed glasses to put Robbins in mind of a graduate student or even a very young college professor. First impressions painted for Robbins the picture of a serious man that did not spend a lot of time smiling.

"Good morning ladies and gentlemen. I am Judge Kazenback. The vast majority of you here today have been selected as potential jurors for this criminal docket. There are forty-four cases on this docket. Not every case will actually be tried. I anticipate it taking three weeks to complete this docket. Now, do any of you possess reasons or problems that will prevent you from serving for this period of time?"

Robbins studied the judge as the judge scanned the crowded room. Evidently two or more persons behind Robbins waved hands in the air.

"Okay, please approach the bench one at a time, starting with you, sir," Kazenback emphasized as he pointed to his left and nodded his head.

The first citizen to the bench was an older man in khaki work clothes. He was followed by an obviously very pregnant young woman who was followed by a middle-aged lady who offered no clues as to why she could not serve. Each conversed with the judge in hushed tones, and each exited the courtroom after doing so.

"The first case on the docket," Kazenback once again addressed the room, "is State of Oklahoma versus David Robbins, CRF 04-2372. If you are not selected to serve on this jury, please report back to the court clerk's office at nine o'clock in the morning.

"In just a moment the court clerk, Ms. Booker, will draw fourteen names from a fish bowl. If your name is called, please come forward to the jury box. Fill the back row first from left to right and work forward to the front row of chairs. The last two names will serve as alternates and will sit in these chairs," Kazenback said as he pointed to two folding chairs just outside and to the left of the jury box.

For the first time since entering the courtroom, Kazenback turned his eyes on David Robbins. His gaze appeared steady and emotionless. "Ms. Booker," Kazenback hailed without averting his eyes from Robbins, "select and call the first fourteen names, please."

* * *

The last name Ms. Booker called was that of yet another woman. Eight of the first twelve and both alternates were female, and all but one of the ladies looked to be in their child-bearing and rearing years. Emerson Bailey smiled at the last women to go up and take her seat but felt like flipping her off.

"Don't worry," Bailey leaned over and whispered in his client's ear. "I'll get rid of some of these women…even the playing field up a bit."

Robbins nodded his head and offered one of his tight little smiles. He was worried, of that Bailey had no doubt, but he wasn't letting it show. Over the past several months Bailey had come to know the man next to him very well. Robbins possessed his share of characteristics that Bailey couldn't relate to nor understand, but he turned out to be a man whom Emerson Bailey held in high esteem. One of Robbins' traits that Bailey admired most, the one he now exhibited, was his calm, laid-back demeanor. Once the traumatic, initial shock of losing his daughter began to subside, Bailey started seeing a Robbins much different than the weakened version who first entered his law office. He saw a much tougher version – one Bailey wouldn't mind having at his side in the worst of times and conditions.

At the moment, in the initial stages of jury selection, times and conditions for a case like Robbins' couldn't get much worse. During a meeting earlier in the week, Bailey discussed with Robbins their ideal juror profile – the type of people Bailey would try to put in the jury box.

"The first thing we need them to be, David," Bailey said, "is male."

"I read somewhere that as a general rule females make more sympathetic jurors," Robbins responded.

"Generally, that may be true. But when you're being tried for the criminal death of a small child, the last thing you want is to be tried by women. Especially women who have children."

Bailey further explained that their ideal male juror would be middle-aged or over. He would not be college educated, and he would be a regularly attending member of a holiness church.

"I thought the idea was to be tried by your peers," Robbins sighed.

"A jury of your peers would hang you," Bailey remembered chuckling.

Now, that didn't seem so cute. Three of the four initially selected men were young professional looking types. The fourth was an older, nicely dressed man who carried himself as comfortably wealthy.

At face value, David Robbins had just drawn a jury of mothers and peers.

* * *

District Attorney Walter Spencer looked at his first assistant and winked. Mike Pierce grinned back at his boss…so far, so good. The way it was looking, the two prosecutors couldn't have handpicked a jury better suited for their needs, and as of yet, Judge Kazenback had failed to snag any of the potential fourteen with his initial questions.

"Do any of you know, or are you related to District Attorneys Mike Pierce or Walter Spencer?" It was Kazenback's sixth question. All the previous ones dealt with familiarity with the judge, his court clerk, or reporter, and about any possible past misdemeanor or felony records. All were pristine.

None of them claimed any associations with the prosecution team.

"Have either of the D.A.s ever tried a relative or close friend?"

All of them evidently came from good stock and chose their friends carefully.

"Have you had any associations whatsoever with the defendant, David Robbins or his attorney, Emerson Bailey?"

No response.

"Are you related to…"

"Uh, excuse me, Judge," the oldest and best dressed man in the box interrupted. "I have shopped in David Robbins' sporting goods store a number of times."

"Come to think of it," said one of the younger men, "I have, too."

"Me, too," chimed in two of the females at the same time.

"Okay," Kazenback said calmly while holding his palms in the air. "Were any of you waited on by Mr. Robbins?"

None were.

"Do any of you feel that the act of shopping in his store has made you incapable of making an impartial decision as to his innocence or guilt?"

None did.

The judge continued with his questions and soon concluded. When none of the fourteen were released by Kazenback for cause, Spencer winked at Pierce again. This one was intended as a "go get 'em" wink because it came to Pierce's turn to question the people sitting to the right of the judge. It was time for him to weed out those who were not highly educated and who had no children. It was time to learn about their religious affiliations and dump those who were not atheist, Catholic, Episcopalian, Presbyterian or Methodist. And if they got really lucky – or luckier – maybe they just might pick up another woman or two.

* * *

"He's in there, goddamnit. I swear to God he's in my fuckin' house!"

Mark Hogue knew both of the big uniformed cops by name. It was Johnson who looked right past him and said to his partner, Finaldy, "I ain't goin' in that shit hole, Mark."

"Fuck it," Mark Finaldy growled. "I ain't either."

"Come on guys," Hogue squealed as he did a little stomp dance on his front yard. "I heard something in there. Please check my damn house!"

"I got some kinda rash the last time I went in that dump, shit-head," Chuck Johnson emphasized with a huge finger thumping Hogue's chest.

"I couldn't get the smell outta my uniform," Finaldy sneered. "Had to throw the sonabitch away."

"You assholes check my house or I'll report you," Hogue insisted in his most authoritative screech.

"Yeah?" Patrolman Finaldy bellowed as he grabbed a handful of Hogue's shirt and jerked him up on tiptoes. "And we'll stomp your maggot ass!"

"Please, Finaldy," Hogue sniffed, "just check my house. If Luke's in there, you guys will be fuckin' heroes. If he ain't, I'll never call again. I swear to God."

"That dude from Shawnee, the little girl's dad, he's still offering a reward, ain't he?" Johnson thought out loud.

"Yeah, ten grand. But could we keep reward money for nabbing that prick on duty?" Finaldy asked, keeping his grip on Hogue.

"Oklahoma-fucking-City can kiss my fat ass if they think I'm giving up my ten thousand dollars," Johnson said as he started for the shack.

"Fuck being a hero, numbnuts," Finaldy said to Hogue as he let go of him and started out after his partner. "I want the money."

"Check it out real good," Hogue called after them. "Be sure and look in the closets…and under the bed!"

In less than five minutes the huge cops lumbered out of the house. Both of the wide faces were twisted into grimaces, and both inhaled gulps of fresh air. Hogue jumped aside when Johnson kicked at him.

"Get out of my way you fuckin' squirrel," he thundered.

"Did you look under my bed?"

Both cops were on their way back to the black and white.

"You think I'd stick this face under what you lay your nasty ass on?" Finaldy frowned over his shoulder.

"Don't call us again, puke," Johnson bellowed without turning around. "The next time I come here, you're leaving with me. On a stretcher!"

* * *

Mark Hogue walked back into his house, shut the door and yelled, "They're gone."

Moments later his brother Luke walked out of the bedroom.

"I don't like doing that," Mark huffed.

"If we keep inviting them here, they won't pay us any surprise visits. Plus, it keeps 'em thinking you're crazy," Luke returned.

"You're the crazy one. If we're ever doing this, and they find you, it ain't my goddamn fault."

"If they ever find me after I've told you to call them, then you're in luck. I won't have your sorry ass killed under those circumstances, and you'll be rid of me."

At one time the thought of getting Luke out of his house and life did nothing but appeal to Mark. That was starting to change. Over the past month or two, Mark grew accustomed to having his older brother around. Sometimes he even enjoyed his company, and when all was said and done, Luke had been no problem at all.

There had been no dope, and when there was no dope, Luke Hogue wasn't all that bad of a guy. About the worst thing he did was get on Mark's ass for drinking so much and for sometimes being a little messy. Most the time, Luke just watched television and never said much of anything. He had never once mentioned the little girl or offered his side of what happened that night in Shawnee. But he constantly scanned news channels and programs, and when there was anything at all on about the girl or her father, Luke paid close attention. Afterwards, he would go into the hole under the bed. Sometimes he wouldn't come out for hours and hours. During those times, Mark could listen really close and hear the sobs. More than once Mark had awakened deep in the night to soul-wrenching screams.

Mark thought about telling Luke that he didn't want him to get caught, but that just wasn't the way of the Hogue men. Instead, he offered his opinion on Luke plopping back into a chair and turning the TV back onto a channel broadcasting the trial in Shawnee.

"Ain't no need in you watching that asshole's trial."

It took a few seconds for Luke to respond, but his response displayed feelings. "He ain't no asshole."

"You ain't thinking about doing something stupid like turning your ass in for that bastard are you?"

Again, Luke remained silent for several seconds. Then he laughed. "Do I look like some kind of fucking idiot?"

* * *

The tiny living room in Robbins' apartment contained only two pieces of furniture – a recliner and the coffee table beside it. Upon entering the apartment, Robbins went straight to the recliner, fell into it, and exhaled long and hard. Judge Kazenback had held his court over until nearly seven p.m. He didn't recess until the rigorous process of selecting a jury had run its entire course.

Of the initial fourteen people placed in the jury box, only three of them survived to the end to make the final cut. A grand total of seventeen people had been selected only to later be dismissed. Eight of those had been dismissed by cause. Five by Bailey and three by Pierce.

Emerson Bailey explained the procedure of dismissal for cause to Robbins in layman's terms as, "giving people the boot who can't be objective because of who or what they are, what they've been, where life has taken them or what they believe in or don't believe in." This definition became clearer when Mike Pierce convinced Kazenback to dismiss one lady because she confessed to being a Biblical literalist. The two people who stood out in Robbins' mind who Kazenback dismissed for Bailey was the man who had once been a Dallas police officer and the woman who had lost a six-year-old daughter in an automobile accident.

The rest of the potential jurors had been dismissed on peremptory challenges. "That's when," Bailey pointed out, "we send them packing because we simply believe that they are not sympathetic to our position." Bailey then emphasized, "However, we only get five peremptory challenges, but then, that's all the D.A. gets, too." Bailey ended up using all his challenges, and Pierce all but one of his.

After turning on the lamp on the table next to his chair, Robbins pulled from his inside coat pocket the notes he'd taken on each juror. He then kicked off his shoes, pushed back in the recliner and started reviewing his written facts and comments.

Collene Manuel was a divorced mother of two boys, one sixteen and the other fourteen. She worked as a registered nurse for a gynecologist. As a member of a Methodist church, Collene only found time to attend on special occasions and holidays.

Dedra Hardy worked as a homemaker with four children ranging in age from four to twelve. Dedra had a business degree from a small college in southern Oklahoma but had not worked outside the home since having her first child. Dedra listed few outside interests.

Those she did have seemed to all revolve around her membership in Shawnee's First Baptist Church.

Kayla Walker was single and the youngest woman on the jury. She worked as a waitress while putting herself through college. Kayla wanted to be a teacher. She also hoped to someday get married and have children. Kayla Walker had not attended church since leaving home three years earlier. Her parents were devout members of an Assembly of God church in Konawa, Oklahoma.

Henry Guedoin made his living as a maintenance man at Shawnee's Medical Center hospital. He would be able to retire in less than two years. Henry and his wife were extremely active in a small Pentecostal church just outside Shawnee. Their four children were all grown and scattered across the state.

The oldest female on the jury was JoAnn Fremont. JoAnn had been married for forty-one years. She and her husband had six children and fourteen grandchildren. JoAnn was a retired grade school teacher and a long-time elder of the First Presbyterian church in Shawnee.

Mark Billings was an unemployed carpenter who had never finished high school. He was divorced but said he visited his three kids as often as he could. Mark said he considered himself to be a Christian but had no need for church because of the type of people who normally attended church. Billings expressed the impression that most church goers were hypocrites. He was one of two jurors selected after Bailey expended all of his peremptory challenges.

Wes Booker was an accountant and a Catholic. He looked to be Robbins' age and had four teenage daughters.

Patty Doonkeen was also Catholic. Patty was six months pregnant with her second child and worked as a hairdresser.

Beverly Barrett and her husband, a Lutheran preacher, had twin girls who just turned five. Beverly had a political science degree and wanted to someday attend law school.

George Harjo was a sanitation employee for the City of Shawnee, and Wanda Blair was a pharmacist. They were the only minorities on the jury – Harjo, a Seminole Indian, and Wanda Blair, an African American. Both professed to be Baptists and attended church regularly. Harjo was married with no children, and Blair was a widow with two grown sons.

Derrick Anglin was the last person selected after Emerson Bailey used all of his peremptory challenges, and the mere fact that he was an atheist was not enough for Kazenback to dismiss him for cause. Anglin had never been married, had no children, and was a drug rehabilitation counselor.

Studying the list of names and facts brought to Robbins' mind the comment he had made earlier to Emerson Bailey, "Only one of these people fit our ideal juror profile."

"One is better than none," Bailey responded. "Not a whole hell of a lot better, but better. Besides, it only takes one to hang a jury."

Robbins tried to keep his apprehension from showing on his face, but Bailey must have picked up on it anyway. "Hey, don't let it get you down," the attorney emphasized with one of his playful grins. "After all, what's a little murder trial for two rich guys who have been through divorces together?"

Robbins simply hated how Emerson Bailey could take a topic bearing not a semblance of humor and make him snicker about it.

SIXTEEN

Channel 4's ten p.m. news had concluded fifteen minutes earlier. Luke Hogue expected his brother home at any time. Luke just hoped Mark did just exactly as he'd been told. Although what Luke had asked him to do was not difficult, Mark had a history of screwing up the simplest of tasks. All Mark had to do this time was find out what kind of car Sid Mitchell drove.

The grand idea had come to Luke in a flash. "Hey, Mark," he had cried out while watching Channel 4's six o'clock news, "hurry, get your ass in here!"

"If you want sandwiches, leave me the hell alone while I'm making 'em," Mark grumbled when he shuffled from the kitchen into the living room.

"The food can wait. I want you to look at this guy," Luke said as he pointed at the television, "and look real damn good."

"Which one?"

"The one on the left."

"So what?"

"Look at him, damnit. Just look at him. Make sure you could pick his face out in a crowd."

"What the hell? I don't like the sound of this bull…"

Then Luke had exploded. "I said fuckin' look at him, goddamnit! Shut your stupid fuckin' mouth and do what I say!"

"Okay. Okay," Mark said with palms exposed to signal submissiveness.

Sid Mitchell sat to the right of anchorman Paul Andrews. Mitchell had been introduced as "one of the city's leading trial lawyers." Paul Andrews pointed out that Mitchell would be a guest analyst for the duration of David Robbins' murder trial. The attorney would be giving a blow by blow of the trial on both the six and ten o'clock broadcasts. Mark Hogue came in as Mitchell explained how – based on the seated jury – Emerson Bailey and David Robbins had "drawn the short end of the stick."

Between the six and ten o'clock news Luke thought out his plan of attack and had drilled his brother over and over on what he needed done.

"According to the phone book, the Channel 4 studio is at Northeast Sixtieth and Hefner Road. There will probably be a guest parking lot. Find it. Park where you can get a good look at anyone coming out of the building.

"When you see this Mitchell dude, get a good look at his car. I need the make, model, color and tag number."

"What the hell are you going to do, Luke?" Mark asked more than once.

"You just do your part, Mark," the older brother responded each time, "and I'll do mine."

* * *

"By God, I got what you wanted," Mark Hogue grinned as he burst through the front door.

"You know what kind of car Mitchell drives?" Luke said as his heart began to race.

"A white BMW with four doors. I can't tell the year of those goddamned foreign cars, but it looks like a new one. The tag is XN 523."

"Did anyone see you?"

"Fuck no, man. There wasn't nobody to see me. Mitchell was the only one to leave the building while I was there. I didn't see no security guards or nothing."

"What time did he come out of the building?"

"I did just what you said, I checked my watch. He came out at exactly ten nineteen."

"Where was the car parked?" Luke asked as he started to pace.

"Just where you thought it would be, Luke. There was this parking lot out front with a sign that said 'Visitor's Parking.' He was parked on the east side of the lot away from the other cars. Probably don't want no door dings on that fancy fuckin' car."

"How many other cars were in the lot?"

"Not many. Eight or ten, I'd guess."

"Is the parking lot well lit?"

"Like a fuckin' Christmas tree."

"Shit," Luke mumbled.

"Now will you tell me what you're planning to do?" Mark whined.

"I been needin' to talk to a lawyer, Mark. Looks like I got an appointment with one at ten nineteen tomorrow night."

"You're going to try to cut a deal?"

"There ain't no deals for me, man. They'll eventually catch me. When they do, they'll either put me in prison for the rest of my life, or put me in prison for a whole lot of years and then pump poison into my veins."

"Hey, Luke, I don't really mind you staying here. If we keep doing what we're doing, hell, they'll never know you're here. They'll never find you."

Luke Hogue looked closely at his younger brother for several seconds. Mark sincerely looked worried. Luke appreciated the offer and almost said so. "This place gets smaller all the time, Mark. Hell, it's just another kind of prison. I can't do prison, man. It's too much like…Fuck, you know what it's like. You know what it reminds me of."

Mark Hogue looked away and practically whispered, "The hole."

Luke Hogue just nodded his head.

* * *

"Mr. Pierce, you may make your opening statement," Judge Hugh Kazenback said to start the second day of David Robbins' trial.

With a small stack of papers in his hands, the Assistant D.A. pushed away from the prosecution table and approached the jury box. Unlike what Robbins had seen on movies and television, Pierce simply greeted the jury, and without theatrics, started reading from a document on the top of his stack.

"In the name and by the authority of the State of Oklahoma, Walter N. Spencer, District Attorney for the 23rd District, comes into court and states upon this affidavit that David Burton Robbins did on April the twentieth, 2012, in Pottawatomie County, State of Oklahoma, commit the offense of Murder in the Second Degree.

"That is to say that the said defendant," Pierce paused long enough to look up from the document and point a finger at Robbins, "did perpetrate an act imminently dangerous to another that evinced a depraved mind, and regardless of human life, although without any premeditated design, did affect the death of one Kayla Marie Robbins."

Having been coached by his attorney, Robbins fought off the overwhelming desire to drop his head and stare at the table top before him. Instead, he turned his gaze from the D.A. to the jury and scanned the faces looking back at him. "Look them in the eyes, and show no shame," Bailey had said. "You have nothing to be ashamed of."

"As a general rule, ladies and gentlemen," Pierce said as he walked back to the prosecution table and carefully laid the document down, "murder cases are very complicated and difficult to prosecute. This case is, however, an exception to that rule. In this trial, the state will prove beyond a reasonable doubt that David Robbins is responsible for the death of his very own seven-year-old daughter, Kayla. We will prove this without having to introduce any physical evidence. We will not rely on forensics or expert testimony. We won't have to try to sell you on any circumstantial evidence."

"What we will do is simply bring up," Pierce looked down at the papers in his hand, pulled a common ball-point pen from his inside, breast pocket and started moving the pen down the page as he counted out loud, "one, two, three, four, five, six, seven, eight, nine, ten, eleven, twelve…" Pierce stuck the pen back in his pocket and moved back to the jury box.

"…We will bring twelve eye-witnesses before you who will testify to the fact that Kayla Robbins did not have to die. You will hear from twelve people who were in the Fellowship Hall of the Highland Street Presbyterian Church on the evening of April the twelfth, twelve people who watched her die a brutal, terrifying death. You will hear from these eye-witnesses…some of whom saved their own children…that David Robbins is responsible for his daughter's death. That David Robbins is guilty of murder."

Very slowly and deliberately, Pierce started to pace before the jury. As he did so, he shuffled a few papers from the top to the bottom of his stack. After just enough curiosity-building silence, he started calling names of witnesses and using what would be the main points of their testimony to recount the events that culminated in Kayla Robbins' death. His adaptation was dramatic, his descriptions horrifyingly vivid, and it took the greatest part of an hour to impart.

"…the bullet that killed little Kayla," Pierce sighed before pausing to take a very deep breath, "entered the skull one half of an inch above her right eye. The force of the projectile completely disintegrated the top two inches of the small child's head."

This time Robbins' head and eyes did drop. Blinking hard, he tried to force away the in-living-color memory that just assaulted his mind. He could feel eyes from the jury box bearing down on him, but he just couldn't look back. Then he felt Bailey's hand light on and firmly squeeze his shoulder. When Robbins turned to look at his attorney, Bailey winked and smiled warmly. That made Robbins remember something else Bailey said during one of the several trial rehearsals. "If you feel pain, let it show. Pain is good. Let's face it, you're still in mourning. By all means, don't try to cover that up."

Mike Pierce made yet another trip to his table, and this time he put down the entire stack of papers. Then he turned to face the jury, sat back on the tabletop and crossed his arms over his chest. "I realize the picture I just drew of what happened on that terrible evening was shocking to say the least. If I offended your sensitivities, then please forgive me. Forgive but don't forget. For one of the things I will ask you to do from time to time is to put yourself in Kayla Robbins' place. If you don't know how frightened she was, if you don't know

how terrifying the man with the gun was, if you don't know how brutally she died, putting yourself in that little girl's place…seeing
through her eyes…might be very difficult to do.

"For, you see, Mr. Emerson Bailey will try to make you believe
that David Robbins had a right to act in the manner in which he acted. Mr. Emerson Bailey is going to try to convince you that David
Robbins' actions are protected by his First Amendment rights to freedom of speech and religion. The state will prove to you that these
rights, as applied to this case, have their limits. Courts across the land
have already established that the practice of these rights cannot and
must not interfere with the responsibility that parents have for safe-
guarding the health and welfare of their children. I submit to you that
just like Christian Scientists must provide life-saving medications and
procedures for their children, regardless of their beliefs, that David
Robbins also had the obligation to save his child's life, and that obligation put limitations on his rights to freedom of speech and religion."

"Therefore," Pierce said loudly and emphasized by poking the air
above his head with an index finger, "when Mr. Emerson Bailey
speaks of David Robbins' rights being violated, put yourself in Kayla
Robbins's place. Look through that little girl's eyes, and you'll see
clearly whose rights have been violated. Please keep in mind that as
for Kayla's freedom of speech, you're the only one left who can speak
for her."

After an almost mumbled thank you, Mike Pierce pushed off the
table, walked around behind it and took his seat. The D.A., Walter
Spencer, leaned over and whispered something in his young assistant's
ear. Then both men nodded and smiled.

* * *

Oklahoma City's Channel 5 carried live coverage of the trial, and Luke Hogue had it tuned in. Mark Hogue had been up and down in and out of the room during the first few minutes of the prosecution's opening statement. He didn't get interested until the D.A. started telling his story of what had happened. Then Mark, like Luke had been all along, became glued to his seat.

When the prosecutor completed his opening statement, the judge called a recess until after lunch. For several minutes the two brothers stared in silence at a soap opera joined in progress. Mark Hogue broke their silence.

"Is that how it really happened, Luke?" he asked in a hushed tone.

"Yeah, pretty much," Luke mumbled without taking his eyes from the set.

"Why'd you go in that church, Luke? Hell, man, why was you in Shawnee in the first place?" It was the first time in the months Luke had been with him that Mark dared to ask questions about the incident.

For seconds Luke didn't respond. Then he averted his eyes to the floor and started to talk. "Until about this time last year, I'd been down in Texas. I was getting my dope off a dude that was running a few crack houses in southern Oklahoma. I got to knowing the dude and pretty soon started pushing his shit for him in Ardmore, Durant, and some of the other towns down south.

"It was going pretty good for awhile, man. I was making some good money, livin' real fine. Then he started fuckin' with me. Accused me of stealing a whole lot more from him than I really was. He started threatening to kill me. Put some bad asses on my case, so I hit the road. I stayed a while in Ada. Went through my money, and that's where my fuckin' ol' car broke down on me and put me afoot. I was hitchhiking my way back up here and that's how I ended up in Shawnee. I was just passin' through, Mark. Just fuckin' passin' through.

"I went into the town thinkin' I'd buy a bite to eat. I was hungry, man, hadn't eaten in probably a day and a half. But I got lucky and was able to score some rock. Used all the money I had on me. I'd gotten in behind some shrubbery at that Presbyterian church so I could smoke my dope. I smoked it all up, Mark, every fuckin' bit, and I was really feelin' some kind of good. That's when the people started showing up with food. Man, they was carryin' enough groceries into that place to feed a goddamned army. I thought they might give me some of it."

Luke looked from the floor to Mark, and Mark saw the tears filling his brother's eyes. The last time Mark Hogue saw Luke Hogue shed a tear was the last time their father had beaten him. Hell, Luke didn't even cry at the old man's funeral.

"And what really sucks, Mark," Luke continued with a quiver in his voice, "is that that man, the one they're fuckin' over in that trial...he asked me if I was hungry."

Luke dropped his head and emitted a single, tortured sob. Then his head bobbed back up. "Fuck, man, he was going to feed me," Luke moaned. Then sobbing through gritted teeth, he hissed, "Then that one bitch went and opened her big fuckin' mouth."

Dropping his head into arms folded across his lap, Luke Hogue started crying loud and uncontrollably. The words and sentences that followed were broken and disjointed.

"...like all those church bitches we used to know..."

"...called themselves Christians..."

"...had the gun for protection, man..."

"...just for fuckin' protection..."

Then all Luke did was cry, hard and loud. His body heaved with the sobs. Several minutes passed before Luke raised his head and once again looked at his brother. "She was a beautiful little girl, Mark. She shouldn't have died that way."

With his head in his hands, Luke lunged off the couch and bolted for the bedroom. Mark didn't have to follow to know his brother was throwing himself into "the hole."

* * *

Unlike Mike Pierce, Emerson Bailey didn't approach the jury box with a stack of papers. Bailey's large, manicured hands were empty. As David Robbins watched his attorney move toward the jurors for his opening statement, he wasn't certain what impact the other contrasts between the two attorneys would have on the jury. It might not help but it surely couldn't hurt, Robbins surmised. One thing was for certain though, Bailey was much more interesting to look at than Pierce.

The assistant D.A. was short and plump. Bailey was tall and powerfully built. Pierce had a pallid complexion and a thatch of unkept hair. Bailey was deeply tanned, and the way he pulled his hair back tightly and neatly into a small ponytail attracted the eye and looked good on him. Pierce had the beginnings of jowls. Bailey's jaws looked chiseled from a substance hard and permanent, and were accented by his perfectly trimmed goatee. Robbins doubted that few if any of the jurors could, without looking, give the color of Mike Pierce's eyes. Robbins doubted if any would ever forget the color of Bailey's. Finally, the prosecutor's ill-fitting suit obviously came from the rack. Bailey's Armani obviously did not.

Bailey didn't use words to greet the jury. Instead, he used a smile so infectious that it produced an epidemic of like responses on each and every face in the jury box. His first words hit before the smiles could fade. The words were metered, and they were forceful.

"Kayla Robbins was killed by a gunshot wound to the head. Not one of the district attorney's twelve witnesses will tell us that David Robbins shot and killed Kayla Robbins. Yes, Kayla Robbins is dead. Yes, she was murdered. But, no, her father did not murder her. Above all else, remember that. Remember that David Robbins did not pull the trigger of the gun that killed the little girl he loved with all of his heart and all of his mind."

Moving close to the mahogany partition running the length of the jury box, Bailey leaned forward and supported his weight by placing his hands on top of the partition. "Be forewarned," Bailey said, lowering his booming voice, "that the D.A. will try to cloud the simple truth that another man, not David Robbins, shot and killed Kayla Robbins. They will do this by employing the complicated legal concept of But-for causation. Simply put, they will by smoke and mirrors try to make you believe it was David Robbins' actions that caused the real murderer to shoot Kayla Robbins in the head.

"Don't be fooled," Bailey said gravely. "The D.A. cannot prove this beyond a reasonable doubt. He can't prove it because he doesn't know; the eye-witnesses don't know; you don't know, and I don't know what the real murderer was thinking when he...not David Robbins...shot and killed Kayla Robbins. We don't know the real reasons he did what he did. More importantly, we don't know what he would have done had David Robbins said the words he was trying to force him to say."

Turning and walking back to the table where Robbins sat, Bailey picked up a large book bound in black leather. He wheeled back around to face the jury.

"David Robbins is not a murderer. He is a born-again Christian. This is the Holy Bible," Bailey said as he raised the book high over head. "David Robbins did not harm his daughter. He had no intent of her being harmed, and, as he will testify, he did not believe she was going to be harmed. The teachings in this book not only would not let Robbins say the words the real murderer wanted him to say, the teachings in this book would not let Robbins intentionally put a child in a position to be harmed. But, something went wrong."

"Can David Robbins be blamed for that? I don't think so. David Robbins is not a murderer. David Robbins is a civic leader, a business leader, a philanthropist, and most importantly a loving, caring, and heartbroken father."

Walking back up to the partition, Bailey started waving the Bible slowly back and forth in front of the jury. "Mr. Robbins is a man who lives his life in accordance with the teachings of this book. Not just the passages that please him and not just in times and circumstances that are convenient for him. Unlike those who will testify against him, David Robbins does his best to live each and every day in the manner prescribed by this book. No matter what your feelings and thoughts are about the Bible, you have to admire his dedication and, by law, you have to protect his rights to adhere to these teachings.

"If you must, then disagree with my client's beliefs. If you are so inclined, go ahead and criticize his practices. But don't blame him for the murder of Kayla Robbins. Lay the blame for this murder where it belongs. Not on Mr. Robbins. Not on this book, and not on the God this book proclaims. Lay the blame for this murder at the feet of the man who pulled the trigger."

* * *

Just as he had the night before, attorney Sid Mitchell crawled into his car, well-pleased with his performances on the ten o'clock news. Unlike the night before, Mitchell now knew what benefits his appearance would bring to the next day: new clients – lots of new clients. Last night's appearance as a guest analyst netted a grand total of eleven misunderstood citizens in need of a defense attorney's services. It seemed too bad, Mitchell thought, that the Robbins' trial wouldn't be a long one. Being at the studio at six and ten was inconvenient, but Mitchell could be inconvenienced for free advertisement that brought that kind of results.

Mitchell started his car, drove the length of the television station's parking lot and started to pull out on Hefner Road when he first sensed something out of order. The road noises – they were too loud and too clear. A quick glance over his shoulder proved they were coming from the right rear passenger's window. Sid Mitchell only had a split second to wonder why the window was down before a hand and arm came up from behind the front seat to wrap around his neck. The strong grip on his throat choked off a scream and discouraged any thoughts of struggle. When a small, blunt point was pressed roughly to the back of his head, Mitchell, thinking he might pass out, stomped on the brakes.

"Keep driving, mother fucker!" an angry voice thundered from the back seat.

"What the hell is this about?" Mitchell squealed, but did as told.

When he obeyed, the hand lifted from his throat, but the object pressed to the back of his head remained in place.

"If you want to live, just do what I fuckin' say," the voice in the back hissed.

"You want money?" Mitchell gasped. "I've got money, man. I've got close to a thousand dollars in my wallet."

"I don't want your money, Sid," the man snapped back.

With the use of his name, Mitchell stole a glance at his rear-view mirror. The outline of the dark figure crouched in the middle of his back seat did not look familiar.

"How do you know my name?"

"Hell, Sid, you're a big fuckin' TV star now, man."

"Shit," Mitchell moaned. He never imagined the down side of free advertisement was attracting weirdos.

"There's an old burned-out warehouse up here on the right. Drive around to the back of it."

"What are you going to do back there?" Mitchell couldn't keep the quiver out of his voice.

"If you keep cool and don't do anything fuckin' stupid, we're just going to talk. If you break ignorant on me, I'm gonna blow off the back of your head."

"I'll be cool. I promise."

The man in the back seat didn't say another word until Mitchell pulled to a stop behind the dark brick structure.

"Kill the engine."

Sid Mitchell winced at the man's choice of words as he fumbled with the ignition switch with a trembling hand. "You're not going to force me in there are you?" he nodded at the creepy building.

"No. We can talk right here. But, you act a dumbass, that's where I'll conceal your body."

"Okay. Okay. Just relax, I'll cooperate. What are we going to talk about?"

"David Robbins."

Mitchell fought back a groan. Crazy people had always frightened him. With a deep breath, he set out to humor the man holding a gun to his head. "All right. What would you like me to tell you about David Robbins?"

"I don't want you to tell me a damn thing about Robbins. I'm going to tell you something…he ain't guilty. You wanna know how I know that?"

If his captor continued talking, Mitchell concluded, he might be less apt to do other things. "How do you know that?"

"My name's Luke Hogue."

It took a moment or two, but the name did register. Prompted by an icy chill that started stomping its way up and down his spine, Mitchell exhaled, "Oh, dear God."

"Does that scare you, Sid?" Hogue snickered.

"Yeah. It does," Mitchell blurted.

"It don't have to. I don't mean you no harm."

The object pressed to his skull fell away. "I need a good lawyer," Hogue said calmly.

No shit, Mitchell thought, but didn't dare say. Instead, he rubbed at the back of his head a second or two and then asked cautiously, "Why do you need a lawyer?"

"I think I got some information that will get Robbins off. I want to give it to you, so you can take it to that judge in Shawnee."

"What information?" Mitchell asked, suddenly very interested in what Hogue might say.

"Information about what really happened, man, and how it happened, and why it happened. I got shit that's going to make everybody feel real bad for doggin' Robbins. Real fuckin' bad."

* * *

"Do you believe me?" Luke asked after telling Sid Mitchell all there was to tell.

"Yeah, I do."

It was too dark in the BMW for Hogue to see the attorney's face, but his tone of voice sounded sincere.

"I mean, since you're not going to turn yourself in," Mitchell said thoughtfully, "and therefore not looking for leniency, then what motive do you have for lying?"

"Like I said, I ain't turning myself in, so you're right. I ain't got no reason for lying. It's the truth, and it's what I want you to tell that judge."

Mitchell cleared his throat, and in a voice that sounded nervous said, "Well, Luke, there's a problem with that."

"What's the problem?"

"It's inadmissible, Luke. It's hearsay. Even if Robbins' attorney would put me on the witness stand, and I tried to repeat what you've told me, it would be an out of court statement offered for the truth of the facts asserted, which is hearsay. The prosecution would object, and the judge would have it stricken from the record."

A solution to the problem came to Hogue in a flash. "Okay, I'll write it all down. Exactly how it happened. Then I'll sign my name to it, and you can sign as a witness, or notarize it, or whatever you have to do to make it a legal document."

"I'm sorry, Luke," Mitchell said in a most apologetic manner, "but that won't work either. It's still hearsay because a prosecutor can't cross examine a written confession."

"You're the fuckin' attorney," Luke growled as the man in front of him cowed. "You tell me just what the hell will work."

"Please don't get pissed at me, Luke. I'm just telling you the way it is. Other than you appearing in person as a witness there's absolutely no way…well, there is another way, but you certainly wouldn't want to do it. The only plausible solution is…"

"What's the other way?" Luke interrupted.

"It's something that was done a few years back in a murder case on the west coast. It just kind of popped into my head, but believe me, it's so crazy that you won't consider it an option."

"Believe it or not, Sid," Hogue sighed, "I've been known to do a crazy thing or two before. So, lay it on me."

* * *

Several other dilapidated buildings sat a hundred or so yards behind the abandoned warehouse. Mark Hogue had situated his pickup between the buildings, so he could see without being seen. When the BMW'S headlights finally came back on, Mark started his engine. He didn't turn on his lights and pull of his hiding spot until the sporty little car was back on Hefner Road.

Mark had pictured wheeling up to where his brother stood, and Luke jumping in the pickup without Mark ever coming to a complete stop. That didn't happen. Mark had to stop, and when he did, Luke took his sweet time getting into the cab.

"Goddamn, Luke, hurry your ass up!" Mark whined.

The look Luke gave him, illuminated by the dome light, was that of a man either very disillusioned or disappointed or both.

"Don't look like it went too well, man," Mark said as he came as close to speeding away as the old truck could manage.

"It went," Luke grumbled.

"I wish the hell you'd just tell me what this was all about, why you needed to talk to a goddamned lawyer anyhow."

Luke stared out his window and didn't respond immediately. "I told you the first night I showed up at your house that I had something I had to do," Luke started without turning away from the window. "The something I have to do is keep David Robbins from going to prison. I gotta right some wrong, man. I wanted to talk to a lawyer about how I could do it."

When his brother didn't say anything else for several minutes, Mark pushed the issue. "Well, hell, Luke, did he tell you how you could do it or not?"

Luke turned his head to face Mark, and the glow of a passing street light momentarily spotlighted a look of bewilderment on his face, "He did, and I don't want to talk about it. I just need some time to think."

The no-nonsense tone of Luke's voice convinced Mark to change the subject. "That guy must know who you are. How do you know he ain't going to the cops and telling 'em you're here in the city?"

"We talked about that," Luke said as he turned his head back to the window. "He has a family to worry about, and he knows I'm fairly good with disarming alarms, like I did on his car, and also…he's pretty much convinced that I'm absolutely fuckin' crazy."

SEVENTEEN

"**N**ow, the real fun begins."

"Forgive me if I don't jump with joy," Robbins whispered back to his attorney.

Judge Arthur Kazenback's bailiff just proclaimed the third day of court in session. Robbins had found the previous two days of jury selection and opening statements stressful and tedious enough. What loomed ahead caused unprecedented anguish.

"Mr. Pierce," Kazenback called out after settling in behind the bench, "I believe we're ready for you to call your first witness."

You may be ready, Robbins thought, but I'm not. Robbins had not seen most of the people Pierce would be using against him since the night Kayla was murdered. However, he had been subjected on three different occasions to chance meetings with some of the people who he once considered not only as close friends but brothers and sisters of Christ. Not a single one of the face-to-face encounters had been pleasant. On the first of such meetings, only days after the funeral, Harold Gains only mumbled hello and then hurried away after practically bumping into Robbins at a service station. Gains and Robbins were golfing partners who had known each other since high school. When Marlene Dolivo and Robbins passed in the aisles of a supermarket, she wouldn't even return his hello. He had known this woman for years, and served with her on numerous church committees, yet, she glared angrily at Robbins until he turned and went about his business. These first two encounters were bad enough, but the third one caused Robbins the most distress.

It was July before Robbins could even consider going near the buildings he related to Kayla's death and funeral. The Sunday school class Robbins attended for years met in the Fellowship Hall, and Sunday morning worship services were conducted in the sanctuary where the funeral had been conducted. On the weekend following the Fourth of July, Robbins concluded that if he were ever going back to the church that played such a key role in his life, then there was no time like the present.

Five minutes before the beginning of the worship service, Robbins walked through the rear doors of the huge, steeple-topped sanctuary and took a seat on one of the back pews. He did not go to Sunday school. For now, the main building of the church was as close as he cared to come to the Fellowship Hall.

By that Sunday morning, Robbins had endured enough experiences with the general populace to know what type of reception he could expect. He hoped it would be different in the church where he served for years as an elder, but he didn't get his hopes up. It was a good thing he didn't. He found the cold shoulders and scornful stares he'd expected in abundance. What he had not expected was to be accosted by Terri Horner within seconds of taking his seat.

With the same brashness and harsh tone of voice the middle-aged woman had used on the gunman moments after he had entered the Fellowship Hall, Horner held no punches. "You have some nerve coming here."

Certainly not wanting a scene, but knowing Terri Horner wasn't a person just to walk away, Robbins looked the woman in the eyes and said as calmly as he could, "I'm a member of this church, Terri."

"You've torn this church apart, David Robbins. You've made it a spectacle," Horner started in a gruff whisper, but her voice started to rise, "You acted carelessly and ignorantly, and now we all share in your shame."

More and more people turned to look back at Robbins, and none of them wore a look of embarrassment or sympathy.

"The best thing you can do for this church, David Robbins, is leave it. You're not wanted here."

If Robbins could have sat there after Horner walked away, if he could have made it through the service, he had to believe that someone would have welcomed him back. At least one of his old friends would have apologized for Horner's behavior, and he would have voiced a different opinion. But he didn't sit there. He left right there and then, and didn't go back.

Now, ready or not, Robbins was about to once again come face to face with those who watched his Kayla die.

"Your Honor," Mike Pierce said as he approached the bench, "the state calls Terri Horner."

* * *

Hours earlier when Luke Hogue finally stretched out on the couch, he'd decided he wouldn't watch any more of the trial. As he drifted off to sleep in the early hours of the morning, he'd done so with the conviction that David Robbins wasn't his problem. He made up his mind, without a single doubt, that he just could not pay the high price that helping Robbins would cost.

Now, as he sat up before the dark and mute television screen, he turned his eyes to the tattered armchair squatted in a corner across the room. In that chair, *she* had sat. Luke knew he was sleeping, and it was a dream, but it was dream from which he had been powerless to escape.

"Please help my daddy," the small voice called out to him from the chair in the corner. Until Kayla spoke those words, Hogue didn't know she was there. Very slowly, he had turned to look at the spot from where the voice sounded. He thanked God the small face and head was hidden in shadows.

"That lawyer said that it might not work," Hogue heard his voice respond.

"But it just might," the little voice pleaded.

"It wasn't my fault, damnit! All he had to do was say the words."

"No, Luke, if he had, you'd really be in big trouble, and you'd hate yourself even more than you do now."

"This is a dream," Luke cried in his dream voice. "You're not really here."

Then the little girl pushed out of the chair and started walking toward Hogue. As she approached a stream of moonlight coming through a window, Hogue tried to look away but couldn't turn his head. He tried to close his eyes, but they wouldn't close. "You're not here with me!" he had screeched.

"I'm always with you, Luke. But if you'll help my daddy, I'll go away. *Forever*."

Then, Kayla stepped into the light, and Hogue screamed himself awake.

It was later, as he lay staring into the darkness, that Hogue changed his mind and decided he would watch more of the trial. He would watch to find out if David Robbins was going to need his help.

If and when it looked like Robbins was going to prison, Luke Hogue would do the one thing he could to try to keep that from happening. He would do it for the father because if he did, he truly believed he wouldn't have to look into the terribly maimed face of the daughter ever again. Never…ever…again.

* * *

This wasn't Henry Guedoin's first time to sit on a jury. In the late seventies he served on a first-degree rape case. That time Henry had done his part in sending the defendant to jail for the rest of his life, and it hadn't bothered Henry one little bit. In that case the man was guilty. There was no doubt about it, and he got what he deserved. That was a cut and dry case. This time, for Henry Guedoin, it looked to be different.

Henry knew his Bible. He read it daily and had taught it on Sundays to junior high kids for over twenty years. The way he saw things, David Robbins had been asked to deny Christ, and Henry knew well what the Good Book had to say about that. In the King James' version – and according to Henry any other version wasn't no version at all – Saint Matthew, Mark, and Luke all quoted the Good Lord as saying basically the same thing – You deny me before man, I'll deny you before God. In the book Henry Guedoin knew and loved, denying Christ was not at all a good thing to do. It could never be an option.

As the young Assistant D.A.'s first witness made her way to the bench, Henry took a small spiral notebook from his shirt pocket and prepared to take notes. Henry's memory wasn't what it used to be, but it was good enough that when the bailiff had Terri Horner raise her right hand, Henry remembered a time before a witness could "swear or affirm" his intention to be truthful. On the last jury he served on, a witness could only "swear" to tell the truth, and they had put their hand on the Bible when they were doing so. It was a sign of changing times. New times when nonbelievers were allowed to "affirm" their intentions of the whole truth and nothing but the truth so as not to offend their sensitivities. These were new times that Henry Guedoin didn't care for at all.

"State your name for the court, please," Mike Pierce said once Horner repeated her "I do."

"Terri Ann Horner."

"Ms. Horner where were you at approximately 7:40 p.m. on the twentieth of April, 2012?"

There appeared no flash or glitter to Pierce, and Henry liked that in a man.

"I was attending our weekly dinner in the Fellowship Hall building of the Highland Street Presbyterian Church." To Henry, Horner wasn't a bad looking woman, but she certainly looked stern.

"Ms. Horner, do you know the defendant, David Robbins?"

"I do."

"Could you point him out for the court please."

It seemed to Henry that Terri Horner's index finger did more than point at Robbins. It jabbed at him.

"Thank you, ma'am. Was David Robbins in the Fellowship Hall at 7:40 p.m. on the twentieth of April, 2012?"

"He was."

With what seemed like too many questions that everyone already knew the answers to, Pierce finally established the fact there were lots of people at the church building, and one of them was Kayla Marie Robbins and another was Luke Wayne Hogue. With another dozen or so questions and answers, Henry learned that Terri Horner was immediately frightened by Hogue's unkept appearance and demeanor. Skillfully, Henry thought, Pierce alluded to, without objections, that Luke Hogue seemed under the influence of some powerful, mind-altering narcotic.

With teeth clenched, Henry listened to Horner tell about how Hogue grabbed her, put the gun to her head, choked her, and finally threw her stumbling into the table. Few things made Henry Guedoin fighting mad, and men who hurt women was one of them. Subsequent testimony on how Hogue pistol-whipped poor Mr. Blevins, and how he placed the barrel of that gun in that fourteen-year-old kid's mouth left Henry seething.

"Tell us, Ms. Horner, what Hogue did once he was finished with the Gains' family."

"That's when he came after me with that gun. He stuck it within inches of my face and called me a filthy name. I had no doubt that if I didn't say what he wanted me to say, he would kill me. So, I told him I worshiped Satan and not Jesus."

"How do you feel about having done that, Ms. Horner?"

"I just repeated words, Mr. Pierce. They didn't come from my heart, and they saved my life."

Henry Guedoin listened carefully and scribbled notes as Mike Pierce progressed to the point of pulling from Horner the things that eleven-year-old Margaret Sugg's mother, Martha, said and did. By the time Pierce finished with his line of questioning, Henry felt convinced that Martha Sugg had most definitely saved her little girl's life by doing what Hogue told her to do. The only point Pierce did not clear up for Henry Guedoin was a matter of theological mechanics. When one was forced to pray to the devil, was it a prayer all the same?

"After getting what he wanted from Martha Sugg, what did Luke Hogue do, Ms. Horner?"

"He turned to David Robbins and said something to the effect that it was his turn."

"What was David Robbins' response?"

"He resisted. He told Luke Hogue he couldn't do it. They exchanged a lot of words that I really can't recall word for word, but it all had to do with David Robbins not doing what the rest of us had already done."

"Did Luke Hogue at any point or time tell Robbins specifically what he would do if Robbins did not meet his demands?"

"I don't remember anything specific. I do remember him hitting David Robbins and grabbing Kayla. Then he stood there with the gun to the little girl's head as he tried to get Robbins to say what he wanted him to say. I don't recall him saying 'I'll do this' or 'I'll do that,' but to me, having that gun to her head said it all."

"So, although there were no specific threats made, Ms. Horner, what did you believe, based on what you had already seen, heard, and experienced, Luke Hogue would do if Robbins did not simply say the words he wanted him to say?"

"I believed he'd do just what he ended up doing. I believed he would kill Kayla."

And that, Henry Guedoin concluded, is exactly what he would have believed had he been there. Turning his eyes to a grave looking David Robbins, Henry suddenly saw everything in a different light. In reality, Henry now believed, Robbins wasn't being forced to deny Christ and worship Satan. He was being forced to lie – to say something with his lips he didn't have to feel or believe in his heart. Lying was wrong, about that Henry had no doubts. But, when it came to Robbins making a choice about lying or saving his child's life, Henry Guedoin strongly believed he should have chosen the lesser of the two evils.

* * *

Juror Beverly Barrett had heard more than one of her husband's parishioners state that David Robbins' predicament stemmed from a conflict between church and state. By doing what was spiritually correct, Robbins violated a man-made law. Thanks to Beverly's political science degree and a strong background in Christian history and doctrine, she didn't perceive a conflict at all. It was the Apostle Paul's guidance to the first century Christians in Rome that put this case in perspective for Beverly. Born-again Romans were to subject themselves to the laws of the Roman government; therefore, born-again Oklahomans were to subject themselves to both state and federal laws. Just as with Rome, the authority of the United States and the state of Oklahoma would not exist if God did not want it to exist.

So, Beverly Barret stepped into the juror box with no Christian worries over having to separate church and state. Her mind and conscious had been clear to do what a juror was supposed to do – determine if a specific law or laws had been broken and if a specific person or persons had broken them. Now, as Emerson Bailey approached the witness stand to cross-examine Terri Horner, Beverly Barrett fought off the feeling that he was doing so in vain. It was much too early in the process, Beverly reminded herself, to already believe that a particular law had been broken and a particular person had broken it.

* * *

"What exactly, precisely, absolutely would have happened, Ms. Horner," Emerson Bailey started off, "if David Robbins would have said and done exactly as Luke Hogue told him?"

Juror Derrick Anglin thought this a superb question coming from the famed attorney, and it produced predictable results. When

Terri Horner got around to opening her mouth, her words and demeanor were not as polished as they had been with Mike Pierce.

"Well, uh, I, uh, couldn't possibly know exactly what would have happened, I just think that…"

"Ms. Horner, are you a criminologist?" Bailey interrupted.

"No," Horner responded coldly.

"Do you have a background in psychology?"

"No," she responded in the same manner.

"Do you have any life experience dealing personally with criminals?"

This time Terri Horner just shook her head while glaring at Bailey.

"I'm sorry, Ms. Horner, the court recorder can't record head motions. Please answer with 'yes' or 'no.'"

With a snarl, the woman all but spit a "No."

"Thank you," Bailey said with a smile Derrick Anglin could best describe as smug. "Now, Ms. Horner, a moment ago you said 'I just think,' then I interrupted you. What is it that you were going to say about what you think?"

Anglin, out of the corner of his eye, caught Mike Pierce springing to his feet. "Objection. Calls for speculation," the Assistant D.A. rang out.

Emerson Bailey wheeled around to face the bench as he threw long arms into the air above his head. "Your Honor," he chuckled, "this entire case calls for speculation!"

"Counsel, approach the bench," Judge Kazenback said evenly.

With the three men talking in hushed tones, Anglin could not catch a word they were saying. He did note that Emerson Bailey did most of the talking and emphasized his comments with aggressive movements of his large hands. Kazenback responded with nods of his head, while Pierce looked to be disagreeing but with no obvious success.

After a pleasant, "Step away from the bench, gentlemen," Kazenback looked to the jury. "Objection overruled." Then to the witness, "You may answer the question, Ms. Horner."

Anglin could tell by the look on the well made up face that Terri Horner seemed leery of a trap and felt more than a little pressure. "I think that had David Robbins done like the rest of us, that Luke Hogue would have spared Kayla's life just like he did the other two children."

"Ms. Horner, in that you have no training, experience, professional or personal knowledge of or on criminal behavior, would it be fair to say you have just provided us with an uninformed opinion?"

"I was there, sir. I know what I…"

"Yes or no, Ms. Horner," Bailey interrupted again.

"Objection. Badgering the witness," Pierce said with some agitation.

"Overruled," Kazenback said patiently.

"Yes or no, Ms. Horner," Bailey smirked.

"Yes," Terri Horner said through gritted teeth.

"Tell me this, Ms. Horner," Bailey said in the next heartbeat. "Where and on what were you visually focused during the majority of the time David Robbins and Luke Hogue were conversing?"

The sudden change in direction caused Horner to pause, then spit and sputter. "Do you mean what was I looking at?"

"Yes, Ms. Horner, where were you looking?"

"Well, uh, mostly at David Robbins' back. He was blocking my view of Luke Hogue."

"You couldn't see Luke Hogue's face then. Is that correct?"

"Not much of it. Occasionally I got a glimpse of it. I guess."

"Would it not be true then, Ms. Horner, that if Luke Hogue was nonverbally communicating a hesitancy or doubt or confusion with facial expressions that you would not be able to see them?"

"That is true."

"Then it is also true, is it not, that David Robbins could have been using different stimuli – that you did not have access to – on which to base his decision?"

"I suppose that's possible."

"Ms. Horner is it true that when you first noticed Luke Hogue in the foyer of the Fellowship Hall, he was standing along-side my client?"

"Yes."

"Were they exchanging angry words?"

"No."

"Were they fighting?"

"No. They weren't fighting."

"Okay. When you first saw Luke Hogue, he and David Robbins were standing peacefully together?"

"I don't know that I would call it 'peacefully.'"

"Why not, Ms. Horner?"

Derrick Anglin couldn't help but feel discomfort for Terri Horner as she mulled over the question with furrowed brow.

"All right," she finally huffed, "they were standing peacefully."

"They were standing peacefully, and that's when you went up and said something to Luke Hogue. Is that correct?"

"Correct."

"And you testified earlier that you don't remember exactly what you said. Right?"

"Right."

"When exactly did Luke Hogue grab you by the hair on your head?"

For a long second or two, Terri Horner just glared at Bailey, then said, "Right after I spoke to him."

"Is it possible, Ms. Horner, that since Luke Hogue was peaceful before you spoke, that it was your words – that you, of course, don't recall – that set him off?"

"The man was obviously taking drugs, Mr. Bailey," Horner said angrily.

"And, therefore, he wasn't stable?"

"Exactly."

"Are you saying Luke Hogue was acting irrationally because he was possibly under the influence of drugs?"

"That's exactly what I am saying."

"Are you saying he was irrational enough to attack you without provocation, but rational enough, calculating enough, to perform an impromptu ritual based on a systematic procedure that resulted in a regimental execution?"

"I, uh, well, Mr. Bailey, I don't know, but I…"

"Thank you, Ms. Horner," Bailey smiled warmly. "I have no further questions, Your Honor."

Derrick Anglin fought off a smile as Emerson Bailey returned to the defense table and sat down. Anglin enjoyed the performance and looked forward to more of Bailey. It would be interesting, to say the least, to see what such a highly acclaimed lawyer could do for a client that, in Anglin's opinion, was so hopelessly destined for a long stay in prison.

* * *

Attorney Sid Mitchell turned from anchorman Paul Andrews to face the camera.

"Yes, Paul, today was a very busy day for the State of Oklahoma versus Robbins. Pottawatomie County Prosecutor Mike Pierce put five of his twelve witnesses on the stand, and the consensus is that it doesn't look good for defendant David Robbins.

"Despite the renowned Defense Attorney Emerson Bailey's hocus pocus of trying to trip up witnesses and confuse the jurors, the facts of the case are still strikingly clear. Growing more and more evident is the idea that David Robbins had the opportunity and means to save his daughter's life but refused to do so.

"I believe, Paul," Mitchell said as he turned back to the anchorman, "that barring a miracle, this jury will have to find David Robbins guilty of second-degree murder."

With that, Luke Hogue got up from the couch and turned off the television.

"You ain't going to watch the rest of it?" Mark Hogue asked from his place in the same chair where the dream ghost sat some fourteen hours earlier. "They're getting ready to show the highlight clips," he concluded.

"I've seen enough," Luke said under his breath. He hadn't missed a second of the day's televised proceedings, and he didn't want to see any of it again. He couldn't disagree with his old friend Sid Mitchell. Even from a layman's point of view, it looked like David Robbins was in big trouble; the time had come for Luke to do something about it.

"Why don't you go outside a minute, Mark?"

"Huh?"

"Go outside. Sit on the porch and smoke a cigarette."

"If I want a damn cigarette, I'll smoke it right the hell here."

"Get outta here before I put you outta here," Luke said with a low but serious tone of voice.

"You ain't throwing me out of my own goddamned house!" Mark bellowed as he stormed out the front door.

With Mark outside, Luke slipped into the bathroom. After removing the top from the toilet holding tank, he reached into the water and pulled out a resealable plastic bag. From the one-quart bag Luke withdrew four six-hundred-dollar bills. The bag and the rest of the money went back in the holding tank, and Luke went to the front door.

"Come on back in now," Luke said after cracking the door open an inch or two.

"I ain't finished my cigarette yet, asshole."

Luke walked back to the couch, flopped down, and waited patiently for his brother to come back in the house.

When he did, Luke waived the cash over head and said, "Come here a minute."

Mark did so without hesitation.

"I want you to take this six hundred bucks and go buy me a camcorder with a tri-pod. Also get whatever kind of wires it takes to hook it to a television."

Damn, Luke, it's nearly seven o'clock," Mark whined.

"The stores stay open to nine, fuckhead."

"What in the hell do you want with a camcorder?"

"It ain't none of your business. So quite being so goddamned contrary, Mark, and just do what I'm telling you to do."

"First you're gonna send me out of my own fuckin' house in the dark of the night to buy something to bring back to my own fuckin' house, and then you tell me what you're gonna do with it ain't none of my business?"

"When I'm finished with the camera, you can have it, Mark."

"Cool!" Mark quipped before grabbing the money and darting out the door.

Luke had never been able to give his brother something nice. Maybe that was the reason he suddenly felt a slight sense of satisfaction, or, maybe, it was because the wheels were now in motion that would eventually square the deal between himself, a good man, and a persistent little dead girl.

EIGHTEEN

David Robbins walked into his apartment, shut the door behind him, and fell back against it. His fourth day in court had gone no better than his third. Standing in the darkness and not caring to move, he closed his eyes and the events of the day came crushing down on top of him.

It had taken until seven p.m., but Mike Pierce finished with all his witnesses, and the prosecution had rested. Nothing new came from the day of testimony, just new ways of introducing the same damaging information over and over. The Gains family had been particularly effective in that arena.

"I still believe he would have killed me," fourteen-year-old Chad Gains said with wide eyes, "if my mom and dad hadn't done what he said."

Amy Gains swiped at tears and blew her nose throughout her testimony, while delivering most of what she said in agonizing sobs. "When he put the gun in my son's mouth, I just knew he was going to pull that trigger,"

"I didn't like saying those words. They hurt," Harold Gains said with emotion. "But I promise you, if I hadn't, my boy would be dead now, too. That would hurt a lot more."

Ted Blevens vehemently resisted taking any responsibility for pushing Luke Hogue too far. "The man was crazy, or on dope, or both. David Robbins watched what he did to me. He should have realized if he'd hurt an old man, he'd hurt a small child."

All the other witnesses chorused verse after verse of "He could have saved her, but he didn't." That, of course, had been the prosecution's underlying theme. Mike Pierce adequately, as far as Robbins believed, underscored the theme well enough to establish a substantial risk to human life had existed, and Robbins had disregarded the risk. In the face of duty to protect his minor child, he had acted by omitting to act and as a result the minor child did, there and then, die a most terrible death.

The jury had bought it. Of that Robbins felt sure. The theme was engraved on their faces and in their actions.

"Watch the jury," Emerson Bailey told Robbins the morning before the opening statements began. "Learn to read them. Find out which ones belong to us, and which ones belong to the D.A. If one of them ever smiles at you, that one is definitely ours. If they nod their head a lot when I've got the floor, they're probably ours. If they stare at you without averting their eyes, and without smiling, they're against us. The ones who will never look you in the eyes also probably belong to the opposition."

Robbins carefully studied the jury, and what he observed was not the least bit heartening. From the very start, he determined that Jo-Ann Fremont, Wes Booker, and Mark Billings were staunchly against him. They would stare, and their looks were hard. Until about halfway through the prosecution's list of witnesses, Robbins felt Henry Guedoin and George Harjo were supporters. Now Guedoin's looks, that had once been amiable, had hardened, and George Harjo had begun turning away abruptly every time Robbins caught him looking.

Beverly Barrett and Patty Doonkeen tended to nod their heads at prosecution-produced testimony. Just the mere data on Derrick Anglin made him the enemy, and the others had never looked Robbins in the eye.

The jury had bought the theme. Robbins had already lost them, and he no longer anticipated what the future held. David Robbins now knew, without a single doubt, he was going to prison. He did not blame the jury, nor Mike Pierce, nor Emerson Bailey. And although the temptation was great and constant, he refused to once again start blaming himself.

"I did not believe he would really hurt her," Robbins moaned out loud into the darkness. "I was getting through to him. It was in his eyes."

Then with a sob that echoed through the small apartment, Robbins placed the blame where the blame belonged. "Damn him, God, damn Luke Hogue to eternal hell, and free me from this consuming hate."

* * *

David Robbins remained in place against his front door until his telephone started to ring, bringing him out of his reverie. Since the trial began, Robbins hoped for a call from his son. Just hearing well-wishes from Kevin could make the whole ugly experience just a little more bearable. It wasn't likely, but just in case it was Kevin, Robbins hit the light switch by the door and moved to answer the phone before his answering machine picked up.

"Hello," he answered without trying to contain his hopeful anticipation.

For a second, maybe two, there was no response. Then, hesitantly, "Hello, David. I hope I didn't wake you. I tend to forget that it's much later back there."

David had been posed to settle into the recliner beside the phone, but the words kept him rigidly upright.

"No..uh, no…Nancy…I wasn't in bed."

"Good, I know this is awkward. I hope you don't mind my calling, but, well, I don't know if you know it, but the trial is big news even here, and although I promised myself I would not watch it, and even though I tried hard not to, well…I've been watching anyway."

Robbins felt as if his mouth and palms had suddenly switched roles. The former was dry as dust and the latter were not, "Nancy, my goodness, Nancy, it's so good to hear from you. Of course, I don't mind that you're calling."

"Well, I hoped you wouldn't. I just thought I'd…well, I wanted to…I don't know how to put this, David, but…" Nancy paused and Robbins could hear her taking a deep breath, "…the trial, David, it, uh, it's not going so well…is it?"

She cared. It was evident in the way her voice trembled. Robbins eyes immediately welled with tears. She really cared.

"It could be going a lot better," he said before placing his hand over the transmitter and sniffing a few times in quick procession.

Then, for the longest, there was nothing.

Nothing until Robbins softly said her name, "Nancy?"

"I don't want you to go to prison."

The words came in sobs.

"Oh, Nancy, please don't cry. Please don't worry, I, uh…" Robbins opted for a lie, "…I haven't given up hope. It's not over. It's still possible that the jury will find me not guilty."

"Maybe," she sniffed, clearly trying to compose herself, "I guess that it's possible."

"I have to know, Nancy," Robbins said as he swiped at his own tears while fearing he was about to bounce up and down on a precarious limb, "If I am found not guilty, is there a chance we can get back together?"

Nancy provided her answer between sobs and sniffles and pauses to catch her breath, "At first, and for a long time, I really thought I hated you. But I don't. I love you. But I'm so, so very angry with you. It all hurt me so badly. Did so much damage.

"I really wanted, really needed something to come from this trial to make me understand why you did what you did. Or something to prove to me that Kayla did not die in vain. That there was some reason, or good, or purpose of logical explanation or, I don't know, David, just something, just anything that could help me to forgive you. But the trial hasn't produced anything that's going to help me do that. And if I can't forgive you, then we're just better off being apart."

"Nancy, couldn't you and Kevin just fly down for…"

"No, David. I can't. And there's something else I can't do that you need to understand. I can't go through this again. It took all I had to make this call. No matter if you are found not guilty…or even guilty, and no matter how much I love you, I won't be calling again."

"Nancy, I want you to know I love you more than ever and I'd be…"

"Good luck, David. May God be with you."

Nancy hung up. As Robbins moved mechanically to put the receiver back in its cradle, he noticed his answering machine registered a single message. Numbly, he watched the red indicator light flash for the longest time. Finally, he absently pushed the play button and sunk into his recliner.

* * *

"Mr. Robbins, I called when I knew you wouldn't be home…"

The recorded voice brought Robbins to his feet.

"…It's hard to hang up on a message. I knew you'd have to hear me out…"

Robbins had only heard this voice once, and only for a matter of minutes, but he would never forget it. He bore it like a scar.

"…I know you hate me, and you got a right to. I'm sure you want me dead. I don't blame you for that either…"

The voice had the effect of a cold hand wrapped around and squeezing Robbins' heart.

"…I can't change the way you feel. I ain't even going to try. But I'd like you to believe two things I have to say…"

Fingernails dug into palms as Robbins hands curled into tight fists. With jaws clenched, he shut his eyes and labored to catch his breath.

"…First off, I didn't want your daughter dead. Second, I've never been sorrier for anything in my worthless life…"

Hot tears started to flow, and it became harder for Robbins to swallow.

"…I can't bring your little girl back. But I might be able to keep you from going to the pen…"

Robbins opened his eyes and turned to glare at the recorder.

"…Someone is going to come and see that attorney of yours tomorrow. They'll have something for him from me. Tell him it's important. Make sure he gets it. If it don't help, well, at least you'll know I tried."

With the message over, Robbins restrained himself from picking up the recorder and bashing it against the far wall. With the pent up energy he saved, Robbins dialed Emerson Bailey's home phone and got the attorney's recorder.

"This is Robbins," he started with a shaky voice, "Luke Hogue left a message on my machine. He's up to something. You better hear it."

* * *

"What the fuck is this for?"

Luke let go of the three hundred dollars and smiled back at his grinning brother. "I want you to take this money and whatever you have left over from the camera money, and go out right now and have a damn good time. Have a night out on the town on me. The way you've helped me, you deserve it."

"Shit, man, I ain't done that much," Mark said with a piss poor attempt at being humble.

"Yeah, you have," Luke humored him. "So, go on and get your ass good and drunk."

"Why don't you go with me?"

"Don't think that would be too cool. But tell you what, bring back a six pack or two. We'll have our own goddamned party."

"It's nearly ten now," Mark grinned. "It'll take me a while to blow this much money."

"When you get back, I'll be here," Luke grinned back. He held the grin until his brother was out the door, then it vanished into a teeth-grinding grimace as Luke set out to do what needed doing.

When the camcorder and tripod were set up and ready, he pushed the record button, and took a seat in front of the camera. Luke forced a smile, and started talking.

* * *

When the doorbell began to ring at a little before eleven, David Robbins rushed to answer it. After looking through the peephole, he jerked the door open, and Emerson Bailey stormed in past Robbins. Jennifer Rhodes was right on his heels.

"I was in Oklahoma City. Just happened to call and check my messages before heading back to Tulsa. Are you sure it was Hogue? Oh, excuse me, I'm sure you remember Jennifer?"

"Sure. Hi, Jennifer," Robbins replied with his brows arched. He'd noted that the reporter had been present during the entire proceedings – doing her job. He didn't know why she was here now with Emo.

"Hello, David," she returned shyly.

Bailey didn't fail to pick up on the awkwardness of her presence, "I guess you didn't know. We're dating."

"Oh," Robbins expressed his surprise. They were not, in his opinion, a likely pair.

"Okay, David, let me hear this message," Bailey said, making a quick transformation to business.

The three of them listened twice to the message without saying a word.

"You're sure it's him?" Bailey asked to break the silence.

"I'm sure."

While the gears of his mind were obviously turning, Bailey scanned the meager surroundings, "Nice place," he mumbled.

"Thanks," Robbins mumbled back.

Then Bailey started to pace. After a moment or two he began to talk. "He says he might be able to keep you from going to jail and says he has something to give me. We have to conclude whatever he has for me can possibly be used to obtain an acquittal for you. I'll be damned if I can think of a single thing that he could provide that would help us."

"Maybe he's going to turn himself in," Robbins contributed. After two hours of thinking about the message, it was all he had come up with.

"I thought about that, and I'm afraid that's probably what this is all about."

"Is that bad?" Jennifer asked Bailey.

"No. Not at all. It's just not helpful, not for our case anyway. You see, Hogue could turn himself in tonight, plead guilty tomorrow, and it would not impact in the least on our case."

"But wait a minute," Jennifer said with an index finger in the air. "If he did turn himself in, would that involve giving you something? I get from the message he intends to give you something tangible."

"Exactly," Bailey agreed. "And that brings me back to my original point...I just can't imagine what in the world it would be."

"So, what do we do?" Robbins sighed.

"Well, we wait to get whatever it is he has for us, but," Bailey emphasized by putting a hand on Robbins' shoulder, "we don't get our hopes up. We just rely on the only real thing we've had all along."

"Excuse me for being nosy," Jennifer said, "but what is that?"

"My key witness," Bailey smiled as he squeezed David Robbins' shoulder.

* * *

Luke found it fairly easy to record his first message. The second and final message would pose a real challenge. First, and real close to being foremost, it would mean stepping back to a place and time Luke Hogue had done all he could to block from consciousness. Just the thought of what lay before him sent Hogue rushing to the bathroom where he heaved up the contents of his stomach. After that, he stumbled back to the bedroom and camera, fell to his knees, and wept bitterly. When he was cried out, Hogue readied the camera and took a seat in front of it once again.

"My name is Luke Hogue. I'm making this recording to try to help Mr. David Robbins. You people are thinking that Mr. Robbins is a murderer, but after I tell you what I'm going to tell you, you'll know that a lot of people owe him more than just an apology."

After taking a breath and clearing his throat, Luke Hogue looked hard into the lens of the camera and took himself back to that spring evening in Shawnee, Oklahoma.

"I was hitch-hiking my way from Ada to Oklahoma City, just passing through Shawnee. I had smoked some crack in the bushes beside that church building. I was hungry. That's why I went in the building in the first place. I just stepped in the door when..."

* * *

"Hello."

The simple word hit Hogue like a brick upside the head. Crack did that to Luke. Whether he was high or not, he hated being startled. With an attitude, he started turning in the direction of the booming voice. For Hogue, crack cocaine sped some things up and slowed others down. It seemed to take an eternity to turn the hundred and eighty degrees, but it did give Hogue time to prepare for what would confront him.

Contempt.

He had watched them file from their cars in their fine clothes and walk the arrogant walk of the wealthy and successful. They were rich people going to their rich church to worship their rich God. He learned long ago the only thing more pious, more condescending, more hypocritical than a poor Christian was a rich Christian. What Hogue would find at the end of his turn would be a scowl – a contemptuous one.

Completing the turn, he learned he was wrong. The man he faced looked an exact opposite of himself, all right. The man was clean, nicely dressed, and well groomed, but he wasn't scowling. The man seemed obviously a member of a higher class, but he didn't wear his status on his face.

"We're having dinner here. Are you hungry?"

For a split-second Hogue thought the dope really messed up his mind, or maybe he wasn't hearing so well. Then the man spoke again.

"Would you like to eat with us?"

Luke was by no means ignorant of the ways of the rich people and their rich churches, but this proved definitely a first for him. This wealthy Christian standing before him had just performed a Christlike deed, and he done so without an audience and without it being during the holidays. This single act of kindness, no doubt intensified by the crack, touched Hogue like nothing had been able to in years. Just when thoughts of letting down age old defenses and reexamining his beliefs on rich people in particular and people who called themselves Christians in general, Luke was startled by a second voice.

"I don't know who you are or what you want, but you obviously don't belong here. *Get out.*"

Luke didn't like being duped. He didn't like feeling foolish. This time he only had to turn ninety degrees to his right, but again it seemed to take forever. The contempt that dripped from the second voice had time to echo in his mind over and over again. The scorn of the words brought pain, and Luke knew only one thing to do with the feelings of foolishness and pain – express them as anger. Showing hurt and embarrassment for these kinds of people would have no effect on anything. However, an exhibition of uncontrolled rage always produced an emotion that brought the high and mighty down to Luke's level. The emotion was fear, and Hogue didn't decide just how much he intended to deliver or just how he'd do it until the moment he looked into the face that owned the second voice.

He'd seen faces like hers before. They were the ones that snarled upper lips and flared nostrils when the less fortunate were up-wind of them. They were the ones that had eyes that looked down noses at people like him. They were the faces on which terror had the most profound effect.

The .357 revolver came out smooth and easy, and the woman's hair felt good in Luke's hand. The way she screamed when the barrel touched the spot between her eyes delighted Hogue as well as pissed him off even more. The bitch acted like it was his fault that she didn't know how to treat human beings. After screaming a few choice threats at the woman, Luke decided to move her into the big auditorium-like room where the others were seated around tables. It was at the same moment he made another decision. He had pulled the gun out of anger and to make a point. As long as it was out, he might as well use it to make a buck or two.

Luke didn't enjoy turning on the kind man, but he couldn't just leave him standing there by the exit. Besides, no one would get hurt, of that Hogue felt certain. Some people were going to get the hell frightened out of them, and some of them were going to lose some cash, but that wasn't something they wouldn't all get over.

"Get in there, you son of a bitch," Hogue forced himself to say to the man, "Get the fuck in there!"

"Please don't hurt her," the man pleaded.

This man looked obviously fearful, so Luke admired him for not just turning tail and hauling ass. Still, Hogue had a game to play.

"Get in there," he said as angry looking and sounding as he could act. For emphasis, as well as just for the fun of it, he yanked hard a couple of times on the woman's hair and added, "I'll blow this woman's head off right here and right now if you don't get your ass in there!" Luke felt relieved when the man did what he said without further delay.

Luke estimated there to be close to a dozen people in the big room. It was by far the biggest job he ever pulled. He had on two occasions robbed lone victims at gun point, and he robbed a liquor store with two clerks. On those robberies he'd simply shown the gun to get cooperation. All his prior victims froze at the sight of it. For some reason, that wasn't happening this time. The people in the big room were going crazy. Screaming. Crying. Some starting to stand, while others moved about frantically in their chairs.

For effect and hoping to frighten everyone into silent submission, Luke wheeled his hostage around, wrapped his arm tightly around her neck, and crammed the gun to the side of her head. It didn't work. They got worse. When he got up to the others, he hoped shoving the woman viciously into the tables would fill the bill. It didn't. The noises and activity intensified. Luke waved the gun in their faces and screamed for them to shut up. They didn't. Then, Luke noticed the teenage boy and an idea popped to mind.

He didn't like the idea. Luke knew what it was to be a boy and be terrorized by a man, but at the moment he didn't have alternatives. He had lost control, and it frightened him. At that moment he had no idea how what he started was going to end. He had to get their attention.

He really believed the way he crammed the boy's head to the table and held it in place with the gun would do the trick. When it didn't and he had to cock the gun, something deep inside Luke came apart. Not once in his life had he ever been so angry. Never had he hated so much. For the people in the room he suddenly felt a hate that even surpassed the worst he ever felt for the Reverend Richard Lee Hogue. The fact that they wouldn't obey him until they thought he would do much more than just hurt, terrorize and demoralize the boy set off in Luke feelings that should have never, ever surfaced. Christians weren't supposed to act this way.

As he looked into their now quiet but horrified, faithless faces and ridiculed them, his hate grew. When he experienced how painfully they separated themselves from their money, it grew even more. After the old man put his money before the welfare of his supposed brothers and sisters, Luke started thinking an unthinkable thought. After the lying old man had the gall to even speak of God's punishment, he came up with a way to either justify or discount the thought that was becoming more thinkable with every passing second.

By the time he came to the bitch who had told him to get out of the building, Hogue *believed* that the thought was a good one. Long before he got to the woman with the little girl, Luke made up his mind that before he left the building, he would kill every adult there. At that point, it was no longer an inclination. It was not a possibility. It was a done deal. Luke possessed more than enough bullets on him to get the job done. He would line the adults up, put them on their knees, and sink one of those bullets into the back of each head. He would spare the children. Luke couldn't even think of killing a child…

* * *

…But a child did die. The sobering thought brought Luke back to his place before the video camera. From that point forward, he would concentrate on recounting the facts and fight with all his might to keep from going back and reliving any more of it in his mind. He had watched the little girl die far too many times already. He could never…would never…watch it again. Staring into the lens of the camera, he went about the task before him and finished his story.

* * *

Mark Hogue sat on the bottom step of his front porch as Patrolman Chuck Johnson walked out of the house and onto the porch.

"Are you sure it was your brother?"

"Hell, yeah, I'm sure. What other asshole would just break into my house and fuck my bedroom up like that?"

"Did a job on it, didn't he," Johnson chuckled.

"You're a prick," Mark mumbled.

"Yeah, but I'm a prick who's going to make some money off this deal," Johnson said as he glanced at his watch. "It's zero six hundred now, and I'm supposed to get off at zero seven hundred. Gonna get some overtime from this one."

"You need me to stick around here for anything?" Mark scowled.

"Nope." Then as an afterthought, "But you know, asshole, we are just here to do the investigation, file the reports and stuff. We ain't cleaning up any of that shit in there."

"I ain't no fuckin' idiot," Mark said as he pushed off the step. "I know who'll be cleaning it up."

Mark made it several yards away before Johnson called out to him. "Hey, why would he break in just to do something like this?"

"You're the cop. You can't figure it out?"

"If I could, I don't guess I'd be askin' you, now would I, jerkoff?"

"It's simple. The bastard done it to get even with me for trying to collect that reward money on his worthless ass."

Mark left the big cop nodding his head, crawled into his decrepit pickup and pulled away from the curb billowing black clouds of smoke. As soon as he drove out of sight of the house, he pulled back to the curb and stopped. Leaning over in the seat, Mark opened his glove box and pulled out the camcorder that now belonged to him. He'd also taken the tripod from the house and hidden it behind the pickup seat. Luke had given the directions to do so, along with other tasks on the first of two recordings Mark found on the camcorder. Mark left four crumpled 8x10 sheets of paper in the glove box. Upon returning home not too many hours earlier in a near drunken stupor, he'd found one taped to the front door, and the other three lying on the living room floor in locations where they could not be missed or ignored. Each said the same thing in bold and capitalized letters, "CAREFULLY WATCH THE FIRST RECORDING ON THE CAMERA."

After coercing the old truck back into gear, Mark set out again. On the first recording, which he'd already deleted, Luke told him to be in Shawnee by seven-thirty. Luke wanted David Robbins' attorney to get the camcorder before the start of the day's proceedings, and before the news media got wind of what had happened in Mark's house. Mark happened to be some kind of pissed at his older brother, but this was one time he did not want to let him down.

By his best estimate, Mark made it within at least twenty-five miles from Shawnee when his truck gave up the ghost. After coasting the jalopy to the shoulder of the interstate, Mark glanced at his watch and started considering his options. It was six-twenty. Mark knew what time Luke wanted him to be at the courthouse with the camera, but Luke had also said the judge wouldn't start court until eight-thirty. Earlier, at his house, Mark had quizzed Officer Johnson about how and when the media would be contacted on the results of the investigation. Johnson said he thought it would be at least nine or ten o'clock before the word started circulating about what Luke had done. With that, Mark concluded he had a good two hours before he had to be in Shawnee. With that much time to work with, Mark wasn't about to walk back to the truck stop five or six miles behind him, and he wasn't so pressured that he wanted to chance hitching a ride with some deviant. So, Mark settled on his third and final option.

First, he got out and raised his hood. Then, he stuck a large "SEND HELP" sign in his back window. The sign was actually a reversible windshield sunscreen. On the opposite side of "SEND HELP" was a reclining blond wearing a tiny bikini and huge sunglasses. Mark picked up the sunscreen at a garage sale a few years earlier for a buck. He had stuck it under his front seat with the idea that it would one day pay for itself.

Having done all he felt he could, Mark settled back behind the wheel and commenced waiting on a highway patrolman. Interstate 40 was busy, and considering how well it was patrolled by the state road cops, Mark didn't expect to wait long.

Besides, Mark could use a little rest. In just a little while, he would be hitting twenty-four hours without sleep. And he sported one hell of a hangover. Also, the ordeal of the recordings had really taken a toll. With a long sigh, Mark laid his head back against a huge pair of sun-faded breasts and closed his eyes.

NINETEEN

"**D**o you swear or affirm to tell the truth, the whole truth, and nothing but the truth?"

"I do," David Robbins replied to the bailiff. Then he turned his eyes on his attorney.

"State your name for the court, please," Emerson Bailey said with a warm smile.

"David Burton Robbins." Despite his lawyer's counsel, Robbins did get his hopes up. Throughout the previous night and all morning long, he hoped for the "someone" to deliver a magical "something" that would make his taking the stand unnecessary.

"What do you do for a living, Mr. Robbins?"

"I own a sporting goods store here in Shawnee."

"How long have you lived in this community?"

"All my life."

Bailey continued to ask his introductory questions, and Robbins returned his answers by rote. While the questions were easy, he scanned the faces in the gallery. Jennifer Rhodes winked at him and smiled encouragement. Hers was the only friendly face he could spot.

"Please describe for the jury, Mr. Robbins…"

During the hours of rehearsal between attorney and client, Robbins learned to key on the "Please describe." It meant the questions and answers were about to take on greater meaning.

"...what the past six months have been like, since the loss of your daughter."

"Objection!" Mike Pierce rang out. "Relevance."

"Mr. Robbins' state of mind at the time of the murder is relevant, Your Honor," Bailey returned immediately.

"His state of mind at the time of the murder is relevant, but his state of mind since then isn't," Pierce huffed.

"The State has alleged that David Robbins' *mens rea* at the time of the shooting was a conscious disregard of a substantial risk to his daughter. The State put on evidence as to Mr. Robbins' state of mind at the time of the slaying, so we have the right to rebut those allegations. In order to do that, Your Honor, this jury is going to have to understand how David Robbins thinks. Mr. Pierce would allow this jury to believe that my client's thoughts can be judged in a vacuum...one thought, at one moment, on one day. What we intend to prove is that anyone who knows David Robbins and understands the way he thinks, knows the conscious disregard of the welfare of his daughter is a thought which never crossed this man's mind, on that day or any other."

"Mr. Pierce," Kazenback said dryly, "I'm going to allow it."

Bailey turned back to Robbins and winked. "So, go ahead now, Mr. Robbins. Tell us what the past six months have been like."

At Bailey's insistence, attorney and client had rehearsed the carefully chosen words of the response over and over again. Robbins found the process distasteful and referred to this and other portions of his testimony as a "canned spiel." Although much of the prepared statement came from his heart, the act of having his words censored, and then practicing the delivery had sullied the end results for Robbins. Bailey responded to Robbins' contempt for the process by pointing out, "Spontaneity is no friend of an alleged murderer testifying on his own behalf."

"They have been awful," Robbins began. "Absolutely awful. My wife left me on the evening after the funeral. We are now divorced. My fourteen-year-old son has just recently started speaking to me over the phone but refuses to see me in person. Even my father has basically disowned me.

"I had to sell my home and deplete my savings to meet the demands of the divorce settlement and pay my legal fees. Revenues from my business have dropped nearly thirty percent since April. That's only one example of the irreparable damage inflicted on my reputation and character. Others include old friends who won't even speak to me, death threats, and the fact that I'm no longer welcome in a church I faithfully served for many, many years."

Pausing to clear his throat, and take a deep breath, Robbins mentally prepared himself for his last words on the subject. Words that, although "canned", had not yet failed to powerfully stir him. "But by far the worst thing about the past six months," he said as he forced himself to scan the jurors eye to eye, "is how terribly I've missed my precious little girl. The way she would laugh. The songs she would sing. How she expressed her curious nature and awe of life in tirades of questions. I miss looking at her. I miss touching her."

"I would give everything I have left, including my life," Robbins concluded with swipes at his eyes, "for just one last minute to hold her in my lap and tell her how much I love her."

As he had planned to do all along, Emerson Bailey stood silently for long seconds and let the silence emphasize the defendant's last words. Robbins appreciated the seconds. He needed them.

"Mr. Robbins," Bailey finally said in an almost reverent tone, "please tell the court why you didn't meet Luke Hogue's demands."

"It simply wasn't the right thing to do, for a number of reasons," Robbins sighed. "At my side was a child I had read the Bible to daily since she was a toddler. All her life, I taught her the ways of Christianity. I always tried to live as an example for her to follow. For years my daughter had heard me talk my religion. In times and situations that demanded no faith or sacrifice, she watched me practice that religion. When that man wanted me to say those words, it put me and my faith to the test. Had I said those words, I would have undermined a foundation I had worked her lifetime to build. Had I said those words, I would have proven to be a hollow man who worshiped a powerless God. A man who said there was a Christ when it was easy to say, but when something great and personal and precious was at stake, readily agreed there wasn't."

"This decision to do what I then and still believe to be the biblically correct thing was greatly supported by a far less spiritual factor. I simply did not believe Luke Hogue would really take Kayla's life. I contribute this to a look in his eyes and the tone of his voice, intangibles I can't really explain. Some people call them gut feelings."

"Mr. Robbins, did you do anything wrong on the night Kayla was shot and killed by Luke Hogue?"

"When that gunshot went off, I was caught totally off guard. I simply did not believe he had any intentions of carrying out his threats. So, yes, Mr. Bailey. I did something wrong. I misread Luke Hogue and his intentions. For that, I've paid dearly."

* * *

First, Luke struck Mark on the side of his head, then he started cussing him and telling him how worthless he was. Then Mark woke with a start and discovered Luke wasn't really in the pickup with him after all. He also discovered it was nearly nine-thirty, and Mark started cussing himself.

With camcorder in hand, Mark bolted out of the pickup. In a stride just short of jogging, he headed in the direction of Shawnee. No longer caring who or what gave him a ride, Mark brought his left arm up parallel with the pavement and extended his thumb toward the east-bound traffic.

As he hurried along, Mark's mind turned to the dream from which he'd just awakened. From the dream about Luke hitting him, his thought arced to the recording intended for his eyes only.

The first part of the message contained nothing but directions — what to do with the camcorder and the other things that Mark didn't care to think about at the moment. It was the last few minutes of the recording that Luke's tendency for violence had brought to mind.

Time and time again in the wee hours of the morning, Mark had rewound the message to the place where Luke's expression melted down from intense to sheepish.

"Hey, uh, Mark, I got one more thing, man," Luke started. "It's, uh, well, it's sort of a confession. You remember those rabbits you had back when you was a kid? The ones whose ears I cut off? If you remember right, I told you that I stomped them to death and then cut off their ears.

"Well, hell, Mark, that ain't exactly how it happened. To tell the truth, I didn't kill those rabbits. They was dead when I found 'em. Something had gotten in the shed and turned over your pen, probably a coyote, or a stray hound. But anyhow, I didn't kill those rabbits. All that was left of 'em when I found 'em was their heads and fur, so I cut off the ears. I thought if you thought I killed 'em, it would be a good way at getting back at'cha for squealing on me about that preacher's daughter.

"I just wanted you to know that." Luke said with an embarrassed-looking grin before concluding, "and, uh, oh yeah, thanks for all your help. I couldn't have pulled this off without you. A guy could do worse than havin' you for a brother."

Now, thinking of the miles of road that lay before him, Mark kicked at a scuffed aluminum can. "You damn straight you could've done worse," he bellowed, "and the next time I catch up with you, I'm gonna kick your ass for all this trouble!"

Five minutes later an old man in a battered Buick pulled to the shoulder and invited Mark to join him.

* * *

After dispensing with the remainder of his questions, Emerson Bailey smiled his confident smile at the jury, strutted back to the defense table, and turned David Robbins over to cross-examination. As Mike Pierce ambled toward the witness stand, Bailey looked once more into the faces of the jury and decided he could no longer postpone the inevitable. When Pierce finished picking Robbins apart, and Judge Kazenback recessed before closing arguments, Bailey would make the admission to his client. They had been beaten.

Bailey knew it wouldn't surprise Robbins. The quiet man Bailey had grown to like and admire was feeling and thinking the same thing. Bailey could see it in Robbins' intelligent eyes. Bailey knew the client, like the attorney, wasn't one to succumb easily to defeat. Now though, it had to be verbalized. It had to be faced. And it was Emerson Bailey being paid the big bucks to do the dirty work.

On that note, Bailey turned his eyes on Robbins. The man on the witness seat wasn't looking back. Robbins had his eyes trained on Mike Pierce. Bailey could just imagine what turmoil raged behind his client's tranquil façade as he braced for the D.A.'s first volley.

"Mr. Robbins could you please explain what acts of violence you watched Luke Hogue perform before he shot and killed your daughter?"

In a calm voice and methodical manner, Robbins described the things Hogue did to Terri Horner, Chad Gains and Ted Blevins. Then he explained how Hogue struck him across the chest with his forearm and elbow. When Robbins stopped and didn't go on, Bailey couldn't help but wince.

"What about when he elevated Kayla by the hair of her head, Mr. Robbins? Did you forget about that?"

David Robbins' eyes twitched, and his jaw muscles tightened. "Well, uh, yes. I, uh, guess I did," he stammered.

Cracks in the façade caused Emerson Bailey's heart to sink.

Mike Pierce looked to the jury with eyebrows arched and head cocked, and for a minute he performed an admirable pantomime of wondering – how in the world could he forget? Turning back to Robbins, Pierce came at him again. "Please explain to the court, Mr. Robbins, how a look in Luke Hogue's eyes, a tone in Luke Hogue's voice and your gut feelings could speak louder to you than all the examples of a violent nature and intent you just recounted?"

David Robbins momentarily cut tortured eyes at Bailey, and then lowered them to stare at his hands. Bailey suddenly felt like a trainer standing hopelessly outside the ring watching his boxer get pummeled.

"It sounds bad right here and now, Mr. Pierce. I realize that," Robbins said without looking up. "But the only answer I can give is that you had to be there and see those eyes and hear that voice."

"Are those the same eyes, Mr. Robbins, that Chad Gains' and Margaret Suggs' parents had to look into. Isn't that the same voice they listened to?"

"The man's demeanor had changed by the time he got to me," Robbins insisted in a strained voice.

"Evidently his intent to do harm had not. Had it Mr. Robbins?"

"Objection!" Bailey emphasized with a pounding fist to the table top. "Mr. Robbins can not testify to the intent of Luke Hogue."

"Sustained," the judge barked.

"Mr. Robbins," Mike Pierce sprang back, "Marlene Dolivo, Trent Carney, and Ethel Rivera testified that they observed you whispering something to Kayla as Luke Hogue was first coming into the dining area. Please share with us what you said to your daughter."

Emerson Bailey was quite accustomed to representing clients that in these situations had no qualms with using the universal, "I don't recall." At the moment he wished with all of his heart Robbins would do the same. But he knew better.

"I was comforting her."

"Do you recall what specifically was said?"

"Kayla asked who the man was. I told her I didn't know. She said she was scared. I told her to pray. She asked me..." Robbins head bowed and his hands came up to rub at eyes Bailey could no longer see, "...not to let the man hurt her. I told her..."

Emerson Bailey shot out of his seat, and Mike Pierce, he observed, all but jumped out of his shoes. The double doors in the back of the courtroom had flung open and hit the walls with such force that it sounded like a gunshot. Two deputies with guns drawn blew by Bailey in the direction of the doors, and Judge Arthur Kazenback looked as though he contemplated hitting the floor. Both Mike Pierce and David Robbins were staring wide-eyed and with mouths gaping at something or somebody behind Bailey.

By the time Bailey turned around, a shabbily dressed man was halfway down the middle aisle of the gallery, and the double doors were swinging shut behind him. With the deputies closing in from every direction, the man hoisted a black, rectangular object high in the air and screamed, "Don't shoot!"

"Drop it!" the deputies chorused.

"It's a camcorder!" the man screamed back.

Seeing this was true, the uniforms sprang at the man. Just before they made contact, the intruder screamed a third time.

"I'm Luke Hogue's brother. Luke's on this camera!"

In the next instance the man was swarmed. As the deputies took him to the floor, he cried, "It's for David Robbins!"

"Your Honor!" Emerson Bailey shouted as he spun to face the judge, "The defense requests a thirty-minute recess to look at that camera. I have reason to believe it contains exculpatory evidence!"

"I object, Your Honor," Mike Pierce practically shouted as he stormed the bench. "This is not procedurally appropriate. That man is not on the witness list, and what evidence could that recorder possibly possess that could prove David Robbins' innocence? Furthermore, this constitutes an unfair surprise for the prosecution!" Pierce was waving his arms about wildly and looked to be in shock.

Judge Kazenback never took his eyes off the tangle of bodies wrestling around on the floor of his courtroom.

"Deputies!" he said before having to clear his throat. "Hold that man until I can get the jury out of here."

The Judge tuned to the twelve wide-eyed people in the jury box. "Ladies and gentlemen of the jury, as you can tell we have an irregularity in the proceedings. It will take a few minutes for the court and council to determine how to proceed. At this time, I'd like to excuse you to the jury room. I will call you back in as soon as I possibly can. Thank you."

"Mr. Robbins," Kazenback said as the jury stood to file out, "You have not been dismissed by the prosecution. However, you can return to your seat until we determine what we have here."

Bailey watched as his client hurried to their table. "What can that thing have on it?" Robbins whispered as he fell into his chair.

Emerson Bailey had absolutely no idea and admitted it.

* * *

"Okay, deputies," Kazenback said after taking the final swig of his third glass of ice water. "Escort your prisoner to the bench, please."

David Robbins noted that the judge's voice had calmed considerably, and that he no longer had the shocked look of a crime victim. The man being brought before him, however, hadn't fared so well over the past five minutes. All that time on the floor under a pile of deputies resulted in a bloody nose, busted lip and torn shirt. The rest of the man's appearance problems, however, could not be contributed to his captors. His shaggy mop of greasy hair, days worth of stubble and grungy clothing looked to be products of a personal grooming deficiency.

"I can walk on my own," the man huffed as he wiggled to free his arms from the deputies on his left and right. It looked to Robbins to be a half-hearted attempt, and it netted no results.

The man didn't open his mouth again until the very moment he was positioned before Kazenback. Then he let it go. "This sucks! I'm a citizen that came here on my own free will to help another citizen, and this is the way I get treated? I ain't never heard of such bull…"

"Shut up." Kazenback said through gritted teeth.

"Yes, sir."

"Now, let me tell you something, Mr. Citizen," Kazenback said in his normally soft, even tone of voice. "You have disrupted my court, and for that I am not at all pleased with you. Any further outbursts or displays of disrespect can only serve to compound my unhappiness and will most assuredly land you in jail for a very long, long time."

"Yes, sir."

"Very good. Please state your name and calmly explain the reason you are here."

"My name is Mark Hogue. Luke Hogue is my brother. You know who he is right?"

"Right," Kazenback responded dryly.

"Well, he made a recording," Hogue said before pausing to look scornfully at the lawmen still standing on both sides of him.

"What specifically does this recording contain, Mr. Hogue?"

"I don't know, sir. See, actually, I was just supposed to hand my camcorder to Mr. Bailey early this morning before court, and then I was supposed to just get out of here, but my old truck broke down on Interstate 40, and I messed around and fell asleep, and then…"

"Where is the camera?" Kazenback asked the deputy to the right of Hogue.

"I've got it here, sir." A deputy from the gallery spoke up.

"Please bring it to me." Then Kazenback turned back to Hogue. "Mr. Hogue, we are going to watch the recording. I'm sure you won't mind waiting patiently with these officers until we are finished. Correct?"

"Do I have to?" Hogue whined.

"You do."

"Yes, sir."

Coming to his feet, Judge Kazenback announced, "Mr. Pierce and Mr. Spencer, Mr. Robbins and Mr. Bailey, please join me in my chambers."

* * *

As Judge Kazenback watched a clerk connect the camcorder to a television in his chambers, David Robbins worked at calming himself. After taking a quick glance at the other four men in the room, Robbins found some satisfaction in knowing he wasn't the only one feeling anxious. Emerson Bailey just rattled change in his pants pockets and rocked back and forth on his toes and heels. For Bailey, however, that seemed quite a display of nerves. Mike Pierce, on the other hand, could have been picked by an uninformed bystander as the one facing the jail sentence. His boss, Walter Spencer, simply scowled, and Kazenback seemed frustrated and impatient with the clerk's efforts to find and play the recording.

"All right, gentlemen," Kazenback finally announced, "gather around. Pull up chairs if you want."

No one did. They all chose to stand in a loose semicircle in front of the judge's desk. Robbins was bracketed by Bailey on his left and Pierce on his right.

After the play button was pushed, the machine whirled to action. For the first second or two the television screen danced with gray, horizontal lines of static. From the static the screen went to a calming robin's egg blue and seemed to stay in that freeze-frame mode forever. Then, an image of a man from the chest up filled the screen.

David Robbins' breath caught in his throat, and his knees all but buckled. The man's hair was longer, and his face thinner, but Robbins had no doubt it was the man who murdered his daughter.

"My name is Luke Hogue. I'm making this recording for Mr. David Robbins…"

Robbins looked into the eyes, listened carefully to the words, and his emotions raged. The first to debut was intense hatred. Shortly thereafter, a deep sadness crept in, but it didn't even come close to crowding out the hatred.

"…when that Horner bitch told me to get out, it just pissed me off, man…"

Hearing Terri Horner's words again, the words Robbins had somehow blocked from memory, made him also mouth the word, "bitch." How different would things have been, he wondered, had that woman offered hospitality in the place of hostility.

Hogue continued with his story, and up to the point where Ted Blevins started lying about not having a wallet, there were no surprises for David Robbins. Though Hogue quickly changed that.

"…when that old man stood there and started telling lies to save his money, you know, I started to think this bastard and everyone else cares more for their money than they do anything else, including each other. That just made something snap in me, man. That's when I first had the thought that I oughta just shoot every really sorry grown up in that room. But at that time, it was just a wild thought, and I didn't pay it no mind."

"After I got finished with the old man, I shoved him and told him to go sit down. That's when he really got to me. The old bastard told me God was going to punish me. And I thought again about using my gun. This time, though, I really thought about it. Just to think that that lying old hypocrite could throw stones at me, just made me go crazy. The crazier I got, the more I thought about killing people. That's when I came up with the plan to help me decide who to kill and who not to kill."

"I figured that on any given Sunday morning that any adult in that room would stand up and confess to being Christians. It looked to me that God had been good to those people, and I reckoned as long as they thought he would continue to be good to them, they'd proclaim him. In other words, while it was good and easy, they'd stick with him. The way I saw it, is that those I could get to deny him during this period of time that wasn't so good, well, they just didn't deserve to live."

Hogue paused and closed his eyes. His hands, that until now had been out of the viewers' sight, came up to vigorously rub his temples. In a few seconds, Hogue opened his eyes, cleared his throat and started up again. "You've heard enough about what I made those people say and do after that. But let me tell you something you don't know. By the time I got to Mr. Robbins and his little girl, I done made up my mind to kill every son of a bitch in there…except the children. No matter what you're thinking right now…because you still don't know everything there is to know…I could never kill a small child. Never."

"Now, let me tell you something else you don't know. Those people didn't live because that little girl got killed. They lived because David Robbins saved them. I know you probably think I'm crazy, and I'm sure you wonder how I could just make the decision to start killing people. Well, all I got to say about that is…I gotta real problem with people who act religious, but aren't. But, that ain't the point here. The point is that if it weren't for David Robbins, you'd had a lot of dead people on your hands. And another point is, you don't know what really happened. But, I'm going to tell you…

* * *

Emerson Bailey had closely studied the events leading to Kayla Robbins' death. He grilled his client over and over again on the minutest details of what precisely had been said and what exactly had been done. He spent hours viewing and reviewing every police report and witness statement. So, as Bailey listened to this new information and combined it with the old, it was not at all difficult for him to play out the action in his mind. He could see Hogue thrusting the revolver underneath Robbins' jaw. He could hear the exact tone of voice Hogue used to say…

"What if you had a gun right now? Would you use it on me if you could?"

"I don't know."

The blow was swift and effective, and Hogue did it because this man had to break. He had to be – no matter how deep down inside – just like the others.

It didn't feel good grabbing the little girl by the hair. Hogue didn't like her screams, but if anything would bring out the real David Robbins, this would.

"Let her go!" Robbins was feeling a fear like none he'd ever experienced.

"If you had a gun right now, you'd kill me."

"I'd protect my daughter!"

"Of course you fuckin' would…" And Luke Hogue found absolutely nothing wrong with that. "…and if you'd blow me away to save your daughter, surely you'd turn your back on God and worship Satan in order to save her…"

But this would be very wrong.

Suddenly Hogue realized he was rooting for David Robbins. Pulling for him in a way not unlike the Patriarch Abraham pulled for the righteous folks of the ancient city of Sodom – pleading with God to spare the city of thousands if only ten righteous men could be found among their ranks. God had agreed to do it. If the Almighty saw fit to spare thousands of wicked because of ten good, then it would be expected of Luke Hogue to spare ten assholes because of one devout man.

God didn't find ten good men in Sodom, and he didn't spare the city either. So, Luke needed to be damn sure convinced that David Robbins was truly a righteous man. "…So, you best get to doing it."

Robbins didn't fail to notice a change in the man's eyes and in the tone of his words, and he took a chance on a gut feeling. "You don't want to hurt my daughter. Please let her go."

"I'm tired of fucking with you, man!" Hogue had to make sure Robbins couldn't be broken. "You got one more chance to tell me there ain't no such thing as Jesus Christ!"

David Robbins looked at the child he loved more than life itself, and her pain made him angry. "Listen, Mister…"

Robbins tuned his eyes up to the ceiling.

Then he closed his eyes.

"…If you absolutely have to use that gun on someone here tonight, then use the damn thing on me!"

David Robbins just offered to make the ultimate sacrifice, and as his daughter started to scream a rebuttal to his proposal, Luke Hogue deemed the man *righteous*. At the same instance, Kayla Robbins wrapped her little hands around the revolver…and gave it a jerk. The trigger collided with Luke Hogue's index finger and Kayla Robbins died...

Emerson Bailey's voice erupted and resounded through the small office, "Autopsy reports revealed gunpowder residue and flash burns on both of Kayla's hands!"

"We thought she had thrown her hands up to cover her face," D.A. Walter Spencer erupted in turn.

"It's all irrelevant anyway," Mike Pierce shouted.

Judge Kazenback hit the pause button and piped, "Gentlemen!"

"It's hearsay and not admissible!" Pierce added in another shout.

Kazenback threw in another impotent, "Gentlemen," and Bailey opened his mouth to give further argument but didn't. The defense attorney realized, at about the same moment as the others, that his client was sobbing.

* * *

David Robbins tried with all his might to hold it in, but he failed. The hate, the sorrow, the pain, and the pity all escaped in torrential tears and heaving breaths of expelled torment. When the four attorneys abruptly stopped their shouting, and Robbins realized all eyes were on him, he went to work with his handkerchief and fought for composure. Bailey placed a squeezing hand on his shoulder.

"I know it must hurt," that big man sighed.

"Yes, Mr. Robbins," Kazenback said softly, "please accept my sympathies. I can only imagine how difficult watching this must have been for you."

Robbins reached up and patted the hand on his shoulder and nodded to Kazenback. "It has been painful, Your Honor, but I'd really like to watch the rest of it."

"I think we should, Mr. Robbins," Kazenback said as he pushed the play button.

Luke Hogue's eyes had started watering about the time he explained how he had grabbed Kayla by the hair. By the time he got to the point where the gun went off, he was weeping. Kazenback had freeze-framed Hogue rubbing at his eyes with fingertips. When the tape started to play again, Hogue dropped his hands, and once again all that could be seen of him was his upper torso and head. After several deep breaths, Hogue lowered his head, shook it slowly back and forth for a second or two, and then raised his head back up and looked into the camera. This time, tears were streaming down his cheeks.

"The little girl died trying to save her daddy. I don't know how to make Mr. Robbins not feel bad about that, but if Mr. Robbins had said the words I wanted him to say, he and every other adult in that room would be dead. I don't think he should forget that. I don't think nobody should forget that."

Hogue wiped at his face, cleared his throat, and continued. "Well, that's all I got to say. Except, one more time, I want Mr. Robbins to know how sorry I am." With that, Hogue lowered his head and started to cry.

Within seconds he raised his head again, and after several sniffs and coughs, he looked back into the camera. "Okay, now, I've talked to a lawyer. I know all about inadmissible hearsay and all that shit. So..."

Hogue sighed long and hard and momentarily looked away from the camera. When he looked back, his eyes looked different. He suddenly reminded Robbins of a frightened child.

"...So, please accept all I've said as my dying declaration."

When Hogue brought his right hand up a final time, it held the big revolver. Robbins watched him put the gun in his mouth and turn his head away from the camera.

Someone in the office spoke for all when they mumbled, "Jesus Christ!"

TWENTY

No one in Judge Arthur Kazenback's chambers spoke. Robbins found the silence rehabilitative, but as life demonstrated over the past six months, all things, good and bad, eventually came to an end. Emerson Bailey shattered the silence.

"I do believe what we have here is some very admissible and highly exculpatory evidence."

"Your Honor," Mike Pierce piped up, "I'm not sure what we have here meets the exception to the hearsay rule."

Robbins couldn't detect the slightest bit of confidence in the Assistant D.A.'s words. Bailey's, on the other hand, were brimming.

"That's ridiculous. A dying declaration always serves as an exception to the hearsay rule."

"All right," Pierce conceded in a near whimper. "It's just that I have a hard time buying that story."

"Moot point," Bailey ho-hummed. "Your Honor, as you well know, the theory of a dying declaration is founded on the rationale that no one wants to meet their maker with a lie upon their lips; therefore, last words are considered inherently truthful."

"We have no true confirmation of death, Your Honor," Pierce emphasized with an index finger wagging over head.

"We watched his head disintegrate, Judge," Bailey bellowed. "I, for one, am willing to bet Luke Hogue is not up and about!"

An extremely red-faced Mike Pierce bellowed back, "But still, we…"

"Your Honor, if I may," the District Attorney Walter Spencer interrupted in a booming voice.

"Please do, Mr. Spencer," Kazenback responded wearily.

Within seconds of witnessing the recorded death, Spencer had plopped down in a chair next to the one Robbins occupied. Now the tall, slender man pushed to his feet and folded his hands behind his back.

"Your Honor, the State of Oklahoma moves to dismiss the charge against Mr. David Robbins."

Emerson Bailey let out a whoop, and before Robbins could do so on his own, the big attorney extracted him from the chair. Numb and weak-kneed, Robbins felt he would have fallen had Bailey not had him in a bear hug.

"But, Walter," Mike Pierce started to object.

"It's over, Mike." Spencer said with a tone that prohibited argument.

"You hear that, David?" Bailey laughed. "It's over. We won!"

It had been a while since Robbins had done any winning. It felt strange, and it felt wonderful.

*　*　*

While David Robbins waited by himself in the small consultation room down the hall from Kazenback's courtroom, he prayed. The thanks and praises came easily. It had been much more difficult, however, praying for Luke Hogue's soul. But to Robbins, even caring to try proved a sure sign that his process of healing had already begun.

When the tapping sounded from outside the closed door, Robbins stood up from his kneeling position. A second later, Bailey stepped into the room.

Robbins extended his right hand, "Thanks...so very much."

Bailey bypassed the hand and for the second time embraced Robbins in a near-crushing hug. When he let go and took a step backwards, the look on his face was one Robbins didn't know Emerson Bailey could make. It looked humble.

"I'd be remiss," Bailey said solemnly, "and feel like a real sleaze, if I didn't admit something to you, David."

The big man took in a deep breath and exhaled it forcibly out pursed lips, "We were getting our asses kicked. Without that tape, you'd most assuredly have gone to prison. I appreciate your sentiment, but I really didn't do all that much."

Robbins placed a hand on Bailey's shoulder and gave it a squeeze, "You didn't have a whole lot to work with."

Emerson Bailey just shrugged his shoulders and then clearly let it go. The confident to the point of cocky bearing quickly reclaimed its rightful place.

"Hey, listen, the media is scrambling around out there in near hysteria. None of them have a clue as to what's transpired, and I'm sure the D.A.'s not real anxious to let them know. So, it's up to us. If you don't mind, I'd like to give it exclusively to Jennifer. You know, let her scoop the others."

"I don't mind, but," Robbins chuckled, "I have to ask, what's up with you two?"

"I think this is the one, David," Emerson beamed.

"The one, Emo? You've been married four times," Robbins teased.

"Trial and error, David. Nothing more."

Robbins gave him a sidelong look.

"Swear to God!" Emerson said, throwing his right palm into the air. "And I know that six months in a serious relationship doesn't sound like much to you, but for me, it's an accomplishment."

Robbins once again extended his right hand and this time Bailey took it, "Congratulations. I couldn't be happier for you."

"Thanks," he laughed happily. "Oh, I almost forgot, there's someone out there that wants a few minutes of your time."

"Who?"

"Mark Hogue."

"Oh, boy," Robbins said, as his smile faded away.

"I can tell him to get lost."

"No," Robbins replied after a second or two of consideration. "I owe him at least a few minutes."

Bailey opened the door and invited Mark Hogue into the room. The man of much lesser means and position looked noticeably uncomfortable behind closed doors with Robbins and Bailey.

"Mr. Robbins, Mr. Bailey," Hogue nodded. "I know you both got better things to be doing than messing with me, but I kinda wanted to ask both of you a question if you don't mind."

"I don't mind," Robbins said and made an effort to smile a kind smile. Emerson Bailey shrugged his broad shoulders and grunted an okay.

"Mr. Bailey, Luke said the police might give me some trouble over harboring a fugitive, and he said I might see if you'd help me out since he helped you out."

"Sure, Mark," Bailey smiled, "I can do that much for you and Luke. If you have any trouble, give me a call."

"Thanks."

Mark then turned to Robbins. "Mr. Robbins, mine and Luke's dad was a preacher, but he wasn't a good man like you. Still, we had a lot of chances to learn the Bible. I didn't take those chances, but Luke did. He studied it most of his life. What little I did learn, I pretty much forgot a long time ago.

"Now, I reckon you know the Bible real well, and I'd like your opinion on something. You see, until recently, I didn't much care for Luke either. But there at the end, I really got to caring for him. What I'm wondering is, after all he's done, do you think there's any chance of him being in heaven now?"

If David Robbins had ever been forced to contemplate a more difficult question he couldn't remember it. Lowering his head and staring at the floor, Robbins thought about everything he had experienced in the past long months.

"Mark, there's a prayer the Catholics pray as part of praying the Rosary. The prayer is, 'Oh my, Jesus, forgive us our sins. Save us from the fires of hell, and send all souls to heaven, *especially those most in need of thy mercy.*' I'm certainly no theologian, Mark, but I'd be willing to bet there's a good chance your brother is now at peace in one form or another."

* * *

"Well, I guess this is it," Bailey said as his limousine pulled into the Gardenview Apartments in Shawnee, Oklahoma.

"Yes, I guess it is."

After a vigorous round of handshaking, Bailey leaned forward in his seat, looked through his window, and gave the Gardenview's grounds a once over. "Damn, I sure hate to see you living in a place like this."

"Hate it enough to give me a refund?"

Bailey turned from the window and back to Robbins with one of those great smiles. "Almost, but not quite."

With a laugh, Robbins pushed open his door and stepped out of the lap of luxury. Then he leaned down to look back in. "That's okay. I won't be here long anyway."

"You know," Bailey grinned, "there ain't no way in hell that I'd bet against that."

"You take care," Robbins said.

"You do the same, friend."

Robbins waved as the long Lincoln pulled away. Because of the darkened windows, he didn't know if anyone waved back.

EPILOGUE

Spring had been long in coming because winter had not wanted to give up its grasp. Six months had passed since the trial. Its effect, unlike the bitter cold of the season past, had not subsided. David Robbins knew it never would.

He ran a finger tip along the smooth surface of the headstone. The piece of granite revealed so little. Just a name along with the day life had begun and the day it had ended.

Some things had changed for the better since the trial. David visited Kevin twice in California. In a month his son was coming home for the summer.

Some things changed for the worse. His business never rebounded, and David lost his store. Leon Beck had died.

Everything else, like most things in life, fell somewhere between better and worse, good and bad. Just before leaving California the last time, David and Nancy embraced. Now they talked by phone often and for long periods of time. Maybe someday she would come home. Maybe she wouldn't. But talking was better than not talking.

And the life David Robbins now had was better than life in prison.

He bent and gently placed a bouquet of carnations at the base of the headstone, then turned and walked away.

It was his first time to visit the grave of Luke Hogue. It would probably be his last.

ACKNOWLEDGMENTS

To Bob Cantrell, a dear friend and very devout man. Many years ago, while teaching an adult Bible class, Bob planted a seed in my mind that resulted in the writing of this novel. Thanks, Bob, for your inspiration and support.

To Henry P. (Pat) Scully of Scully and Associates for the cover design. Pat, thanks yet again for the work of art that draws the eye to my novel.

Last, but certainly not least, to Sohail Liaqat for formatting and editing. Thanks, Sohail, for doing the part that takes the most expertise.

ABOUT THE AUTHOR

Keith Remer is a retired Army colonel. After thirty-two years of service in the Army, he taught various courses as an adjunct professor before buying a horse ranch. He has to date written twelve novels and is the recipient of the *International Indy Book Award for Best in Fiction* for his thriller, *The Hiding Place of Thunder*. Keith lives on his horse ranch in rural Oklahoma City where he writes his novels and tends his horses.

To connect with Keith, visit his Facebook page @KeithRemerAuthor, or his webpage: keithremer.com